# ACCORDING TO THE POWER

Quin Arrington

Now, That's a Word! LLC
Montgomery, AL

Copyright © 2022 by Quin Arrington.

All rights reserved. No part of this publication may be reproduced, distributed or transmitted in any form or by any means, including photocopying, recording, or other electronic or mechanical methods, without the prior written permission of the publisher, except in the case of brief quotations embodied in critical reviews and certain other noncommercial uses permitted by copyright law. For permission requests, write to the publisher, addressed "Attention: Permissions Coordinator," at the address below.

Quin Arrington/ Now, That's a Word! LLC
P.O. Box 211372
Montgomery, AL, 36121
www.nowthats-aword.com

Publisher's Note: This is a work of fiction. Names, characters, places, and incidents are a product of the author's imagination. Locales and public names are sometimes used for atmospheric purposes. Any resemblance to actual people, living or dead, or to businesses, companies, events, institutions, or locales is completely coincidental.

The Holy Bible, New International Version®, NIV Copyright© 1973, 1978, 1984, 2011 by Biblica, Inc.® Used by permission. All rights reserved worldwide.

Book Layout ©2017 BookDesignTemplates.com
Cover Design: The Book Cover Whisperer | ProfessionalBookCoverDesign.com
Photographer: Weezo Photography

According to the Power/ Quin Arrington. -- 1st ed.
ISBN 978-1-7371225-4-8 (Print)
ISBN 978-1-7371225-5-5 (eBook)

*God, thank you for showing me that there was more to me than I could have ever imagined.*

# ACT I

## SPRING 2003—SAVANNAH, GEORGIA

"Go ahead, Emily, power up!" Victoria Brown taunted Emily as she inched closer with a sinister look on her pretty, yet ugly face. All eyes on the playground were on Emily and Ms. Prissy Vicky. Emily had just landed the biggest swing-jump performed by any kid in the 5$^{th}$ grade that entire year. Just minutes before Victoria started provoking her, Emily was swinging sky-high on the swing set.

Mrs. Maxine, their P.E. instructor, was too busy scolding another student to see that she had swung dangerously high on the ancient metal swing set that threatened to give any of the students tetanus if they were ever cut by it. "Emily, you're so high! Your head nearly touched the top pole!" said Stacey Young, Emily's best friend.

"Aaahhh! I know!" yelled Emily, bubbling over with adrenaline and excitement. "I'm about to jump! Count me down!"

"5 ... 4 ... 3 ..." Emily didn't wait for Stacey to finish the countdown before she jumped. She leaped from the swing, high on dopamine and fearlessness, but as soon as Emily released, she briefly became fearful when she noticed just how high she was in the air. Emi, as her dad affectionately calls her, has nothing but dirt and patches of grass on the ground to catch her if she misses her landing.

*"Too late to be scared now,"* Emily thought. Emily steadied her flailing limbs and found her footing mid-air, focusing on where her feet will touch the ground. Behind the red string was where she was silently praying that her beat-up Vans would land. The red string represented the highest swing-jump recorded that school year. Reggie —Reginald Jones, the promising football

player with stellar athleticism—had set the undefeated record at the top of the school year back in September.

It was now the top of May, the end of the school year, and no one had yet come close to beating Reggie's record. That little red string remained secured in the ground with makeshift nails constructed out of paper clips and silly straws. As Emily stretched her legs out for landing, her feet hit the soil with a hard thud.

As anxious as she was to see if her feet had landed ahead of or behind the red string, Emily didn't dare open her eyes. Like a college kid too nervous to open an acceptance letter, Emi was too apprehensive to look. But Stacey's shriek coerced her into tearing her eyes open. "OMG! OMG! Emily, you did it! You did it!"

Emily looked down to see that her black and white Vans had sure enough landed just a hair above Reggie's undefeated red-string-noted record. Emily's eyes widened in disbelief before she burst out in a victorious laugh, displaying a set of beautiful pearly white teeth inherited from her dear old dad. "I'm the BEST! I am the BEST! When you address me, address me as the BEAST that I am because I am THE BEST!" she gloated in her classic competitive nature.

Emily had tried all year to beat Reggie's record. It made no difference that he was a boy, and she was a girl. Emily loved a challenge. Especially a challenge she was not supposed to beat. She dabbled in sports herself. She took gymnastics, starting when she was five years old up until the age of nine. Emily was the top gymnast of her class and had several plaques and trophies to prove it. She knew with every fabric of her being she would've remained as the top gymnast if her family's finances hadn't suffered.

Daddy temporarily lost his job, which resulted in Emi having to put sports on the back burner. Benjamin Waters hated to see either one of his girls miss out on what they enjoyed because of his self-proclaimed temporary failure as a father. His wife, Elena, rebuked him harshly when he blamed himself for a lack of funds when it had been his employer of 15 years lack of integrity that caused their financial bind. However, he couldn't help but feel responsible for Emily's disappointment when he told her she would have to temporarily stop gymnastics. It was just as hard to tell Estella, his youngest daughter, that ballet would have to be postponed.

But Benjamin wasn't out of a job for long. He was resourceful. Less than three months later, he found a better paying job with better benefits. "God is good," he said in the car after he was hired on the spot. After a few more months of playing catch-up on past-due bills, Benjamin couldn't wait to tell his baby girls they could start practicing gymnastics and ballet again. Estella was ecstatic to restart ballet, but in the extra three months it took for Benjamin to get his ducks in a row, Emily had lost her excitement for gymnastics. She liked it but she'd never loved it. She loved the competitiveness of the sport more than the sport itself.

That's why Emily had tried virtually every day to beat Reggie's record. And that's why, now that she had beat it, she couldn't keep calm about it. In Emily's mind, she had just won gold in the Playground Olympics. "Put. Some. Respect. On. My. Name!" Emily playfully shouted while throwing her head back in a stance that emulated a character powering up from a videogame.

Just as she threw her head back, her ponytail holder broke. Wooly, ginger-brown curls scattered across her head. Although the coils separated into sections, because her hair tended to defy gravity, some parts of it stood straight up. Still standing in her videogame character pose, Emily resembled a melanated Super Saiyan, which led to Victoria Brown's onslaught of insults.

"Girl, please!" Victoria said as she rolled her cat-like eyes. "You look stupid with your hair sticking up all over your head. You act just like a boy!" Being a girl but looking anything like a boy was the ultimate no-no in Ms. Prissy Vicky's opinion. Clad in pink, white, and gold clothing with matching glittery gold nails accompanied by perfectly coiffed long black hair, Victoria Brown exemplified all things feminine. Hence, Emily and Stacey's secret nickname for her—Ms. Prissy Vicky. If only her heart matched the beauty of her appearance.

"You may as well be a boy since you beat a boy's record. Go ahead, Emily, power up! Power up to be the tough little boy that you think you are!" Emily couldn't decipher which one had more venom—Victoria's words or her face. Both revealed such a severe disdain for her. She had never understood why Victoria seemed to hate her so much.

"Leave me alone, Victoria," Emily said as she walked away. Emily's parents always taught her to avoid unnecessary confrontation. Fighting of any sort was frowned upon in their home. Once Emily and her little sister Estella had gotten into a physical altercation. Being three years older than Estella, Emily had the upper hand and unfairly bruised Estella's shoulder after shoving her to the ground. Estella, hurt in body and pride, ran into the house to tell Daddy.

Yet, Benjamin Waters didn't punish his girls in the way one might expect. He didn't yell at them. He didn't whip them. Nor did he take their things away. Instead, Benjamin made his girls study together. They were to come straight home from school, complete their homework, and then study a subject of Daddy's choosing for a week. Daddy had just so happened to choose the Bible—a children's Bible, to be fair—as his subject of choice.

At the end of the week, the girls had to submit a team effort book report on what they had learned. If Daddy didn't approve of their report, it would cost them another week of studying until they were in A+ standing. The girls ended up studying for two weeks and completed two book reports as they had been ignorant of Daddy's high book-report standards.

Emily never knew how Daddy might discipline them if they acted up. She definitely didn't want to have to write a book report on Noah and the ark or Jonah and the giant fish on account of knocking Ms. Prissy Vicky's head off. So, Emily opted to walk away ... but Victoria just wouldn't let up.

"I said power up, Emily!" Victoria shouted as she pushed Emily's shoulder hard from behind. The shove caused Emily to stumble a few feet forward. She had to catch herself from falling to the ground. Emily paused. She stood straight up and slowly turned around.

"Victoria ... don't put your hands on me again ..." Emily said, slowly and deliberately accentuating every word through clenched teeth.

"Or what?!" Victoria asked, staring Emily down with her hands on her hip. Emily ignored Victoria's question, turned around, and proceeded to walk away once more but was caught off guard when she felt a sharp tug at the roots of her hair.

"Don't turn your back on me when I'm talking to you, *Emily!*" Victoria had grabbed a handful of Emily's coarse curls and yanked her head backwards. Once Emily realized what had happened, she had a fleeting moment to think before she acted.

*"Should I walk away, or strike back?"* Emily thought about the consequences of her actions. She thought about the possible school suspension and whatever random punishment Benjamin would place her on. Ultimately, Emily decided that school suspension and whatever punishment her dad conjured up wouldn't be all that bad.

Emily turned back around to face Victoria who had a nasty smug look on her face. Emily decided she was going to make sure Ms. Prissy Vicky would never look at her like that again. She balled up her right fist, tilted it backward, and lunged it straight forward into Victoria's pursed-up lips. Victoria fell backwards and hit the dirt. With a look of sheer bewilderment and terror in her eyes, she began to cry. Her sidekicks, Chelsea and Dana, dared not allow Emily to hit their dear friend. They both set eyes on Emily to attack and settle the score. Emily's friend Stacey was more of a peacemaker than a fighting comrade, so, she ran to get Mrs. Maxine.

In the meantime, Emily had to stand her ground. She turned towards Chelsea and Dana and steadied herself for the onslaught. Chelsea attacked first. Emily was quick on her feet and ducked her wild swing. Chelsea swung so hard that she did a 180 when she failed to connect. Dana didn't wait for Chelsea to do a complete 360 before she decided to take a swing at Emily. When Chelsea turned back around, she hung back to give Dana an opportunity.

Emily dodged Dana's punch and countered with a right of her own. Apparently, Emily's punch packed power. She assumed gymnastics training had something to do with that. Or maybe it was her compact physique that held natural strength. Either way, down fell Dana. So, far her one-hitter-quitter was two for two ... but Chelsea refused to give her three for three.

Like a raging bull, Chelsea ran at Emily with all her might and tackled her. They both hit the dirt hard, but Emily hit it the hardest as she landed on her back. Chelsea proceeded to throw an array of punches towards Emily's face. While Emily was still thrown off guard from the tackle, Chelsea landed clean hits to Emi's apple-shaped face. When Emily came to, she immediately threw up a defense, guarding her face with upturned forearms. With her guard up, Emily was able to refocus. She acted quickly and tucked-and-rolled Chelsea underneath her. With Chelsea now beneath her, fire shot from Emily's head. The only thing she saw was red and revenge. She was determined to punish Chelsea for the hard tackle and ambush of punches.

"What on earth! Emily Waters, stop it right now!" yelled Mrs. Maxine as she ran across the playground to stop the fight. Emily didn't hear her teacher and proceeded to plunder Chelsea with punches, only stopping when Mrs. Maxine pried her off. Once Emily looked up at Mrs. Maxine, she snaped out of her rage. She looked down at Chelsea and instantly felt a surge of regret as she noticed the swelling on her forehead, mouth, and cheeks. She glanced over at Victoria and Dana who had regained their composure. They both had matching contusions on their mouths. *"Yep,"* Emily thought, *"I'm in deep trouble."*

"To the principal's office now!" directed Mrs. Maxine.

Emily was suspended from school for a week. Her mom didn't say anything to her as they drove home from the parent-teacher-principal meeting. Elena didn't understand Emily sometimes. She was such a smart girl. A straight *A* student with an inquisitive mind since birth as far as she was concerned. But sometimes her firecracker ways tended to overshadow her intellect. The only thing Elena could think to say to her daughter was, "I'll let your daddy deal with you when we get home." Benjamin seemed to be able to get through to Emily better than she could most of the time. That's just the way it was with Benjamin and Emily. They had a special connection. An unbreakable daddy-daughter bond.

Though he never told Emily, Benjamin loved her spunk and tenacity. Whenever anyone said Emily was too rough or too this or that to be a little girl, he would firmly tell them, "No, she just has more grit than you're accustomed to seeing in little girls" or "Strong girls turn into strong women." He prayed to God all the time that neither he nor his wife would discipline Emily's personality away. Benjamin knew that her grit made her special. It just needed cultivating.

So, when Elena broke the news to Benjamin about the fight, he took it easy on Emily. He reasoned that it was important to stand your ground when someone was mistreating you. He also put himself in Emily's shoes and concluded that he would have 100% succumbed to a brawl as well. "But fighting was and will always be frowned upon in this home," he said as he calmly talked to her in her trophy-studded room. She silently nodded her head and accepted her punishment.

Emily was placed on punishment for one day but her reputation at school far outlasted 24 hours. From the day of the 3-on-1 scuffle onward, Emily was known as the record-breaking girl who was not to be trifled with. She never had a problem with Ms. Prissy Vicky or anyone else ever again. She knew she'd always had grit but breaking the red-string record and putting an unfortunate whipping on Victoria, Dana, and Chelsea in the same day loudly announced her grit to everyone else too.

# WINTER 2019—SAN FRANCISCO, CALIFORNIA

Emily snapped out of her 5th grade brawl daydream when the light turned green. She couldn't believe that she had just ran into Chelsea Stark at Honey's Boutique on Broadway Boulevard. Emily had dropped in to purchase a brand-new pair of croc-skinned stiletto boots. She thought they might pair nicely with her cream pants suit she'd purchased last week. But she would have never imagined running into an old classmate, especially not on the West Coast.

"Emily Waters? Is that you?" Chelsea asked from across the small luxury boutique, walking closer to ensure that her eyes weren't deceiving her. Emily turned around from checking out a chiffon piece on the clothing rack. Her eyes meet Chelsea's and she tilted her head in honest surprise. "Chelsea? Hey, girl. What a surprise … What are you doing here in California? Are you vacationing for the holidays?"

Emily had moved to California shortly after graduating high school. In her teenage years, she'd decided she was going to start a life anywhere in the US besides Savannah, Georgia. She didn't hate her hometown per se, she was merely eager to explore the world on her own. Emily was accepted into McQueen University in San Francisco straight out of high school. Apart from birthdays, holidays, and the occasional random visit home, she pretty much stayed in Cali. She loved being a Californian. She loved the life and career she had built there. But she had never ran into anyone from her past until now.

"No, I actually moved out here about two months ago. My husband's job relocated us, so here I am," Chelsea said smiling brightly. "What are you doing here?" she asked. Emily checked Chelsea over for a second before she responded. She looked different. Granted, her appearance hadn't changed much since the last time Emily had seen her in high school, but something was different about her. Perhaps it was her countenance or the way she carried herself. She couldn't quite put her finger on it. Emily supposed Chelsea may've thought the same about her.

"I live here ... I have lived here for about eight years now. I'm a real estate agent for Hassen's Realty" Emily stated.

"Hassen's?" Chelsea said an octave higher. "Oh, my! Well, look who's come out to California and made a name for themselves." Chelsea returned the gesture of glancing Emily over. Emily had traded her bushy brown curls for a more stylish, curly pixie cut. Her amber-colored eyes shone with fire and resolve just as they had when she was younger. Chelsea had always thought Emily was pretty but never thought she would grow up to be stunning.

"I've done alright for myself I suppose," Emily humbly admitted. She had never aspired to be one of the most sought-after real estate agents at one of San Francisco's top-rated realty companies. Before graduating from college, she had taken on a position as a real estate assistant at Hassen's. She loved the work environment, and her work ethic was noted and praised by her superior. Eventually, this superior causally mentioned her superb communication skills in earshot of Ms. Cathy Rugsby, the owner of Hassen's. Cathy Rugsby always knew when she came across someone who had the ability to sell, and Emily was one of those people.

Although Ms. Rugsby knew real estate wasn't likely to be Emily's aspiration, she nevertheless dropped a bug in her ear about her sales potential. Emily, who had never lost a touch of her grit or competitiveness, figured she could earn a few extra bucks while she finished her last semester. Once she'd learned the art of selling an igloo to a polar bear, she racked up her six-figure salary rather quickly. Though it had been unexpected, Emily could confidently say that her job at Hassen's was her dream career.

"Oh, don't be modest. Hassen's is the one of—if not *the*—top-rated realty companies in San Francisco. I should know as much as I badgered Henry about picking a good realtor company before our move," Chelsea said, tossing her slick tresses back from her face. Emily couldn't help but think of Ms. Prissy Vicky and the crew. Chelsea and Dana had always fit right in with Victoria. Chelsea was statuesque with smooth chocolatey skin. Emily couldn't help but compare her own less-than-perfect skin to Chelsea's. Normally, Emily's caramel face was clear but her last one ... or two or three ... guilty pleasure trips to Fat Burgers had caused a small pimple to formulate on her lower chin. She hoped Chelsea didn't notice.

"Yeah, I guess I'm doing better than alright," Emily responded.

"Of course, you are in your beautiful yellow DeLois dress. I've been dying to get into one of those. Where'd you get it? It looks so good on you!" Chelsea said as she grabbed Emily's hand and twirled her around for a full view of her outfit. "Yessss, Emily. You better wear this dress!" Chelsea said, making Emily laugh at her flattery. It had taken venturing out to California for Emily to find her beauty and style. But now that she found it, she reveled in it.

"Girl, you're so crazy," Emily laughed. "I got it from Margaret & Jessie's. They have some good stuff in there."

"Oh yeah?" said Chelsea. "Well, maybe we can go shopping there one day or catch lunch. What's your number?" she asked as she dug in her purse for her phone.

"Absolutely we can do that one day," Emily agreed. Chelsea handed Emily her phone to save her number.

"I'll text you. Save my number when I do," Chelsea said. "It's good to know there's a familiar face in town. I'll hit you up soon. Talk to you later," Chelsea said as she swished away.

"Okay, it was nice seeing you. Looking forward to your text," Emily said as she waved, made her way to the register, purchased her items, and left.

Emily made way to her car and sailed down the boulevard. She glided down the Golden Gate Bridge and zoomed all the way home in her red convertible BMW. With Cali's #1 radio station for hip-hop and R&B playing as her background music, she sped past and jumped in front of all the Sunday drivers, displaying the rear end of her car that read "G R I T" on her license plate. Emily couldn't wait to get home. She was beat.

Earlier that day, a family had entered Hassen's looking for a new home. Emily happily set the family down to review budgets, credit scores, expectations, and the likes. She was sure she could help them find a great place, but the type of home the wife wanted was out of their price and credit range. Emily was never the one to sugar-coat facts and gave it to Mr. and Mrs. Donahue straight. However, Mrs. Donahue also had a 'straight-no-chaser' attitude and quickly refuted Emily's assessment of their possible future living arrangements.

"Aren't you Ms. Emily Waters, the best of the best? Surely you can work with our budget and credit," Mrs. Donahue said with a stern look and a slight roll of the neck.

"Of course, I can. I'll only do my best for you, and my best usually lands my clients in a home that they love," Emily reassured her. Yet

Emily didn't know if Mrs. Donahue thought she was a really good realtor or a really good magician with her absurd request.

"Usually?" Mrs. Donahue retorted before Mr. Donahue cut in on the conversation.

The rest of the consultation continued with a mixture of Mrs. Donahue's aggressive behavior and Mr. Donahue attempting to sooth his wife's quick tongue and temper. Emily's day hadn't started off so grand either. Between spilling coffee on her shirt, receiving the finger from someone who cut *her* off in traffic, getting the wrong order at lunch, and the lovely Mrs. Donahue, her day was less than fantastic. All she wanted to do was crash and watch a little TV.

Emily pulled into her condo driveway, grabbed her things, and headed inside. She relaxed with a hot shower and threw on her favorite luxury robe. Then she whipped up a quick meal, stretched across her plush sofa, and clicked on the TV. "What to watch? What to watch?" Emily sighed as she flipped through the channels. She decided to watch a drama series on the OWN network for a spell. Her phone lit up. Missed call from Stacey.

*"Ugh, I'll talk to you tomorrow, Stace,"* Emily thought. She and Stacey had never stopped being friends. Though they lived miles apart, their bond had never changed. She loved Stacey like a sister, but right now, she just wanted some alone time. Emily also thought about the missed call from her mother earlier that day. She had called when Mrs. Donahue was giving her a mouthful. *"I'll call her back tomorrow too,"* Emily thought, but for the time being, she just wanted to catch up on her show. She turned up the volume and tuned in.

*The water below crashes and churns. I'm floating again. Suspended above the rushing waves. The dark billows stretches out as far as my eyes can see. Black and gray clouds loom over me. There's a strange stillness in the atmosphere. Time drifts slowly. The sound of the ocean beneath is that of a deep moan ... as if it is weeping. The clouds above roll sluggishly. The elements are speaking. But I can't decipher its language. I have no control over my body. I only float between the heavens above and the ocean below.*

*As I hopelessly float, the ocean calms. The frothy foam dissipates. The once rushing waters now resemble a navy-blue mirror. I peer into the ocean. Something moves. The silhouette of a colossal creature appears just below the surface of the waters. My heart stops. A lump forms in my throat as I panic. I try to move. It's of no use. I'm stuck. I have no choice but to look at the ocean. So, I look and pray that I make it out alive.*

*I peer harder at the glassy water. The creature shifts its position. Its silhouette is now clear. It has wings and talons. It stretches out its wings under the dark, blue marine. Is it a pterodactyl? It must be. Or some other sort of prehistoric bird. Nothing in the modern-day world has a wingspan that large. I gasp for air as I examine its size. My God, what will I do if it emerges from the water? But it doesn't emerge. It only shifts again.*

*Is it stuck? Yes, I think it is. A muffled caw cries out from the ocean. No, I don't think its stuck ... I know its stuck. I examine its long talons. One of them is oddly turned downward toward the ocean. Something is pulling it. I can't make out what's holding it captive. All I can do is float. Float as the helpless creature squawks. Float as the clouds above silently roll. Float as time continues to stand still. All I can do is float. Float and pray.*

A sweet sunrise melody floats into Emily's head while she floats and prays. She slowly drifts back into consciousness and opens her eyes. She reaches down in-between the sofa cushions to turn off her phone alarm. She had fallen asleep on the couch and never woke up to go to bed. *"Goodness, I must've been more tired than I thought."* She lays there for a few more minutes. *"Why do I keep having this dream?"*

She must've had the same dream at least three times by now. *"It's so weird. Why am I dreaming about a dinosaur bird stuck in the ocean?"* Emily sat up on the sofa, still puzzled about the dream and the fact she had fallen asleep and stayed asleep all night on the couch. *"Whatever,"* she thought. She opened her Bible app to read the verse of the day, whispered a quick prayer, and hopped up from the sectional. *"Now, what's for breakfast?"*

Emily strolled into Hassen's with a seasonal peppermint truffle coffee. *"Maybe it'll give me a little holiday cheer,"* she thought as she placed her order at the quaint coffee shop on the way to work. She sipped her coffee and scarved down an omelet wrap as she zoomed down the freeway. She arrived at work, punctual as usual, and strode through the front door. Emily may've not felt Christmassy, but her office made up for her lackluster holiday spirit. In the foyer stood a 12-ft tall Christmas tree with a mini train surrounding it, along with faux presents. Many of her co-workers had their offices decked out in garlands, lights, and wreaths. The office looked like a mini wonderland. Christmas was two weeks away and she had yet to put a tree up in her home, let alone decorate her office.

"Peach!" yelled Tony Myers from the breakroom as she glided by. Tony Myers was probably one of the most charismatic, attractive men she'd ever met. Which is why she'd agreed to get to know him better over a year ago. He affectionately nicknamed her Peach on account of her being from Georgia, the Peach State. She'd thought the nickname was cute at first, but that stopped after she found out that Tony was a very married man.

Tony conveniently never wore his wedding band to work or any other place for that matter. She only discovered he was married because one of her co-workers told her when she saw them flirting with one another. Emily immediately shut Tony down from that day forward. She wasn't desperate for a man. If one came to her, so be it. But finding love wasn't on the top of her priority list.

"Good morning, Tony," Emily said through a fake smile. She could be cordial, but Tony always pushed it. "You going to the Christmas party next weekend?" he asked with a devilish grin on his face. Last year's Christmas party was a night filled with a tad too many spirits—and not holiday spirts. She and Tony had talked, texted, and flirted on the phone on and off for months. They also went on a few sporadic dates prior to the Christmas party. So, she was quite comfortable with him by the time the annual work holiday party occurred.

She and Tony both displayed light public affection towards one another at the party. She had a great time. Perhaps too great of a time. Emily, along with a few other co-workers, wasn't in the best condition to drive home after the festivities were over. So, Tony volunteered to carpool a few people home, including Emily. And he just so happened to make Emily his last stop.

When they arrived at her house, Tony asked if he could come in to use the restroom. She was hesitant. Emily had decided she would try her hand at celibacy after her last relationship. She had stuck to it even while randomly dating Tony. But she knew inviting him into her home would be playing with fire.

Yet, she let him in. They talked for a while before Tony did the inevitable. Initially, she had no willpower to stop his advances. He had on a tantalizing cologne, and he'd cleaned up more nicely than usual for the Christmas party. His dazzling smile, easy banter, and her one-too-many drinks almost caused her to break her celibacy. Almost. Emily stopped the escapade before it went too far. She was so glad that she did. The following Monday at work, Emily discovered that she would have laid with a married man.

Tony made his excuses. He said that he and his wife were estranged and that they lived separately. Emily never bothered to figure out if any of it was true, but Tony never stopped telling her that it was. And with that slick smile on his face, Emily could tell he was wishing they could pick up where they left off at the last Christmas celebration. "*Wishful thinking, Tony,*" Emily thought.

"No, I don't think so," Emily said as she kept walking. It wouldn't be Tony if he didn't follow and flirt with her for few minutes and on cue, he strolled out of the breakroom and walked alongside her. She rolled her eyes and breathed deeply as she waited for Tony's rebuttal. "Oh, come on, Peach. It'll be fun. Didn't you enjoy the last Christmas party? Or the events afterwards?" Tony bent down and whispered the last question so no one else could hear.

Emily stopped and faced him. "Tony, let me make this abundantly clear to you," she said in a firm yet quieted tone. "What happened between us was a mistake. And it won't ever happen again as long as I live, so help me God. Got it?" Emily glared at him with all the 'I ain't taking your mess' attitude she can muster. Tony backed up, hands in the air in a surrendered position.

"Got it," Tony said as he winked at her and smoothly walked away down the hallway. Emily was instantly upset with herself when his wink nearly made her knees buckle. "*Why does he have to be so fine?*" Emily sent up another quick prayer, "*God, I'm going to need you to help me keep that vow. I said never again, so help me God ... so help me God, help me.*"

On her lunch break, Emily remembered her missed calls from her mom and Stacey. She knew a conversation with Stacey would likely last longer than her lunch break, so, she opted to call her mom. "Hey mom. Sorry I missed your call. Everything alright?"

"Hey baby. Yes, everything is alright. I was just calling to see if you're coming home for Christmas." Elena Waters spoke into the phone with her soft-toned voice.

Emily had never missed going home for Christmas, but her mother asked her the same question every year. "Yes, ma'am I'll be there," Emily said.

"How long are you staying this time?" Elena asked.

"Only a week, Mom. You know I have to get back here to work." Sometimes Emily regretted spending limited time with her family, but no one was going to build her career for her. Sacrifices had to be made. Benjamin seemed to understand that more than Elena did.

"I know, I know Emi. But I can be hopeful, can't I?" Elena said with disappointment in her voice. "Hold on Emi baby." Elena yelled away from the phone "... What, babe? Yes, it's Emi ..." Elena returned to the phone. "Emi, your daddy wants to talk to you." Emily grinned from ear to ear. She loved to hear from her dad. He had a way of making her light up. She always felt like a little girl again whenever she spoke to him or when she was in his presence.

"How's my baby girl doing? You own half of California by now?" Emily laughed at her dad. He'd always told her she could be whoever she wanted to be if she worked hard at it. He'd quote Proverbs 14:23 to her. "All hard work brings a profit, baby girl, but mere talk leads to poverty." His words constantly played in her head like a radio. She attributed much of her success to his encouragement and belief in her.

"Not quite, Daddy, but I'm working on it. I'm doing good. Just working as usual. How are you? You been taking care of yourself?" Benjamin had been diagnosed with diabetes a year after Emily moved out to California. Benjamin wasn't too keen on change, especially a change in his diet. He continued to eat burgers, soul food, pasta, and anything else his tastebuds wanted when Elena wasn't around to stop him. He was retired but Elena worked part time as a substitute teacher. So, Benjamin had more than enough time away from his wife to indulge in his guilty pleasures.

"Yes, I'm taking care of myself, and I don't need you to hound me about it like your mom does." Emily knew he was likely lying but she didn't press the issue. "Mom's not hounding you, Dad, and neither am I. We're just checking in on you, making sure you're okay," Emily said.

"Well, I am, thank you very much, Nurse Waters," he answered sarcastically. Changing the subject, he asked "Any knuckleheads on the West Coast I need to rough up for messing with my daughter?"

Emily could hear her mom in the background. "I sure hope there's one ... She hasn't brought anyone home since Roger." Elena made her way closer to the phone, unaware that Emily had overheard her. Roger was her first and only real relationship. They were together for three years. They even talked about marriage. But Roger was given the opportunity of a lifetime to pursue his dreams in Chicago.

Emily encouraged him to go. Sometimes she wished she hadn't, but that was the past. Last she checked, he was in a relationship anyway. None if it mattered now. She didn't want to try the long-distance thing like Roger had suggested. She figured it would only prolong the ending of their relationship. She preferred a quick hit to the heart instead of a long drawn-out one.

"Oh, yes, Emi. Are you bringing anyone with you?" her mother asked.

"No, no one's coming home except me, Mom." Emily said, obviously annoyed.

"Good," Benjamin cut in before Emily could say anything else. "Now I don't have to clean the shotgun." Emily always thought it was funny how Dad threatened to be aggressive with his daughter's potential suitors but was nothing short of well-mannered when she and Estella brought their boyfriends home. She guessed it was just his way of illustrating his love for his girls.

"Well, I'm finishing up lunch. So, if I don't talk to you guys before I land, I'll see you in two weeks." Emily was ready to get off the phone before her mom asked her about her dating life. Her parents said their goodbyes and the call ended. Emily thought about her trip home. She was looking forward to seeing her family. Although she wasn't half bad in the kitchen herself, she couldn't hold a candle to her mom's southern home-cooked food. She couldn't wait to sink her teeth into her mom's delectable mac and cheese and red velvet cake. She could finally feel a slither of the holiday spirit seeping to her core, and she didn't mind it one bit.

# CHRISTMAS SEASON 2019
## SAVANNAH, GEORGIA

Nostalgia flooded Emily's senses every time she came home. Estella had picked her up from the airport roughly half an hour ago and they were now parked in front of their parents' home. Emily told Estella she could've rented a vehicle so as to not burden her. Estella was five months pregnant but insisted that she was pregnant, not handicapped. Surprisingly, she was not waddling like a penguin the way Emily had imagined, but she did have that beautiful, healthy glow that baby boys superstitiously give their mothers. Emily couldn't believe her little sister was having a baby and that she was a pending aunt. *"Crazy how time flies,"* Emily thought.

Emily gazed at the two-story house she and her sister grew up in. The porch steps led up toward two wooden rocking chairs that flagged the right and left side of the front door. The Spanish moss tree stood slightly off to the left of the house as it always had. A jovial wreath dotted with classic silver bells and ornaments hung on the door. Icicle lights dripped all around the perimeter of the house. Emily imagined Benjamin had complained about hanging the lights, while nevertheless hanging them to Elena's precise expectation.

Good times and good memories washed over Emily. She had never wanted for anything as a child. God had given her a great childhood and outstanding parents. She thought about how blessed she was as she watched the front door open and both parents stepped onto the porch with huge matching smiles on their faces. "There go your parents," Estella said with a grin. "Now, they can gush over you for a few minutes instead of me and their precious grandbaby to be". Emily returned the grin and stepped out of the car.

Her mother ran towards her as if she was the prodigal son. "Emily, baby. You look so good!" her mother said, embracing her tightly. They were cheek to cheek and Emily could feel the love oozing from her mother's pores.

"Thank you. I missed y'all," Emily said with her eyes closed, taking in her mother's sweet perfume.

"Oh, you know we missed you more, baby," Elena chuckled. Benjamin stood behind Elena, waiting for his turn to embrace Emily.

"Hey, Daddy," Emily said as she laid her head on his chest.

"Hey, amber eyes," he responded.

Emily recalled how her dad would occasionally mention her eyes when she was younger. He'd say, "Your eyes shine like jewelry... they look like ambers." Ignorant of what ambers were and finally wanting an answer to her lingering question, Emily asked, "Who is Amber?" She remembered how her dad let out a good hearty laugh before he'd said, "No, baby. Ambers are stones. They're honey, golden-colored stones and your eyes like look them." He'd showed her pictures of ambers on their desk-top computer. "Oh," was all Emily could utter at her new discovery.

"Well, let's get settled inside," Benjamin said after releasing Emily from his grip. "I'll bring the luggage in. Y'all go on in."

"Let me help you with that, Pops," yelled Reggie from the front door. Emily would have never guessed that her old classmate, Reginald Jones, would grow up and marry her little sister. They had been married for four years now. She liked Reggie. She thought he and Estella were a good fit for each other. Emily and Reggie had a comedic relationship. She always brought up beating his red-string record in some form or fashion.

"Take it easy now bro-law. We don't need you trying to set any luggage-carrying records that I'll end up breaking," Emily smirked at Reggie before jokingly punching his chest.

"Go head on now, Em. It's too early for all that." He laughed Emily off and gave her a quick hug before helping Benjamin. The women make their way inside, out of the cool air. As soon as Emily stepped inside, a waft of homecooked food assaulted her nostrils. It was only the day before Christmas Eve, but Elena made it her business to cook quality meals as often as she could when her family was united.

"Mmm," Emily said. "What you cooking today, Ma?"

"Chicken pot pie. And we're having peach cobbler with vanilla ice cream for dessert," Elena said proudly.

"Oh, goodness Mom," Emily said.

"Look at God!" Estella exclaimed, "I get first dibs... I'm eating for two."

"Whatever, sis. As long as I get my share, we're good," Emily said as she looked over at the kitchen table. As per usual, Elena had it superbly set for their holiday dinners. Bright red poinsettias sat in the middle of the table. Jazzy Christmas music played softly from the living room. It felt good to be home.

Benjamin and Reggie trucked through the front door with Emily's luggage. She'd brought a vast amount of her belongings with her. Her plan was to stay until Monday, which would make one full week. Christmas was Wednesday and she would have flown back on Friday for work, but her cousin Julianne was getting married on Saturday. Julianne had planned her wedding around the holidays to ensure most of her family could come. It seemed to work. Her husband-to-be apparently had a huge extended family like theirs. Their guests list ended up being 300 people—and that was after final cuts were made.

Emily wanted to show her support, so she decided to fly back Monday morning. She also wanted to visit her childhood church home. Benjamin and Elena were still faithful members at the same congregation. She'd never joined a congregation in California. She frequented a few churches that she liked, but she'd never found a place she considered home. Maybe it was because she wasn't in the habit of attending church every Sunday like she did as a child.

Emily attended church services when she felt so inclined, but she usually opted to play gospel music at home on Sunday mornings while she cooked brunch. Sometimes she would catch a broadcasted sermon. Church in pajamas wasn't half bad in her opinion. Yet, she thought it would be nice to feel at home again in her old church.

"Dang, Em. Did you pack your whole house or just half of it?" Reggie asked as he burst through the door, struggling to carry Emily's luggage.

"I mean, Reg... I carried them to Estella's car no problem. Sounds like you need the champ's help," Emily retorted.

"Here y'all go," said Estella as she rolled her eyes with a small smirk on her face.

"I ain't studyin' you, Em," Reggie said as he hauled her luggage up to her old room. Elena had kept the girls' old bedrooms in mint condition. The girls knew that if hard times ever hit, they'd always have a place to stay.

A few hours later, the family dug into dinner and dessert. They finished the evening watching classic Christmas movies. Emily excused herself to speak to Stacey on the phone for a few minutes before she was off to bed. Stacey was also in town visiting her parents for the holidays. Emily had returned Stacey's missed phone call back in Cali and they'd agreed to have a girls' night out on Friday evening. Food, drinks, the movies, or maybe a night club. They still hadn't decided.

Stacey lived in Florida with her boyfriend of two years. She had managed to establish a reputable cupcake business in Orange County. Stacey's boyfriend, Walter, was a lawyer. Emily didn't know too much about Walter, but she did know he was always too busy with work. And when he wasn't working, he seemed aloof—or at least that's what she'd gathered from conversations with Stacey. Emily thought Stacey could do better, but Stacey loved him, and that was good enough for her.

Emily ended the call with her friend and turned off the light. Her gymnastics trophies remained in their same places. In high school, Emily ran track, and those medals were hanging in their respective places as well. She sighed. Although she was excelling in her career, sometimes she thought there was more of herself that she could offer. There was an itch on her soul that she couldn't quite scratch. She felt as if her competitive spirit needed to offer more to the world besides working at Hassen's. She knew there was more in her than what was coming out but had no clue as to what that might be. Her thoughts ran through her mind as she drifted off to sleep.

# THE WEDDING

Christmas Eve and Christmas Day went along as it traditionally did. The 3 E's and the B—Emily, Elena, Estella, and Benjamin, as Reggie called them—all exchanged gifts and ate a spectacular dinner on Christmas Eve. On Christmas Day, the extended family—aunts, uncles, cousins, and more—all came together for a grand southern Christmas gathering. They played games, exchanged more gifts, talked, laughed, and ate to their heart's content. It was as great as expected except for a small cousin Julianne issue.

Julianne was a ball of nerves on Christmas Day. She was noticeably stressed. There was a problem with her caterer, which caused a normally docile Julianne to transform into an unyielding bridezilla. Emily hoped her bachelorette party had taken some of the stress away. Julianne invited Emily to her bachelorette party on Christmas Day. Emily hated to cancel on Stacey at the last minute, but Julianne needed all the comforting she could get. Stacey was disappointed, but she understood.

The bachelorette party turned out well. They drank champagne, ate fancy sandwiches, and played wholesome bridal games. Cousin Melinda called it bougie. "Y'all ain't got no strippers?" Melinda asked with not a shred of tact. Emily shook her head and tried to stifle a giggle at Melinda's shamelessness. Melinda was Melinda.

"Can't pick your family," Auntie Paulina whispered in Emily's ear. There was genuine love amongst the family, just differences in opinions and the occasional squabble. Emily was putting on the final touches of her makeup and wondered how Julianne was doing at that very moment. The wedding was 45 minutes away.

"Come on Emi, let's go! We're leaving in the next few minutes." Benjamin yelled up the stairs.

"Coming!" Emily yelled back. She tossed her lipstick into her clutch and made her way down the stairs.

"Well, aren't you a sight for sore eyes," Benjamin said as Emily floated down the stairwell. Estella let out a flirtatious whistle.

"Okay, brickhouse!" she exclaimed. Emily blushed at her family's comments.

"Thank you," Emily said as she playfully curtsied in her pastel purple dress. "Y'all don't look half bad yourselves."

Everyone had on their Sunday's best. Talks of Julianne and Joseph's wedding had gone on for months. It was a black-tie 'Winter Wonderland' themed wedding and was expected to be the most extravagant family event of the year. Apparently, Julianne had married into money and her soon to be mother-in-law was willing to break the bank for her only child's wedding.

"Lucky Julianne," said some heckling family members to Julianne on Christmas Day.

"No, she's just blessed," Emily retorted while sashaying away from the gossiping huddle.

Emily and the family piled into their cars and make their way down to the cathedral where the ceremony would take place. They arrived and filed in line with a few other guests who were making their way up the steps to the massive building. Once inside, Emily gasped. It was breathtakingly beautiful. She had never seen a space so gorgeously decorated. *"As if it needs decorations?"* Emily thought.

The architecture of the cathedral was remarkable. The height of the ceilings, the vastness of the building, and the antique workmanship made a grand statement on its own. But the flowers, candles, crystalized embellishments, and glitzy winter white trees that reached towards the ceiling took the ambience over the top. Everyone had expected extravagance, and no one was disappointed.

The family made their way over to the bride's side and took their seats. A violinist stood to the side of the wedding arch playing a romantic tune as everyone waited for the wedding to begin. Light chatter hummed under the lulling music. Emily scanned the room. She recognized most, if not all, of the bride's side. Glancing over, she could see there were just as many people seated on the groom's side as the bride's side. It appeared that all 300 members on the guest list showed up. She looked back toward the entrance and watched as a gentleman sat down toward the back on the groom's side.

Emily didn't realize she was staring at him until he made eye contact with her. She quickly turned her head, hoping he didn't see her gawking at him. He was handsome. Tall. Dark. He had a certain air about him that caused her eyes to linger a little longer than they probably should have. Estella snapped her out of her thoughts. "I keep looking all over this place too. It's stunning," she said.

"Yeah, downright beautiful," Emily replied. Yet, Emily's comment was more about the beautiful man in the back than it was about the building or décor.

The ceremony was lovely. When Julianne walked through the door, Emily shed a tear. She was such a beautiful bride. Her husband-to-be Joseph also shed a single tear as she walked down the aisle towards him. They exchanged vows and rings and said, "I do". The bride and groom were whisked off in a Cinderella-style carriage pulled by two majestic Clydesdales. It was a true fairy-tale wedding.

Everyone was now at the reception, mingling and eating hors d'oeuvres until the bride, groom, and wedding party arrived. Emily nursed a cocktail while talking to a few of her family members, including her unashamed cousin Melinda. "I ain't going to lie," Melinda said, "I think this was over the top and siddity. But if I had it like them, I'd have a wedding just like this too. Girl, how much you think they spent on all this because, honey, I know all this costs a pretty penny."

Emily sipped her drink before she responded. "I honestly don't know. $40K maybe? But hey, mother-in-law wanted the best for Joseph, so who are we to count their expenses?"

"Child, me!" Melinda exclaimed. "Shoot, I'm trying to count their expenses so I can see just how good they have it. I mean, they must have some *mon-ey*." Melinda said rubbing her index and thumb together as if she had cash in her hand. "Y'all sure Joseph don't have a brother?" she asked.

"Girl, no!" Emily said as she playfully slapped Melinda's shoulder and walked away from the group toward a tray of delicacies she'd been eyeing.

"I was just asking," Melinda cackled from behind her. Emily shook her head and shooed her. She turned her head back around and there he was. The beautiful man from the back of the church. She'd caught herself secretly looking for him this entire time but hadn't found him. It was like he had disappeared after the ceremony. She thought maybe he hadn't come to the reception, but there he was sitting on a bench just outside the reception area by himself.

"*Surely he's here with someone,*" Emily thought. She moseyed around the room pretending to be in pursuit of appetizers and good wine. She needed to see if anyone might interact with her new-found interest. No one approached him from what she could see, but her investigation was interrupted when the DJ announced it was time for the bride, groom, and wedding party's grand entrance. When she turned back towards the bench, he was gone.

Everyone had backed away from the entrance and made a path for the guests of honor. It was easy to lose someone in a crowd of 300 people. Besides, Emily knew she wouldn't approach Mr. Beautiful even if she did lay eyes on him again. "*He's just eye candy,*" she reasoned. So, Emily danced and laughed the night away with her family. Even Benjamin and Elena hit the dance floor for the Electric Slide. She did catch one more glimpse of the beautiful man in the navy-blue suit as everyone was leaving, but that was it.

Emily was ready to get out of her clothes, shoes, and makeup so she could hit the sheets. "Church in the morning!" Elena yelled as they entered the house. "Get some rest. Service starts at 10." Sometimes Elena talked to her and Estella as if they were still little children. Not in a disrespectful way, just in an assertive motherly tone. Emily and Estella always responded as if they were still the same little children their mother had carefully raised.

"Yes, ma'am." Emily, Estella, and even Reggie responded. If momma said church started at 10:00 a.m., then doggone it, Emily had to be at church at 9:57 a.m. on the dot. "You need three extra minutes to get yourself together in the car," Elena always said. So, Emily made ready for bed. She sent up a quick prayer, buried herself beneath the covers, and drifted off to sleep.

## SUNDAY MORNING

Emily woke up to the smell of bacon and the sound of gospel music. She glanced at her phone. It was a little past 7:00 a.m. She wanted to stay in bed a little longer, but the promise of a tasty breakfast hanging thick in the air was too tempting to ignore. She rolled out of bed, took a quick pitstop at the bathroom to freshen up, and headed downstairs.

"Good morning, Emi," Elena said as she reached in the oven for a pan of hot buttermilk biscuits.

"Good morning, Ma. You need help with anything?"

"You can finish setting the table ... and get that orange juice out the fridge too, baby." Emily hopped to Elena's request. As she set the table, Estella came bounding down the stairs.

"What can I do, Momma?" she asked. "You can sit down and feed my grandbaby in about two minutes," Elena said as she smiled at Estella.

Estella gave up on her declaration of being able-bodied and simply said, "Yes, ma'am." Reggie came down the stairs shortly after, followed by Benjamin. Benjamin headed towards the kitchen and wrapped his arms around Elena's waist. "What you got cookin' this morning, Mrs. Waters?" he asked as he kissed her cheek. Elena blushed. Emily and Estella hated to see Benjamin and Elena's public affection when they were younger. They would stick their tongues out in disgust and beg them to stop.

They thought differently now. It was encouraging to see a couple stay together for 30+ years and still maintain a youthful-like fondness toward one another. A few years ago, Emily and Estella had thrown a 30-year wedding anniversary celebration for their parents. Every so often, Emily would watch the video on her phone of her parents slow dancing to Al Green's *Let's Stay Together*. Emily adored their relationship. If she couldn't have a love like theirs, she didn't want love at all.

"Sit on down, Benjamin," Elena smiled as she swatted Benjamin's hand. "We're having biscuits or pancakes ... or both ... Whichever y'all would prefer. Bacon or sausage, and grits, and eggs ... Just a little something to put on y'alls' stomach before service."

"A little something?" Reggie questioned. "This is a whole lot more than a little something, Mom." A couple of yeses and head nods followed Reggie's statement.

"It was no bother," Elena said as she threw up her hand in protest. "I just needed to make sure everyone had options. Y'all go ahead and eat before it gets cold."

Very light conversation occurred as everyone passed jellies, syrups, and dishes across the table. Everyone needed to shower and get ready in time for service. With only two bathrooms in the house, little time could be spent lollygagging. After breakfast, Emily, along with the rest of the family headed back upstairs to get dressed. Once everyone was ready, they all trucked out the door for Sunday service.

Emily stepped into the familiar old-fashioned church. The building had undergone some remodeling, but the atmosphere remained the same. If the people at Healing Rose didn't know how to do anything, they knew how to make people feel welcomed, and they knew how to praise God. As soon as the Waters family stepped into the church, they were greeted by First Lady Peoples. First Lady Peoples was a powerful prayer warrior with a bubbly personality. Her bubbliness was a stark contrast to Pastor Peoples.

Pastor Peoples was as bold as a lion in the pulpit, but he was usually as quiet as a church mouse under ordinary circumstances. He always seemed to be in deep thought, and it appeared he deliberately contemplated all his responses before he responded to anything. "Oh, my goodness. Well, looka here!" First Lady said as she walked toward Emily with open arms. First Lady was, as the old people say, 'casket sharp' in her classic church hat embellished with intricate designs and a sparkling brooch.

"Emily, don't you look beautiful. It's so good to see you ... and Estella I couldn't be happier for you and Reggie on your new addition. You are glowing! ... Sister Waters, Brother Waters, it's good to see y'all as always. I know y'all are glad to have your children in town." First Lady Peoples continued with her greetings and hugs. Several other members greeted them before it was time for service to begin. Emily was glad to see everyone. She was looking forward to the singing and the message from Pastor Peoples. They took their seats towards the front of the church as Elena led the way.

The worship and singing were like medicine to Emily's bones. Though she didn't realize she was thirsty, her soul was quenched. She closed her eyes, clapped her hands, and swayed to the praises that filled the building. Right before Pastor Peoples was due to take the podium, a young man sang a song so beautifully, so full of adoration towards God, that Emily had to excuse herself from the sanctuary once he ended the song. He sang a rendition of *Hosanna*. Emily had heard the song before, but she had never heard anyone sing it quite the way he had.

The young man sang as if only he and God were in the room. He sang it truthfully, from his heart. There wasn't a soul in the building who could deny how he ushered the spirit of true worship into the room. Once he finished the song, Emily rose from her seat to wipe her tears in the restroom. On the way out, she saw him. Mr. Beautiful. There he was on the backrow with his hands raised toward the ceiling in full out worship.

"Glory Hallelujah to your name, Jesus! We give you praises God! Hosanna in the highest, oh God!" he shouted out in a clear baritone voice. Emily continued out the backdoor and made a beeline for the restroom. She looked in the mirror. Her eyes were bloodshot red, and her eye makeup was running. She reached into her bag and pulled at her travel-sized makeup kit for a quick touch-up. *"What are the odds of him being here?"* Emily thought as she grabbed the door handle to exit the bathroom. But she didn't give it much more thought. She had to hurry back to catch the sermon.

When Emily stepped back into the sanctuary, Pastor Peoples was reading a familiar passage. She tiptoed her way up the aisle and sat back down next to Estella. "What's the scripture?" she whispered to her sister.

"Psalm 91," Estella replied.

*... If you say, "The Lord is my refuge,"*
*and you make the Most High your dwelling,*
*no harm will overtake you,*
*no disaster will come near your tent.*
*For he will command his angels concerning you*
*to guard you in all your ways;*
*they will lift you up in their hands,*
*so that you will not strike your foot against a stone.*

> *You will tread on the lion and the cobra;*
> *you will trample the great lion and the serpent.*
> *"Because he loves me," says the Lord, "I will rescue him;*
> *I will protect him, for he acknowledges my name.*
> *He will call on me, and I will answer him;*
> *I will be with him in trouble,*
> *I will deliver him and honor him.*
> *With long life I will satisfy him*
> *and show him my salvation."*

"If I had to choose a title for today's sermon, it would be called 'You Will Tread', Pastor Peoples said as he peered out into the audience. "I've come to realize, at my ripe old age, that life isn't always pleasant. Sometimes we will suffer. Sometimes we will have pain ... and if we were to be honest about it, sometimes we question our afflictions and we question God's decision to allow the afflictions." A couple of 'uh-huhs' and 'Amens' rose from the crowd.

Pastor Peoples continued, "We wonder why God places these burdens on us. Some of you have been betrayed. Some of you have been lied on. Some of you suffer from depression. Some of you have lost loved ones. Yet, others have wayward children or perhaps you are battling sickness." Pastor Peoples paced the pulpit slowly and spoke even slower. "And some of you just don't understand why. You don't get God. You don't understand how a loving God could allow such terrible pain." Emily listened to Pastor Peoples, but she admittedly also had Mr. Beautiful on her mind.

She wanted to turn around to get another glance at him but decided it wasn't the best idea. Instead, she turned her attention back to the sermon. "And if I was to be honest," Pastor Peoples continued, "I can't answer your question in great detail." He paused and surveyed the congregation. "Maybe some of you are being tested. Recall Abraham was tested by God. Maybe some of you are being set up for a comeback. Remember how Joseph was sold into slavery and thrown into prison as a mere launching pad to be second in command over all of Egypt."

Pastor Peoples stopped again and rested his hands on the podium. "Oh, but if I was to be honest ... some of us are going through trails of our own doing."

"Preach, preacher!" someone yelled from the audience.

"Some of us, and I do mean us—I have to include myself in that number because I've been there ... I haven't always been saved," Pastor said as he comically widened his eyes from behind his glasses. There were a few chuckles from the crowd.

"Some of us are very much so like the children of Israel. We keep sinning against God. But when we are faced with the consequences of our sin, we wonder why we are going through hard times." Pastor Peoples said with a stern look on his face. But his stern look quickly turned into a giant smile. "Oh, but God! God is faithful and just enough to forgive us of our sins. Every time the children of Israel cried out to God, He delivered them."

"God's love and His grace is from everlasting to everlasting. What greater love than a man to lay down his life for us, especially when we were yet sinners? If Christ died for you, surely, He's willing to deliver you." Pastor's voice echoed throughout the building. His passion showed as he preached. By this time, he had stepped down from the podium and was pacing the floor at the front of the church. "All you must do is repent! Repent and be baptized for the remission of your sins!"

"Now, let's be clear. I am not insinuating that everyone who is going through hard times are struggling because of sin. We all know Job was a perfect and upright man. Yet, he lost everything." Pastor's eyes were burning with fire. Sweat had started to form and fall down from his brows. He wiped the sweat with a white handkerchief one of the deacons had handed him earlier. "What I am telling you is that no one is exempt from tough times. God Himself endured the cross! Are you not to bear your cross too?"

"But listen to me. Regardless of the reasoning behind your struggle, whether it's by your own hands or by God's intentional design, you can tread. You will tread. We see here in the scripture that God said we would tread on the lion and the adder. The adder ain't nothing but that snake. It's Satan, your #1 enemy. But somebody ought to praise God in here because God said you can tread on that great deceiver. You will tread! You are more than a conqueror, and if God is for you, who can be against you?" A slew of 'Amens' and 'Hallelujahs' echoed around the building.

"God said because you have chosen to set your love on Him, He will rescue you. Because you acknowledge Him, He will protect you. God said He will be with you in trouble." Pastor was pointing his index finger towards the congregation. "Did you catch that? God said, *in trouble* He would be with you ... which means there will be trouble. Oh, I know you don't want to hear it, but it's the truth. In this life you, you are going to have your fair share of troubles. But praise be to God, as long as you have God by your side, you will tread."

Pastor continued with his sermon. It was concluded with an uplifting congregational hymn. Announcements, tithes, and communion proceeded as scheduled. A little after lunchtime, service was over. Emily, her family, and the congregation, all spilled out of the sanctuary into the vestibule. More hugs and greetings from old faces were given and received after service. After chatting with an old roommate from vacation Bible school, Emily went to the restroom for a quick moment before the family headed out for lunch. They had all agreed to dine at a local soul food restaurant.

As she made her way back up the hallway from the restroom, she heard someone call her name. "Emily, Emily Waters, right?" Emily turned around. It was him. Mr. Beautiful.

*"How on earth does he know my name?"* Emily thought before she responded.

"Yes ..." she replied with an arched eyebrow.

"Hi, I'm Angelo Heights. Aren't you from Cali?" Emily eyed him suspiciously. He spoke again before she could respond. "I recognize your face from a couple of advertisements back home in San Francisco. I'm stationed there. You helped one of my old comrades close on a home ... You may remember him, Louis Sanchez?"

"Oh, yes! I remember Louis. That was a few years back," Emily said. She remained wary of him. Why did he recognize her face and name from a few ads in California and from a client she'd had almost five years ago? And how was it that he was a Californian but conveniently in Georgia at the same time she was back home?

Angelo spoke again. "I'm sorry. This may be a little awkward. I'm actually looking for a home back in Cali and you come highly recommended in the Bay Area."

Emily eased at his confession of searching for a home. She even managed to give a smile, though she still found it odd that he was in Georgia the same time that she was there.

"Well, I can absolutely help you with your home search," Emily responded. She was tempted to reach into her purse and grab her business card, but she held off until she'd posed a few questions. Though he was mysteriously attractive, who was to say stalkers and psychos weren't charming and good looking?

"Odd that we both live in California and are both here in Georgia at the same time, don't you think? If I'm not mistaken, I saw you at a wedding yesterday. How do you know the couple?"

Angelo gave a quick smile. "Yes, one may say it is odd. I'm in the army and served in war with Joseph while in Iraq. I thought it only fair to witness him tie the knot."

"*Umm,*" Emily thought, "*Julianne did mention Joseph touring in Iraq ... I guess his story checks out. But let me dig a little more. He said he was stationed in San Francisco. There's a burger joint close to the military base that I want to try out one day. He should know the general area if he's really stationed there.*"

"Well, that's nice of you to fly out for their wedding. So, where exactly is the military base in Cali if you don't mind me asking?"

"Oh, I don't mind at all," Angelo answered. "It's near 1st Street, close by B.A. Burgers and that jazz lounge. I think it's called Adeline's." "*Okay, I think he's legit. I guess it's safe to show him a couple of empty houses without concern,*" Emily thought.

"Oh, yes, that's right. B.A. Burgers is close by the base. Well, here's my card. Call me and I'll be happy to help you find a new home." Angelo took her card and placed it in his pocket.

"Thank you, I'll be in touch."

"Well, enjoy the rest of your day," Emily said. "I have a group of hungry family members waiting on me."

"You as well, Ms. Waters," Angelo said as he nodded a farewell.

"*Umm, looking for a home in Cali ... military man. I wonder what's his story? Married? Children?*" Emily walked out the door to catch up with her family. As she climbed in the car, she saw Mr. Heights walking out of the church. His last name suits him well she thought.

He was at least 6'2 and he walked with a certain measure of authority. Shoulders back, head up. There was a seriousness about his demeanor. He seemed disciplined. More disciplined than most soldiers she'd come across. "*I'll learn more about Mr. Angelo Heights when I return to Cali,*" Emily thought. But for now, it was time for some good ol' southern soul food with her family.

Tears rolled down Emily's cheeks from laughing at her dad. She was trying to finish her sweet tea but was afraid she'd choke if she took another sip. Benjamin was a great impersonator, and he was acting out a scene from a classic comedy. Emily could hardly catch her breath. Everyone at the table was boiling over from laughter at Benjamin's performance.

"Whoa! Goodness, Daddy! You're so crazy," Estella said as she grabbed the bottom of her rounded belly.

"Benjamin, you need to stop before you send my daughter into premature labor," Elena said as she caught her breath from giggling.

"Man, Pops, what are we going to do with you?" Reggie said.

"You just gonna have to put up with me," Benjamin teased. He'd decided to let his family take a break from their gut-wrenching laughter when the waitress made her way back to the table.

"Are you guys having dessert?"

"Yes, I think I'll have some banana pudding," Benjamin stated. "Y'all getting anything?" Everyone was stuffed from the meal and declined.

"Okay, one banana pudding coming up," the peppy waitress said as she grabbed empty plates from the table.

She quickly returned with Benjamin's dessert. He scooped a spoonful of whipped cream, pudding, and cookies into his mouth. "Mmm, y'all don't know what you're missing," he said. He closed his eyes in food heaven as he continued his dive into the dessert. Then suddenly, Benjamin's eyes started to water. He grabbed at his chest as if he was struggling to breathe. Emily hopped up in a panic.

"Daddy, what's wrong?!"

Elena had already sprung into action. She dialed 911 from her cellphone. Estella and Reggie rushed to Benjamin's side, unsure of how to assist.

"Yes ... yes...we're at the soul food restaurant off of Decatur Street," Elena said into the phone. "Please hurry," she said as she ended the call. "The ambulance is on the way, baby, just hold tight," she said to Benjamin.

"Mom, what's wrong with him?" Emily asked, barely holding herself together. Elena seemed too calm, given the circumstances. She continued to reassure Benjamin as if she hadn't heard Emily's question.

"Mom! What's wrong with Daddy?" Emily shouted. It wasn't her intention to yell, but she was distraught and wanted to know why her mother was not. Elena took a deep breath and exhaled slowly. "Your father is having a heart attack, Emily. We were told to be prepared for the worst, and it looks as if the worst has come."

## ACT II

"Prepare for what? And what do you mean the worst has come?" Emily asked, overcome with anxiety. Elena looked from Emily to Estella and back to Benjamin. She lowered her eyes to the floor as she girded herself to divulge the truth. "Your dad has kidney failure. His diabetes took a turn for the worse earlier this year. He started dialysis about two months ago." Although he was writhing in pain, Benjamin tried to grab Elena's arm. Elena knew he was trying to silence her. "No," she said. "They need to know what's going on."

"He normally goes three times a week. But he didn't want y'all to see him after treatments. Dialysis takes so much out of him. No parent wants their children to worry about them." Elena paused while she fluttered back tears. "So, he decided to miss treatments this week and start again next week."

"Daddy ..." was all Estella managed to say.

Emily chimed in and finished saying what Estella couldn't. "Daddy, are you crazy? And Mom why didn't you stop him? Why would you miss your treatments? And why didn't y'all tell us about any of this? We are not babies anymore. Why wouldn't you tell ..."

"Watch your tone, Emi" Elena interrupted while giving Emily a stern look.

Emily took in a short breath and proceeded an octave lower. "Why didn't y'all tell us about this Momma?"

Elena tossed up her hands. "You know your daddy," she replied, "He didn't want y'all to see him like that, in a weakened state." Reggie made Estella sit down and take deep breaths.

"No point in the ambulance being here for the both of you," he reasoned. Seated in a chair with Reggie rubbing her back for ease, Estella asked, "And what do you mean by prepare for the worst, Momma?"

Elena looked at Estella and then down towards her swollen belly. She took another deep breath. "I called the doctor and asked him about side effects of missed treatments ... He said the symptoms could be bad."

"How bad?" Emily asked, bracing herself for the answer.

"It could lead to fluid build-up, stroke, heart attack..." Elena trialed off. Estella and Emily remained silent as their eyes darted back and forth between their mother and father. Neither sister wanted to ask the unthinkable. They didn't dare ask if it could lead to their dad leaving this earth. That was too much to think about.

"Where is that ambulance?" Emily yelled in frustration.

"Calm down, Emily. They're own the way," Elena tried to soothe her.

"Let's just get Daddy to the car. I can get him there quicker than waiting for the ambulance," Emily said, determined to do something, anything. She felt hopeless as she watched her dad in agony.

"No," Elena said. "Let's wait for the ambulance so they can help him on the way to the hospital. It'll be okay, Emily. Just calm down." Emily tried to take her mom's advice, but she couldn't.

"I can't take this," Emily said as she stormed out of the restaurant.

She paced back and forth in the brisk wind outside. Her mind drew a blank as to what she could do to help. Fear crept up her neck and chilled her bones.

*"Pray."* She stopped mid-stride. She hadn't thought about praying, and she had no clue where the thought came from, but she didn't waste another second in contemplation. *"Dear Lord, please help my daddy. Please Lord, I can't do this without him. I need him here, Lord. Please help him ... please ...please ..."*

Emily's head popped up at the sound of sirens. The ambulance was coming.

"Oh, thank you, Jesus! It's about time ... Now please, let him be okay," she whispered with her hands folded tightly in front of her chest. She waited for the first responders to hop out of the truck before she rushed toward them. "My mom called you. I'll show you where he is."

They followed Emily inside the restaurant toward Benjamin. They immediately checked his vitals, hauled him onto the stretcher, and made their way back to the ambulance. Elena climbed in the back with Benjamin. Emily, Estella, and Reggie rushed to the car. They followed the ambulance to the hospital and prayed for a good report the entire way there.

The doctor walked towards Elena, Emily, Estella, and Reggie. Emily was unknowingly holding her breath as the doctor walked towards them. She felt faint and was certain she was close to passing out. She grabbed her mother and Estella's hands for support. Reggie stretched his arms across their backs in an attempt to provide some sort of security.

"He's going to be okay," the doctor said.

Emily exhaled. "Oh, thank God!" she exclaimed. Elena hugged her firmly as Reggie embraced Estella.

"I told you not to worry, Emily," Elena whispered in her ear, "God is always with us, be it good or be it bad." Emily always thought her mom was dainty, frail even, but today, she saw her in a different light. Her mother was a rock.

"But Mr. Waters will have to remain on his regular scheduled dialysis treatments. He can't put himself in danger like this again. Have you all given my other suggestion any more thought?" the doctor asked.

"He said he wants to stick with dialysis for now," Elena said quickly.

"Okay, but please consider it. Dialysis can be taxing on the body long-term. Give him a few minutes and you guys can go in to see him." The doctor gave a tight smile and walked away.

"What does the doctor suggest, Momma?" Estella asked.

Elena was tired. Emotionally and spiritually, she was just tired. It was hard trying to take care of a husband who refused to be taken care of. It was equally frustrating trying to explain to her children that she couldn't make a grown man do anything, no matter how much she tried. Through it all, she still smiled, took care of home, and continued to be a mother because that's what mothers do. But she was tired.

Elena rubbed her fingers across her forehead and temples as if she was trying to rub the stress away. "Girls, if you don't mind, I just need a minute, okay?" Emily and Estella knew what Elena meant. They were putting her under pressure, and she needed a 'mommy minute' as she used to say when they were children. They backed off and waited in silence to be called in to see Benjamin.

"He's ready," a nurse said to them as they waited in the holding area. They made their way down the cold corridor and walked into the room. Benjamin was reclined in the bed with multiple plastic tubes extending in various directions from his body. Besides a common cold or a case of the flu, Emily had never seen her dad down. She didn't realize it until that very moment, but she thought of her dad as invincible. Seeing him in this condition was a chilling reality check for her. Her parents were getting older. The need to spend more time with them came over her like a flood.

"Hey," Benjamin croaked out. He tried to sit up to maintain some of his dignity.

"Lie down, Benjamin," Elena said in a somber voice. "You don't have to pretend to be strong right now." Benjamin twisted his face in discomfort. It was hard to tell if it was from physical discomfort or emotional embarrassment.

"We're glad you're okay, Pops," Reggie said.

"Yes, Daddy," Estella added. "We just want what's best for you. We need you to take care of yourself." Emily walked over to Benjamin and peered down at him. Words wouldn't formulate on her tongue.

"Aw, Emi, don't look at me like that," Benjamin said. "Get all of that pity out of your eyes. I'm okay." Emily knew she should probably wait to ask, but she needed answers. She needed her daddy to be present as long as possible, and if there were other options that he refused to consider, Emily needed to know why.

"Daddy, the doctor said there were other options that he suggested you consider. What are they?"

Benjamin looked at Emily, then scanned the room to observe the rest of his family. Against Elena's request, he sat up in the bed to speak. "He suggested a kidney transplant," Benjamin said giving Emily direct eye contact, "but if you think I'm letting anybody cut on me, you can think again." Emily stared hard at her dad. She had never stood-off in a confrontation with him before, but she was about to today. She gulped and straightened her posture before she took her stance. She knew he could be stubborn, because she was stubborn and had inherited the trait from him. This wasn't going to be an easy task.

"Daddy, the doctor said long-term dialysis isn't ideal. What are you expecting? To live on dialysis for the rest of your life?" Emily searched her daddy's face, hoping he would give a logical answer.

"It isn't ideal for whom?" Benjamin responded. "Because what is *not* ideal for me is to allow someone to cut me open like some sort of science project." He managed to find the strength to protest. "No, what's ideal for me is to remain intact the way God made me."

"Would God have you ignore a procedure that could possibly extend your life?" Emily questioned him. Benjamin glared at her.

"Would God have you stand in my face and disrespect *my* decision on what to do with *my* life?" Benjamin was angrily pointing his fingers toward his chest.

Estella chimed in, "Daddy, she doesn't mean any disrespect and you know that, but your decision doesn't affect just you. It affects all of us."

"I mean, Daddy, c'mon." Emily continued, "We can't base current decisions on things that went wrong in the past."

Benjamin's mother, Grandma Hope, had died in the hospital after having open heart surgery. The family had initially pursued a lawsuit against the hospital. Grandma Hope's death could have been prevented if her doctor or attendants had listened to her complaints after the surgery, but the hospital staff had ignored her pleas. She died two days after surgery while being 'monitored by the physician' per the medical records. Eventually, the family dropped the lawsuit. The red tape and legalities only prolonged their grief and deepened their debt. Benjamin had never let that experience leave his psyche.

"Oh, we can't?" he asked sarcastically. "I beg your pardon, but that's exactly what I am doing and will continue to do. That's just plain common sense to me. If something goes wrong in your past, you're supposed to learn from it. And I learned that sometimes people who look like us don't get the best care in places like this." Benjamin pointed around the hospital room. "So, you'll just have to excuse me Emi for doing what I think is best for me. Besides, there are many people who have lived long, fulfilling lives while on dialysis ... And that was something the doctor didn't tell me. I had to find that out with my own research."

Emily looked over at her mom for assistance in the debate against her dad, but Elena only threw her hands in the air. She had had the same arguments repeatedly with Benjamin. There was nothing else she could say. She looked at Estella, who walked over and stood next to her sister.

"Daddy, I need you here for your grandson. This is the boy you never had. Treatments for the rest of your life will not give you the best quality of life. We need you at your best. Please, at least consider it."

Benjamin breathed deeply. "I intend on being here for my grandboy, and I intend on God giving me the grace to have the best life I can have without surgery." He grabbed Estella's hand and rubbed it as if his statement brought reassurance.

*"My goodness, am I this stubborn?"* Emily pondered. She decided to up the ante with her next declaration. *"Maybe this will set a fire underneath him,"* she thought.

"Well, maybe I'll just set up an appointment to have them take my kidney. Will you do it then?" she asked in desperation. From Benjamin's facial expression, Emily knew she had crossed the line.

"Have you lost your mind? Did you not hear anything I've said to you? Them people ain't cutting on me! And I don't want them cutting on you or anyone else in this room either. But you're a grown woman. You do whatever you want to do. Just know that if you give up your kidney, it ain't going in me."

One of the machines in the room beeped. The argument had caused Benjamin's blood pressure to rise. A nurse entered the room shortly thereafter and asked the family to let him rest uninterrupted. They exited the room at the request.

Out in the hallway Estella asked, "What are we going to do?"

Elena shook her head. "Nothing we can do, baby. You can't make someone do something if they don't want to do it. All we can do is pray and put it in God's hands." That wasn't what Emily wanted to hear, but she knew her mother was right. Prayer was their only solution.

Emily didn't know what to do. She was scheduled to fly back to California the next day. She was due to close on a home with one of her clients the following day. She was also scheduled to show homes to Mr. and Mrs. Donahue amongst other tasks that day. Yet, she couldn't abandon her family in a crisis. There was a possibility that Benjamin was going to be released tomorrow, but there were no guarantees.

"Ugh!" Emily yelled out loud in her old bedroom back at her parents' house. She was sitting on the edge of the bed contemplating. A sea of emotions encompassed her. She was angry at her dad for his stubbornness, but she was also saddened by his sickness. Thinking of the worst-case scenario frightened her. She also thought about the extra expenses her parents were taking on in medical bills. Emily wanted to pitch in as much as she could with financial and physical support. Helping financially would be easy but being a California real estate agent with a sick parent in Georgia would prove difficult.

Emily's thoughts were interrupted by a knock on the door. She didn't want company, but it could've been news about her dad. "Come in," Emily said.

Estella walked into the bedroom and joined Emily on the bed. They sat in silence for a moment, weighing out the reality of what had happened in the last five hours. Estella broke the silence. "I was talking to Reggie about how quickly things happened. How one moment we're all laughing at Daddy, and the next moment we're shedding tears because he's in the hospital." She paused, "And it scared me. It scared me to think about how unpredictable life is. How at any given moment we can be on the verge of something beautiful or on the verge of something terrifying."

Emily remained silent as she listened to Estella think out loud. She had learned that sometimes her little sister didn't necessarily want to converse. She just needed someone to vent to. "What are we supposed to do with that?" Estella asked. Emily sat up. She knew this was a question Estella wanted an answer to.

"What did Reggie say?" Emily asked unsure of how to answer.

"He said life has never been predictable. We just assume it is because our lives usually go on as planned. And that sometimes God will show us just how unreliable our situations are, just to show us how reliable He is." She paused again, "And he said whether we are on the verge of a beautiful moment or a frightful one, God has the power to keep us through them all." Estella looked at Emily and waited for her response.

"Sounds like Reggie might know a thing or two," Emily said.

"Yeah, I guess so," Estella said. More silence. "Are you flying back tomorrow?" Estella asked.

Emily stood up and walked over to the mirror. Her reflection revealed her weariness. She turned back towards Estella. "If Daddy isn't back home tonight, then no."

"You know Reggie and I are staying. You don't have to cancel your flight if you don't want to. We can keep you posted."

"Right, so I should just fly back to confirm to y'all that I love my career more than I love my family?" Emily retorted. She knew her family didn't agree with how she poured herself into her career at the expense of family. They just never said it.

"First of all ... where's this attitude coming from?" Estella asked, crossing her arms. "It sounds like you are projecting your own feelings as ours." Estella then backed off from a possible argument. The day had been stressful enough. "We know you love us, Emily, but you've also built a life that involves a demanding career. So, if you need to fly back, you can."

"So, you really think I'd fly back to California while my daddy is laid up in a hospital bed?" Emily questioned.

"Emily, you're reading into this. This isn't about what I think ..."

"But what *do* you think, Estella?" Emily cut in. Emily and Estella were always completely honest with each other, even if their honesty was hard to hear. Estella didn't want to argue, but now that the question was in the air, she knew Emily wouldn't back down unless she told her exactly what she thought.

"Emily, I think if guilt wouldn't eat you alive, you'd fly back to Cali. I think you are considering going back because the doctor told us Dad would be fine. But you don't want to fly back right now because it would look just like you love your career more than your family." Estella examined Emily's face. Her poker face showed no emotion, but Estella knew her sister. The barely noticeable shift in Emily's body language confirmed that Estella's assessment was correct.

Emily struggled for words. What could she say? Estella was right, and she felt terrible about it. How could she even consider leaving while her dad was still in the hospital? What kind of daughter would do such a thing? Maybe she did put her career over her family. Emily's mind was overloaded with thoughts.

"Emily don't overthink this, okay," Estella said as she walked over to her sister. "Daddy will understand either way. He's expecting you to take over Cali, right? You can't do that if you hang around in Georgia too much."

"Estella, the only reason I work as hard as I do is because Dad made me believe I could do anything. I miss family functions and don't come home as often as I should because Dad taught us that sacrifices must be made, but this is one sacrifice I'm not willing to make. I'm staying." Prior to speaking it out loud in that very moment, Emily was undecided as to what she would do. A big part of her hated that she even had to think about it.

She walked out of the room, jogged down the stairs, and stepped outside into the backyard. She needed to call in a work favor. She couldn't disappoint her client by pushing back their home closure, and she definitely couldn't afford to reschedule showing homes to Mr. and Mrs. Donahue. She had a reputation to keep, and she refused to tell her boss that she needed help doing her job. Ms. Rugsby didn't need a reason to think that she was slacking off or not handling her own business.

She pulled out her phone and called the only co-worker she knew who was just as efficient as her and wouldn't gossip about her putting her work on someone else.

"Hey, Tony. How are you?" Emily hated to call him this late. It was after 10:00 p.m. but she was desperate.

"Hey, Peach. What's up?"

Emily shook her head at herself. *"Can't believe I'm doing this,"* she thought. "I need a huge favor."

"I'm all ears," Tony replied.

"I'm in Georgia and a family emergency came up. I have a closing and a showing the day after tomorrow. Can you do those for me please? I'll send you all of the paperwork and details." Emily held her breath for his response. She was certain he would do it only if she agreed to go out with him.

"Is everything okay? Are you good?" Tony asked. Emily was surprised at his response. He seemed to actually be concerned.

"Yes, I'm fine. I just need the favor." Emily didn't want to give any details or rehash her day. She was drained.

"Okay, sure Peach. I got you." Emily waited for the rest of his response, but she was met with silence. "Hello, Peach? Are you there?" Tony asked.

"Yes, yes, I'm here. So, you'll do it?" Emily asked, unsure of what to make of Tony's lack of flirting.

"Yeah, I said I got you Peach. Just take care of what you need to take care of."

"Okay. Thank you, Tony, I appreciate it," Emily said.

"No problem, and whatever it is, Peach, try not to stress out about it. You're strong. Chin up, you got this." Again, Emily went silent. She had forgotten that Tony had showed concern for her when they'd dated. He was kind too. But memory of all those attributes went out of the window when she found out he was married. Thinking about his marital status induced Emily to rush off the phone with him. She didn't want to catch an attitude with the same person she needed help from.

"Thanks again, Tony. I need to get back now."

"Alright then. Take it easy, Peach. Let me know if you need me to cover anything else for you," said Tony.

"Will do. Thank you. Talk to you later." Emily hung up and headed back in. On the way to her room, she saw her mother sitting alone at the dining room table. She walked over to her. "You okay, Mom?"

Elena glanced up from her daze. "Oh, I'll be okay, baby. You go on up to bed. Get your rest so you don't oversleep and miss your flight." Elena tried to put on a smile, but the corners of her mouth barely rose.

"I'm staying until Daddy gets home," Emily said. She was hurt that Elena hadn't even asked if she would consider staying. Elena had automatically assumed she would fly back. Yet, Emily didn't fault her mom for her realistic prediction.

"Oh, you are? You don't have to. He'll be out tomorrow. I just got off the phone with the hospital about 20 minutes ago," Elena said.

"He is? Oh, thank goodness. Why didn't you tell us, Mom?"

Elena shrugged her shoulders. "Still taking everything in, I suppose," she said rising from her seat. Elena didn't move as quickly as she used to.

*"When did they start aging?"* Emily thought. "So, you don't have to cancel your flight, baby. Go ahead and handle your business."

"No, I'm staying, Mom. I think this is more important," Emily replied. Elena walked over to Emily and grabbed her face.

"You know your Daddy and I love you no matter what you decide. I never faulted you for loving and chasing your career, Emily, I just wanted you to remember to cherish your family above it. Because no matter how much time and effort you devote to it, your career will never love you, but we will always love you."

Elena hugged Emily sweetly and Emily fell like putty into her embrace. "I know, Momma." She laid in her arms a few more seconds before breaking away. "I'm headed up to bed. You should get some rest too," she said to her mother.

"I will. You have a good night," Elena replied.

"Good night," Emily said while climbing the steps.

She wanted to drop by Estella's room and apologize for her snappiness, but the bedroom door was shut and the lights were out. Emily decided she'd talk to her in the morning. She entered her room and instantly crashed on the bed. She was exhausted in every way possible. She just needed some rest.

*Déjà Vu'. I'm floating again. Floating between the dark clouds and foamy sea. The rolling clouds threaten to break open, but they never do. The ocean below churns and moans. Forming waves, attempting to tell me it's deepest secrets. But I don't understand it. I just float and stare as it rages.*

*Time drifts. Silence ensues as the waters calm. The ocean stills into a navy-blue mirror as it has in times past. The clouds stop rolling. Everything around, above, and below me quietens. The elements freeze...anticipating the coming of something I cannot foretell. I wait and watch.*

*Something shifts in the water. I panic. I want to leave, but I'm forced to float. The water shifts again. I see the winged creature. It's*

*stuck, struggling for liberty. It spreads its wings under the sea. I am again awed and frantic at its wingspan. My anxiety is as high as the sky above me. It pulls and yanks, trying to escape its entrapment.*
*Dread seeps in. What if it breaks loose? Instinctive prayers fall from my lips. I pray against the fowl's freedom for the sake of my own safety, but my prayers are not answered. The beast pulls back one last time and snaps away from captivity. My heart stops as I watch in terror. The massive silhouette rises and breaks the surface of the ocean.*
*As it emerges from the water, a lump catches in my throat.*
*It is divinely beautiful, yet terrifically unsettling. It's not a prehistoric bird after all. It's an eagle or at least it appears to be ... yet far more majestic than any bird seen with human eyes, dead or alive. It's at least double, maybe even triple, the size of a normal eagle. Aside from its size, the beauty of the bird is purely hypnotizing.*
*Its feathers flicker with whimsical hues of emerald, turquoise, violet, honey yellow, and coral. The tip of each feather appear to be dipped in gold, and each feather is embroidered with a thin trace of gold around the outer circumference. At the top of each wing is a color-coordinating jewel. Every emerald feather is graced with an emerald stone. Every turquoise feather donned a beryl stone. Citrine for every honey-yellow feather. Amethyst for every purple feather. Morganite for every coral feather.*
*I float in astonishment as the bird fully stretches out its wings. I am so overwhelmed by its beauty that I barely notice the jagged scar on its left wing. Crimson blood drops from a nasty gash right above a beryl stone. That explains why it's hovering so closely to the ocean's surface. But suddenly, it gains its strength. It rises up and flies straight towards me. I am petrified. I try to escape once more but it's of no use.*
*As the bird draws closer, its face comes into view. The feathers on its face are dark brown with speckles of gold. The sunlight breaking from the looming clouds reflect its glinting radiance. The closer it gets, the more beautiful it becomes, and the more frightful I become. My knees would have buckled underneath me if I wasn't floating in mid-air. It's coming straight towards me at missile speed. This is it. I brace for impact ... Deep breath in, deep breath out. Knock, knock, knock ...*

Knock. Knock. Knock. "Emily are you up?" The knocks on the door interrupted her dream. Disheveled, Emily reached for her phone on the nightstand. 8:50 a.m. Knock. Knock. "Emily, Dad should be here in 10 minutes or so. Mom and Reggie went to pick him up."

Emily shot up. "I'm up. Come in!"

Estella cracked the door open and peered in. "Are you decent?" she asked. Emily shot her a look.

"As if you haven't seen me indecent before," she responded.

Estella stepped into the room. "Well, that was years ago, and I didn't want to see you exposed then, and I don't want to see it now." Estella walked over to Emily's bed with a playful expression on her face and sat on the edge of the bed.

"Estella, I wanted to apologize for…"

Estella threw up her hand to cut Emily's apology off. "No need to apologize for expressing your feelings. I know if push comes to shove, you'll pick family over career. I know that sometimes you have to make sacrifices. I ain't mad at you for that, Emily … nobody is. I'm actually proud of you and how determined you are. We're all proud of you." Emily looked at Estella with an overly exaggerated face of appreciativeness as she fluttered her eyelashes rapidly.

"You're proud of me?" Emily asked in a babyish tone, while hugging Estella tightly around her shoulders.

"Eww, girl get off me. You huggin' all up on me and you ain't bathed or brushed your teeth or nothing," Estella said as she got up and headed for the door while trying to maintain a straight face. "I'm cooking us breakfast. Be downstairs in ten minutes."

"Alright," Emily said as she got up from bed.

Emily thought about her dream for a fleeting moment before she freshened up to head downstairs, but that was the least of her worries. Her mind was on her dad and his well-being. She was also worried about his weekly treatments and how she would manage frequent trips back home with her busy work schedule. *"No way he's going to be okay with dialysis treatments three times a week for the rest of his life,"* Emily thought, *"Something's got to give.*

She could hear his voice from the stairs before she saw his face. Benjamin sounded in good spirits.

"Emi! Baby, why aren't you in California taking over? The doctor told y'all I'd be okay. Don't be missing work because of little ol' me." Benjamin flashed his beautiful trademark smile at his daughter. She flashed a smile back.

"California will be subdued when I return to it, Daddy. More pressing matters are at hand now."

"Pressing matters? Man, I swear y'all making a mountain out of a molehill. I'll be fine. I'm fine," Benjamin said in protest. "Estella up here cooking a vegan meal, knowing full well I need some beef or pork or something. Your momma been looking at me like the Grim Reaper is standing right next to me. And here you are, forsaking your career as if I need round the clock care or something." Benjamin shook his head. "I'm okay, y'all. I really am."

"You had a heart attack, Benjamin," Elena said, clearly irritated that Benjamin was not taking his health seriously. "Please stop acting like we are crazy for showing concern."

Reggie joined the conversation to ease the tension. "Yeah, Pops you know we're just looking out for you. But I agree with you ... Estella could've at least gotten us some turkey bacon or something. I mean, a brother ain't gonna make it on avocado toast and a smoothie, you know what I'm saying?" Reggie fist bumped Benjamin while they both laughed.

"Ha, ha, I know that's right, son!"

"Okay, okay," Estella said. "Maybe I shouldn't have fixed a vegan meal, but we all need to start making better eating habits. I can't tell you guys how much better I feel since I started eating healthier."

Emily sipped on the green smoothie Estella had made. "I agree, sis. I have way more energy and I feel really good since I started eating better. You don't have to be a raving health nut from day one. Just do a little at a time. Substitute soda for water or fried for baked. Eat more fruits and veggies, you know. Small changes, bit by bit."

"Yes," Elena said, "which is exactly what I've been telling y'all daddy for the past several months." Elena glanced at Benjamin with an 'I told you so' face.

"Y'all ain't telling me nothing I don't already know," Benjamin said. "Believe it or not, I have started making small changes. I know if I want God to heal me, I need to do my part. So, I've been doing better." Emily smiled at her dad. It was encouraging to hear him acknowledge that changes needed to be made.

"So, I reckon I'll give this here healthy breakfast a spin," Benjamin said. He sipped his smoothie and crunched into his toast. "Not half bad Stella," Benjamin said while examining his food.

Estella smiled. "Glad you like it, Dad." Though Emily was happy to see her dad attempt to eat more healthily, she wished he had started years ago. Then maybe they wouldn't be in this predicament.

*"If he's willing to budge on eating healthier, maybe he'll change his mind about a transplant,"* Emily thought. Emily was too good at sales to not come up with the ultimate sales pitch to help her dad. She had to make another attempt to convince him. *"Yeah, I'll come up with something,"* she thought as she watched him enjoying a meal she thought he would never consider. She'd get her dad to make the most logical choice one way or another.

## JANUARY 2020—CALIFORNIA

Emily peered at Angelo Heights, waiting for him to answer her question. He had just arrived at Hassen's about five minutes ago. She didn't keep him waiting and escorted him into her office shortly after his arrival. She was still weirdly intrigued by him and wanted to know why. What was so magnetic about him? Though he was just as attractive as she had remembered, he wasn't as dapper as he had been the last time she saw him. She didn't expect him to arrive in a tailored suit as he had at church or the wedding, but she expected more.

He was dressed in sweats and a baseball cap—not fashionable athletic sweats, just regular old sweats. Emily's office window faced the front parking lot, so she saw him emerge from his vehicle when he arrived. He drove an old blue Chevy pickup truck, which was not the typical mode of transportation for a bachelor in San Francisco. Emily had assumed he was the pretty-boy type. Maybe even the flashy type. He certainly had the looks for it. But it appeared Emily's assumptions were wrong. So, now her interest was even more so piqued by Mr. Heights.

"I'm looking for a spacious house," Angelo said. "Four bedrooms, two baths with a decent-sized backyard." Angelo waited for Emily's response. His eyes were enigmatic. They looked as if they had one thousand stories to tell. But from his militant presence, Emily wondered if anyone really knew him or his story. *"Surely someone knows about him. Who would be in this spacious place with Angelo? Is he buying a home for his family? Where is his wife?"*

Emily looked at his hand. *"No wedding band ... maybe he's single,"* she thought. *"Tony didn't wear a ring either and look where that got you. Plus, why would a single man need a house with four bedrooms? It doesn't matter, Emily. Focus! He's your client, not your potential new boo. Get it together!"* Emily interrupted her own thoughts and cleared her throat. "Four bedrooms, huh? Okay, we can arrange that. Need the extra room for your children?"

*"Why did you ask that? Mind your business Emily! Just do your job and make the sale."*

"No," Angelo replied. "I don't have any children."

"Oh, okay. So, the wife just needs a little extra space then, right?"

*"So, you really just going to pry into this man's life, huh?"*

Angelo smiled and Emily's heart dropped into her stomach. He had such a brilliant smile. Only God could create such a gorgeous facial feature.

"No, no wife either," Angelo replied. "I don't necessarily need all the space right now. I'm thinking about the future."

*"Maybe he's in a serious relationship... or maybe he's engaged and plans to have a big family soon, hence the need for all the space."*

"Okay, I understand that. Nothing wrong with preparing for the future," Emily said, wondering if she was right about his relationship status.

"So, I see you were pre-approved for a rather generous amount," she continued. "House hunting should be rather fun for you. I have a couple of areas in mind that should meet your standards. We can start searching today if you'd like." Though Emily loved to show relatively nice homes to her clients in great neighborhoods, she wondered how Angelo had been approved for such a large amount.

He said he was in the army, but to her knowledge people in armed services—no matter their rank—never made *that* type of money. He had to have another healthy income stream from somewhere. But that was none of her business, and she dared not meddle in his personal finances. Even her inquisitive mind knew better than to ask that. *"Maybe he's an entrepreneur too,"* she thought.

"I appreciate the offer, but I can't go house hunting today. I need to get back and handle a few things," Angelo said, adjusting his hat. "Plus, I promised Guardian I'd take him for an overdue walk today, and I like to be a man of my word."

"Guardian? Oh, I like that name," Emily said. "What kind of dog do you have?"

"He's a Bernese Mountain Dog," Angelo replied.

"Oh," Emily said. "Those dogs get pretty big."

"Yeah," Angelo said. "He's about 115 lbs. He's smart and protective. We get along quite nicely."

"Isn't that sweet. I always wanted a dog, but my dad's allergic to dog hair. I never thought to get one as an adult," Emily said.

"Well, who knows? Maybe you'll end up with your own one day," Angelo said. Though he was very much so inscrutable, Emily figured he must have a soft side to be a dog lover. She also remembered how he was enthralled in full worship at church that Sunday. She didn't know much about him, but she knew his worship was sincere. No one could fake the type of praise he was sending up that day.

"Yes, maybe I'll take on the responsibility of being a dog mom one day," Emily responded. "So, when is a good day for us to start your house hunting journey, Mr. Heights?"

"You can call me Angelo, and how about next week sometime?" Emily had thought he would say sometime this week as it was rather early in the week. "*Maybe he's a busy man,*" she thought. "Okay, next week should work. What day and time?" she asked, looking at her schedule.

"Can I call you and let you know? I don't have an exact answer for you right now." Emily never had a client put off house hunting. It was the most exciting part of buying a home besides closing day. She was confused that he didn't jump on the hunt as soon as possible.

"Sure, that's fine," she said. "Just give me a call and we can work out a time."

"Okay great," Angelo said as he rose from his seat, standing at his full height and exuding masculinity. He was, as some say, 'all man'.

"I hate to leave so abruptly Ms. Waters, but I must go." Emily rose from her seat as well.

"Oh, no need to apologize, and you can call me Emily. I'll just scope out some nice homes for you until we meet again. Let me see you out."

"No, that's okay. I can see myself out. Thank you so much for your time," Angelo insisted.

"It's my pleasure," Emily said as he walked out of the door.

She watched him as he climbed into his vintage pick-up truck and pulled off. "Mr. Heights, Mr. Heights," she said out loud in her office. Emily hadn't been allured by a man like this since... well, she had never been attracted to a man in this way. Although he was incredibly easy on the eyes, that wasn't the magnetic pull she felt. It was something else. Something was drawing Emily to Angelo like a moth to a flame. She just hoped her allurement wouldn't burn her.

Emily hopped in her drop-top convertible and cruised down the street to grab a bite to eat after shopping. She and Chelsea had spent most of their Saturday indulging in retail therapy. Chelsea was fun. She had a big personality and seemed to live her life to the fullest. Emily couldn't remember the last time she had laughed so much. Between the exhaustion of the usual grind at work and her recent commitment to fly home to Georgia every other weekend to check on her dad, Emily needed and very much appreciated this friend-date with Chelsea.

It was well into the afternoon and they both agreed to call it quits for the day, but not before they ate and had a cocktail or two accompanied by a little girl chat. They walked into the chic restaurant and ordered drinks while they waited for their food. "Whew, girl. I know Henry is going to fuss if he sees me walking in the house with all those bags. I may need to hide them in my trunk until I can sneak them in the house," Chelsea said while sipping on a martini.

"Now, Chelsea, that's a shame. You gonna run that man pressure up," Emily teased.

"Honey, listen. Henry and them doggone kids done ran up my pressure a gazillion times. He ought to be glad I use shopping as a release. Otherwise, I'd lose my mind trying to keep everything afloat." Emily had learned that Chelsea had four children from ages 2–10. Chelsea and Henry were high-school sweethearts and had their first child together when they were only 17 years old. Emily remembered how Chelsea missed prom and graduation. She was also unable to graduate on time due to a few missed credits. She had her baby one month before graduation day.

A couple of years later, Henry asked Chelsea to marry him, and the babies just kept rolling in. Chelsea eventually received her GED and even completed a few semesters of college. She tried to finish school, but it never worked out. Finding affordable daycare was impossible, and online school wasn't ideal with the needs of small children. She just wasn't dedicated to the effort it required of her.

Henry, on the other hand, was able to graduate high school and college. It took time, but about a year ago he finally landed a job in an industry that gave his family the lifestyle he always wanted them to have. So, Chelsea took advantage of every opportunity she had to splurge and enjoy her life.

"Well, girl, I know we can't go by appearances, but it looks like you are keeping everything afloat to me," Emily said, "I mean, look at you. You're in better shape than me and I haven't pushed out any children. You've done it four times. How do you do it?" she asked.

"If you had seen me a year ago, you would be singing a different tune," Chelsea said. "I felt like my life was spiraling out of control. We really don't have any outside help with the kids, so I barely get a break.

I felt so overwhelmed, and I just needed to be able to control at least one aspect of my life. So, I started exercising. I put my all into it, and BOOM ... look at me now," Chelsea said confidently.

"Yes, girl. Look at you! You look good, and you should be proud of yourself. Cheers to you," Emily raised her glass toward Chelsea's and they clanked them together.

"Thank you, girl. So, what's your plan to coerce your dad into the kidney transplant?" Emily hadn't thought she would tell Chelsea about any of her personal problems, especially since it was their first time hanging out, but she was glad to have a listening ear. She told Stacey about the chaos on the phone, but it was good to have someone to talk to in-person.

"Coerce is a harsh word. I would say I just plan to apply pressure." Emily took a bite of the food the waitress had just served her. "My dad is as stubborn as an ox. I can't get him to change his mind by mere talk. I know I can't. But if I take some action ... maybe I can get him to bend." Chelsea waited for Emily to continue but Emily just stared off into space in deep thought.

"Soo... what are you planning to do exactly?" Chelsea asked.

Emily pushed her food around her plate. She was unsure if Chelsea would call her crazy or even stupid for her 'plan'. She decided it was best to talk to Stacey or even Estella about her possible course of action. "I'm not sure yet, but I'll think of something," she said. Chelsea studied Emily's face and shrugged her shoulders.

"Well, whatever you do, I hope it works out."

"Yeah, me too." They ate in silence for a few minutes. Emily contemplated the Chelsea that sat across from her and the Chelsea she had known in high school. Granted, she hadn't known much about her back then, but it appeared she had changed. Chelsea and Ms. Prissy Vicky had remained thick as thieves throughout school. Emily was never fond of either one of them. They both had condescending attitudes and talked trash about any and every one they didn't like, which seemed to be almost everybody. But the Chelsea who was before her now wasn't the same girl.

Emily would've been repulsed by her company ten years ago. She guessed that time and having children had changed her heart for the better. "This was nice, we should hang out more," Chelsea said while wiping the corners of her mouth.

"I agree. I could use the girl talk and escape from my hectic world," Emily responded.

"Cool, let's link up again soon," Chelsea said. Emily agreed and was optimistic at having a potential new friend. They paid for their meals and left.

Once settled in her home, Emily called Stacey. She almost felt guilty hanging out with Chelsea all day. That was supposed to be her and Stacey a few weeks ago. She FaceTimed Stacey from her couch. "Hey chick. What's up?" Emily asked when Stacey answered. From her surroundings, Emily saw that Stacey was at her cupcake shop. "Nothing much. Just whipping up this order for a party. What's up with you?"

"Okay, so don't be mad, but I feel like I cheated on you. I had a girl's day with someone else today," Emily said biting her lower lip.

"Oh no ma'am. Who's the heifer?" Stacey said holding a rolling pin up as if she was going to fling it through the phone.

"You actually know her, Stace," Emily said amused at Stacey's reaction.

"Who? Who is the heifer?" Stacey asked with her hands on her hips.

"Chelsea Stark," Emily replied.

"Chelsea Stark? Chelsea Stark from school? How in the world did that come about? And why exactly would you be on an outing with her of all people?" Stacey's face said it all. She disapproved, and Emily understood why.

"Well apparently Henry—she and Henry are married with four kids by the way—apparently Henry landed a job here in San Francisco. I ran into her shopping one day, and she suggested we hang out. I agreed, and surprisingly I don't regret it. She's actually pretty cool."

"Pretty cool, huh?" Stacey's words dripped with sarcasm. "Well, hey, if you like it, I love it. I guess time can change people."

Emily nodded her head. "Yes, that's exactly what I was thinking… but there is something a little… I don't know… different about her." Emily twisted her face trying to explain what she meant.

"If Chelsea Stark is cool enough to hang out with, then of course she's different," Stacey reasoned.

Emily smirked at Stacey's cynicism. "I think I may be reading into her tiredness. She mentioned how she just needs a break sometimes, and that I don't know how good I have it to be able to come and go as I please."

Stacey made a face. "Yeah, that could be it. Just feel her out some more. Maybe you'll find out what's up with her."

Emily pressed her mouth together in thought. "I don't get bad vibes from her or anything. Like I said, she's cool. Honestly, I don't know what to call it. She just seems... I don't know. Can't put my finger on it."

Stacey gave her another look. "Um, is that right? Well, I'm glad you had fun. Just don't get too close to her. You only have room for one best friend. Don't make me fly out to Cali to remind you," Stacey said.

"Yeah, yeah, I got you. Your jealousy is actually cute BFF," Emily smiled. Stacey smiled back and rolled her eyes.

"Anyway, how's your dad?" Stacey was just as upset over Benjamin's sickness and stubbornness as Emily. Benjamin had been like another dad to her growing up. She and Emily were practically sisters.

"He's doing okay. Those treatments are kind of tough on him. But he's been eating better from what mom says," Emily paused. "Hey, I have a question. And be honest with me," she said seriously.

"Okay, ask away," Stacey said.

"Do you think it's crazy of me to see if I can be a donor for my dad? I know he said he wouldn't take my kidney if I donated it but maybe he's bluffing. Maybe if I took a drastic step, he would feel obligated to have the surgery... but then again, I would hate to pressure him like that. But I know he can't live forever on treatments. Some people can have a decent life while on dialysis, but it doesn't seem like he can ... I don't know. I don't know." Emily stopped venting and sighed deeply.

"Emily," Stacey said in a calm comforting tone. "If it was my mom or dad, I'd do the same thing." Emily exhaled at Stacey's answer. Stacey always had a way of making her feel comfortable. She was such a good friend and listener. "But you have to be emotionally prepared if you go through with it and it doesn't go in your favor. Because what if he isn't bluffing? Worst case scenario, your kidney could go to someone else in need, but you'd still be in the same predicament you are in now, just with one less kidney."

"Yeah, I know and that worries me," Emily confessed. "I just don't know what else to do."

"Nothing you really can do," Stacey said with a face full of concern. "You can't make someone do something that they don't want to do. Just pray about it." Stacey hated that Emily had to go through this.

"Trust me, all I've been doing is praying about it," Emily replied. "Well, I'm going to let you get back to baking, Stace. Love you girl."

"Love you too, girl. Keep me posted."

Emily hung up and felt better about her radical plan. She'd run it by Estella for a second opinion. Yet, even if Estella didn't agree, Emily was sure she'd go through with it. She had already considered the worst case scenario and thought her kidney donation would be a good deed whether it went to her dad or not. She'd always wanted to contribute to society or anyone for that matter in a big way. If her dad refused her kidney, giving her organ to someone else would absolutely count as contributing to someone in a major way. She just prayed that her contribution would be to her dad.

# FEBRUARY 2020—CALIFORNIA

Emily stared at the screensaver on her monitor in dazed disbelief. She couldn't believe what had just happened. She had never been questioned about falling behind at work. Yet, roughly an hour ago, Ms. Rugsby visited her office to discuss her unusual January numbers. "I'm just concerned as this is uncommon for you Emily. Is everything okay?" Ms. Rugsby had asked.

Emily wasn't necessarily warned or even lectured to do better but having Ms. Rugsby question her work was a huge disappointment to say the least. She had known that flying back and forth from California and Georgia might have some negative consequences, but she didn't think it would affect her work. She imagined she may be tired, even irritable at times, but she hadn't anticipated a decrease in sales and leads.

*"What was I thinking?"* Emily thought, *"I can't pull this off"*. Her commitment to flying home every two weeks meant that she missed at least two or three days of office work the week she traveled. Although she kept her laptop and business materials handy while she was away, it proved both difficult and insensitive to work while in the company of her parents. In addition to the missed days, the jet lag she experienced managed to roll over into the days she was present to work. Her fatigue and difficulty concentrating was evident in her January numbers.

"I'm in the middle of a family crisis back home in Georgia. I've been traveling back and forth, which has resulted in my subpar numbers last month. I just need to figure out a system. I'll have those numbers back up in no time," Emily explained.

"Do you need to take some time off?" Ms. Rugby had asked. There was no such thing as paid time off in real estate. You either worked to get leads and sales or you didn't get paid. Emily's bills wouldn't have understood her crisis. Plus, she wanted to pitch in to help her parents' finances a bit more. Time off wasn't an option.

"No," Emily responded, "I'll manage. Everything will be fine. I just need to work on my time management." Now that Emily was alone in her office rehashing the conversation with Ms. Rugsby, she didn't know if she could uphold what she promised her boss. *"How can I possibly keep up my numbers with less time working? I can't consistently miss the mark. It'll ruin my representation."* Doubt began to settle into her mind.

*"What happens if I can't manage? Should I cut traveling back home to once a month or maybe every other month? But that's not enough time spent with mom and dad. I need to be more present because what if..."* Emily exhaled deeply at her next thoughts, *"what if these are dad's last days? I'd hate myself if I didn't spend as much time as possible with him."*

Emily felt a migraine coming on. Her thoughts ran around her head in a chaotic whirlwind. It was impossible for her to choose what was the best course of action. The way she saw it, she was in a lose-lose situation. A light knock at her door broke her train of thoughts. She quickly put on a smile to mask her inner turmoil.

"Come in," Emily said. The door cracked open, and Tony peeped his head inside. *"I don't need this crap right now,"* she thought. Yet, Tony had rescued her when she needed his help. She knew she needed to be thankful and courteous towards him for his generosity.

"Hey Tony," Emily said. "What can I do for you?"

Tony stepped inside her office and shut the door behind him. "I saw Ms. Rugsby leave from here. Is everything okay?" Ms. Rugsby wasn't the kind of boss who visited her employees' offices often, but when she did it was normally either for good reasons or bad reasons—there was no gray area.

"Yeah, I just didn't make my numbers last month and she was a little alarmed. Nothing too terrible. She just knew something had to be wrong," Emily said unable to hide her frustration.

"Awe man, Peach. Don't beat yourself up about it. I mean you're the best," Tony said as he sat down in the chair facing her desk. "She had to see what was going on if you didn't make your numbers. That just doesn't happen to you," he said adjusting the button on his blazer.

"Yeah, I know," was all Emily could say.

"You know I can help if you need it, Peach," Tony said as Emily fumbled with a pen.

"I can't ask you to help me with my work, Tony. Otherwise, it'll be your work. It wouldn't be fair if I received commission from your work," Emily said frankly.

Tony didn't have a rebuttal for Emily's response. She was right. He decided to segue into another topic he wanted to discuss. "You may be right. Can you look at this file for me?" Emily looked at the manila folder Tony slid onto her desk.

"Tony, I don't even know how I'm going to handle my own work and you're asking me to look at yours? I mean, I know I owe you the favor, and I'll return it, I promise. But right now…"

Tony interrupted. "So, if you owe me the favor just look at it. It won't take long."

Emily sighed and grabbed the folder. She opened it and looked at the first page of a small stack of documents. It was finalized divorce papers. She looked up at Tony. He wasn't smiling in his usual flirtatious way. Instead, he held a serious disposition.

"I wanted to show you that I am officially divorced. I also wanted to prove to you that I was separated from my wife when you and I were involved with one another. In fact, we separated and divorced because of her infidelity, not mine. We were living separately and only speaking through our attorneys. Everything you need to know is in that folder."

Emily looked back down at the paper and closed the folder. "Even if that is true, you shouldn't have approached me until you were legally divorced. You didn't give me the option to choose if I wanted to be involved with someone who was still married. You intentionally withheld information from me, which is the same as lying in my eyes. You mislead me, and these papers can't deny that" Emily said, handing the folder back to Tony. He took the folder, got up from his seat, and placed it back on Emily's desk.

"You're right," Tony said, "and, for that, Emily I do apologize. I'm sorry that I didn't consider that you wouldn't be okay with that. That was bad judgment on my part. It wasn't my intention to lie to you or mislead you. I just really wanted to get to know you." Tony shifted his feet as he stood. "I didn't want to wait to approach you because I didn't want to risk the chance of someone else getting you," he said as he sat back down across from Emily.

"Men don't come across women like you often Peach," he continued as he leaned forward in the chair. "If I had waited until my divorce finalized, I knew it was possible that I could've missed out on you. And that just wasn't a risk I was willing to take." Tony glared into Emily's eyes. Emily looked into his eyes for a moment before she dropped her eyes back down on her desk. He seemed so sincere, and his words were filled with passion. *"What if I misjudged Tony? What if he really isn't a liar?"* she thought.

Tony grabbed Emily's hand while she was in mid-thought. "All I'm asking is that you think about what I'm saying. I never meant to hurt you, Emily. I really like you. I can see myself easily loving you one day if you'll let me. I think we'd be good together. Just think about it." With that, Tony got up from his chair and headed for the door. He turned around and looked at her one more time. His eyes pleaded for a second chance before he closed the door shut.

Tony's cologne lingered in her office after he left. She could still feel his firm, warm grip around her hand. The intensity of his eyes and words were etched into her brain. It didn't help that he was always incredibly easy to look upon. Emily didn't know what to make of this whole ordeal. She had enough on her plate dealing with her job and Dad's health. Now, she had this to add to her confusion.

Emily reached into her purse for a Tylenol. She needed to focus and get some work done, but Tony's proposal lingered in the back of her head, just as his cologne had lingered in the room. She was going to need something stronger than over-the-counter medication to help solve her dilemmas. "Jesus, be a Tylenol for all of my headaches," she said as she logged into her computer to catch up on her overdue work.

Emily stepped into the foyer of what she thought was the perfect home for Angelo Heights. It was a big, spacious place, just as he had requested. There was a dual winding staircase that led upstairs to four bedrooms. There was an extra guest room downstairs. Emily thought the extra bedroom within Angelo's price range would be a great selling point. The open concept floor plan, French windows, and vaulted ceilings made the home appear larger than life.

She looked down at her watch. He should be arriving any minute now. Emily was never nervous to show a home. On the contrary, she thoroughly enjoyed this part of her job. But something about Angelo put her a little on edge. She wanted to impress him. She smoothed down her pencil skirt and checked her hair in the mounted mirror one last time. *"Okay, Emi. You've done this a million times. You got this."*

The rumbling engine of a pick-up truck prompted Emily to step away from the mirror and glance out of the window. Angelo parked on the road and made his way up the walkway. Emily scurried over to the entrance, took a deep breath, and opened the door.

"Why hello, Angelo! Come on in," Emily said with a ginormous smile on her face. Angelo greeted her with an equally large smile.

"Hello, Emily. How are you today?"

"I'm great, thank you. So, what do you think of the neighborhood? Do you like it?" Emily wasn't short. She was 5'5 and had on four-inch heels, yet Angelo appeared to be at least five inches taller than her. She lifted her chin towards his face for his response.

"It's lovely. Seems nice and quiet. The outside of the home looks amazing too. I approve so far."

"Great, great. Alright. Well, let's start the tour, shall we?" Emily asked.

"Let's," Angelo responded.

Emily walked over toward the open floor kitchen/living room area. Angelo followed suit. "Before we go any further, Angelo, I'd have you know that this house was built from the ground up a little over six months ago. Should you choose this place to be your new residence, you and your family will be the first people to live within these walls."

Emily intentionally mentioned a family, hoping Angelo would confirm or deny any plans of having a family in the near future, but he said nothing. He just walked over towards the kitchen island and observed the granite top.

"Brand-new home, huh?" he finally stated.

"Yes, sir. Brand spanking new," Emily said as she studied him. After she glanced over his broad shoulders and formed arms, she noticed a scar on his right forearm. It was healed and appeared to be from years ago. She imagined how bad a wound it must've been when it was fresh. It was a pretty large scar. *"Is that a war wound?"* Emily thought.

"Is the furniture just for show?" Angelo asked.

"Yes and no," Emily said. "I actually have a business partnership with Mac & Sons' Furniture. Occasionally, they agree to show pieces in homes that I am showcasing. If the client likes what they see, they can purchase the fixtures at a discounted price." Angelo studied the sectional and dining room pieces in the living room area.

"Awesome. I will need new furniture, and I do like what I see here."

"I'm glad to hear that. Usually, they only allow me to fix up one room with their furniture, but they are receiving a massive amount of inventory due to tax season and needed to clear out some space in their warehouse. So, I was able to deck out this entire house with fixings and furniture," Emily said. "It appears you lucked up, Mr. Heights.

"I wouldn't call it luck… more like divine intervention," Angelo said as he winked at her.

*"Did he just wink at me? Oh, goodness. He just winked at me. He's too fine to be winking at me. Focus, Emily."*

"Okay, divine intervention, I like that," Emily said, hoping Angelo didn't notice how his wink had momentarily frazzled her. "Just down that hallway is the first-floor bathroom. I'll wait here while you take a gander." Angelo made his way down the hallway to the bathroom. Emily needed the quick moment to compose herself.

"Wow, this is nice!" Angelo shouted from the bathroom. "I love the walk-in shower."

"Well, you're going to love the bathroom upstairs," Emily said. "If you're ready, we can head up there after you view the bedroom right across the hall from where you are." Angelo crossed the hallway and stepped into the bedroom. Emily made her way down the hall to ensure that he checked out the closet space.

"Yeah, this is nice. I'm liking this. I'm ready to see the rest of it."

"Follow me this way." Emily guided him back down the hallway and up the stairs.

"That chandelier is amazing," Angelo said.

"Yes! I love it. It's my favorite fixture in the house. It adds a sense of elegance to the place. Okay, here we are. These are the bedrooms." Emily stepped aside and allowed Angelo to walk in front of her. He made his way into the rooms as Emily followed and sold the rooms on their size and modern flare.

"I see you went above my expectations. There are five rooms instead of my requested four… I'm impressed," Angelo said in a satisfactory tone.

"That's my goal. I aim to please," Emily said. "And as you can see from outside this window, the backyard is a nice size as well. Plenty of room for Guardian to run around and play. There's also a patio area if you're ever interested in hosting a nice outside gathering." Angelo peered out of the window and nodded his head.

"Nice, very nice," he said.

"I'm glad you like it. I think it's an excellent choice. But I think it's wise if I show you a few more options," Emily said.

"I agree," Angelo complied. They made their way downstairs, through the foyer, and out of the front door. Emily locked the door and faced him. He had his arms folded across his chest checking out the neighborhood. He had his legs far apart as he looked, in a standard military stance.

"You said you were in the army, correct?" Emily asked.

"Yes, ma'am. I am," Angelo said, facing her.

"Are you a lieutenant or captain?"

Angelo unfolded his arms and attempted to look like a regular civilian. "What gave it away?" Emily smiled. "You just have more of a military demeanor than other serviceman I see."

Angelo blushed. "I'm a major. I'm used to keeping an eye on my battalion. Two things I take seriously—God and my servitude. My dedication to my assignments spills over in my daily interactions sometimes. Please excuse my disposition if it appears hardened at times."

"Oh, no need to apologize. I think its commendable that you stand for something, and I thank you for your service," Emily said.

"It's my pleasure," Angelo replied.

They made their way to their vehicles, and Emily showed two more homes to Angelo in the San Francisco area. After the third one, Angelo suggested they call it quits for the day.

"You selected beautiful homes, Ms. Waters," Angelo said. "I'll get back to you with my decision as soon as possible. In the meantime, if I'm not being too forward, would you care to join me for lunch?"

Emily was thrown off by his question. *"What about your fiancé and soon-to-be family?"* Emily thought. *"Well now you have the opportunity to ask him about that. Go out with him."*

Angelo noticed her hesitation. "No fraternization will ensue, I promise. This is just lunch," Angelo said.

Emily offered a smile. "Of course, that's fine by me. I am hungry."

Angelo clasped his hands and smiled. "Great, do you like burgers?"

Emily loved burgers. Occasionally, her dad used to take the family out on Friday evenings to a hole-in-the-wall burger joint back home in Georgia. She didn't know if she loved burgers because of the taste or because of the nostalgia they brought her. Either way, a burger sounded delightful.

"Yes, I do," Emily said.

"There's this burger joint close to the base that has the best burgers in San Francisco called B.A. Burgers. Have you tried them?" he asked.

"No, I haven't. I've heard great things about them though," Emily replied.

"Well, I'd say you're in for a treat." Angelo smiled at her and walked toward his car. "I'll meet you there."

Emily hopped in her car and took a minute to find a good playlist for the ride. She looked in her rear-view mirror and noticed Angelo still waiting in his truck. *"Oh, snap. He's waiting for me. He must think I'm so rude."* She put her car in reverse, backed out of the driveway, and stopped parallel to Angelo's antique truck.

"I'm so sorry. I thought you pulled off already," Emily said.

"That's no problem. After you," Angelo said.

Emily pulled off and headed toward the burger joint. She hadn't been able to find a good playlist before she drove off, so she opted to listen to the radio. She was annoyed with all the commercials and kept flicking through the stations. The ads finally ended just when she pulled into the parking lot of the restaurant. *"Oh, now you want to play music… and I love this song too,"* Emily thought as she got out of the car and walked toward the entranceway of the burger joint.

Angelo parked his truck and was right behind her. Emily reached for the door.

"No, let me get that," Angelo said as he opened the door for her.

"Why thank you. Chivalry is not dead I see," she teased.

"No, ma'am it's not, "Angelo said.

Emily walked into the restaurant and smiled. They were tuned into the same radio station she had been listening to in the car. She nodded her head to the song. "I was just annoyed that I wasn't able to listen to this song in the car. Glad to hear them playing it."

The sultry voice of Anita Baker floated through the restaurant in conjunction with the smell of fresh fries and burgers.

"So, you like this song, huh?" Angelo asked, amused at Emily's blatant enjoyment of the music.

"You don't? Who doesn't like Anita Baker?" Emily asked as she hummed the lyrics to *Angel*. "This one and *Caught Up in the Rapture* are my favorites," Emily said. "Are you not a fan? Because if not, I simply cannot eat with you. I simply cannot dine with someone with such poor taste in music," she joked.

Angelo chuckled. "I like her. She's soulful. Is she your favorite singer?"

Emily's face scrunched into a thoughtful frown. "Umm, I don't know. It's hard for me to pick a favorite singer, but she's definitely in my top five. What about you? Who's your favorite?"

A young man approached them. "Welcome to B.A. Burgers. You guys can sit wherever you please. Let me get you all a couple of menus, and I'll be right over." They settle into a booth toward the back of the restaurant.

"I don't think I have a favorite artist either," Angelo said, "but I do like real music. You may find this odd, but I can listen to instrumental music all day. I love good gospel music too." Emily thought about Angelo praising God in the church again.

"Yeah, gospel music is great. It has a way of uplifting us."

Angelo nodded his head. "Agreed, but I really love the praise and worship aspect of it."

"You know, it's rare to see a man confess his love and devotion to God nowadays. Where are you from?" Emily asked.

"I'm originally from up north, but I've been all over. My father was, well, still is, the top-ranking commander of his troop. So, that equated to moving around often," Angelo said. The waiter brought out their menus, and they placed their orders. "And as far as my love and devotion to God, that just comes naturally. Aren't we all created to praise Him?" Angelo asked.

"Yes, I think so," Emily said, "but many people don't do it so freely or even publicly." Angelo sipped his pomegranate mocktail.

"Why do you think that is?"

Emily pondered his question. The waiter brought out their food and it looked as promising as Angelo had stated.

"I think sometimes people don't feel the need to praise God. Some people are suffering... struggling. Some people have so much trauma and heartache. It's hard to praise God when you're going through it, you know?" Emily took a bite of her burger.

"Oh, my goodness. This is for sure the best burger in San Francisco," she said as juices and sauce dripped down from her sandwich.

"Told you," Angelo smiled confidently. "But don't you think, regardless of struggles, God is still God?" Angelo asked. "Our pain doesn't negate the fact that He created the heavens and earth. No suffering will ever change that He is the Great I Am. He is always God, and because He is always God, He is always due praise."

Emily chewed and contemplated.

"I agree, but sometimes I don't think it's that simple. It's hard to praise God in the midst of turmoil." They ate in silence for a few seconds.

"Struggles don't last, but God does. I believe it's only right to hold on to what will last," Angelo said. "It's important to remember that God never said troubles would not come. In fact, He said troubles would come, but He also said He would be near the brokenhearted and give beauty for ashes. If we can remember that, we'll be okay." Angelo spoke with enthusiasm. He was leaning forward in his seat. His mysterious eyes burned with fervor.

"You really love Jesus, huh?" Emily said.

Angelo laughed. "I do, no shame over here."

"I need to do better. I know I do," Emily said. "It's like I have a slight disconnect with God. I love Him, and I know He exists. I just don't feel connected the way I know I should be. The last time I really felt His presence was back home at church."

Angelo wiped the corners of his mouth. "Why do you think that is?"

Emily glared at Angelo. She didn't know if he was being sarcastic or genuine.

Emily read her daily devotions. She prayed. She didn't know why her spiritual life was lacking. And she really hadn't given it much thought until Angelo posed the question. Life was good to her. She was successful, established, young, and beautiful. She was single by choice and enjoyed the life she had. Yet, there was a nagging in her spirit that left her feeling unfulfilled at times. The recent turn of events in her life revealed just how unfulfilling her life could be at times. She never considered that it may've been her disconnect with God.

"I don't know," Emily said.

"Sometimes there's too much noise around us to fully connect to God," Angelo said. "Sometimes we need to silence the world so that we can hear from God."

Emily sipped her drink and glanced Angelo over. *"He sure is preachy and has a lot to say about God,"* she thought. *"I wonder, does he live the life he preaches about? I've seen my fair share of hypocritical believers. Let's see if I can get him to answer a few questions."*

"Speaking of silence, once you move into your new place, you'll have all the quiet time you want... unless Guardian interrupts it of course," Emily said. "Are you converting the extra rooms into different spaces? An office? In-home gym? I'm just curious about what you will do with all the room."

Angelo smirked at Emily. "It is a lot of house for just little ol' me, huh?" Angelo said. "No, I don't plan on converting the rooms into anything. But I do have a plan for the house."

Angelo dipped a fry in ketchup and didn't offer a further explanation, so, Emily asked for her own clarification. "Are you being proactive? Planning to move a family of your own into it one day?"

Angelo asked the waiter for the check. "Something like that," he said as he reached for his wallet.

"Oh, you don't have to pay. I'll cover it," Emily said.

"No, I asked you here. Let me take care of it," Angelo insisted.

Emily obliged but his answers did not please her inquisitive mind. She wanted a clear-cut answer to his relationship status, and a clear answer as to why he needed so much space. But it wasn't her place to ask. *"Client. He's your client. That's it. It doesn't matter why he needs the house, and it doesn't matter if he's with someone or not because he's your client."*

"Are you seeing anyone, Emily?" Angelo asked.

*"...didn't see that question coming,"* Emily thought. She thought about Tony. She'd read the divorce paperwork he'd given her, and his story checked out. But she was still hesitant about him. He'd withheld vital information and that wasn't right.

"No, I'm not," Emily said. Angelo nodded his head in approval.

"Good, maybe you should keep it that way for now," he said.

"Maybe I will," Emily replied.

They left the restaurant, and Angelo walked Emily to her car. "Thank you for joining me, Emily. And thank you for doing you due diligence in selecting homes for me. I appreciate it."

Emily looked into his eyes. No sign that he would hug or kiss her goodbye... although Emily thought either one would have been nice. *"Of course there's no sign of that, Emily. He's your client. This was just lunch. No fraternization remember?"*

"Oh, no, thank you for the invite. I really enjoyed the food and conversation," she said, still standing there waiting for something, anything to happen.

"Same here. Well, I'll see you later Ms. Waters. Enjoy the rest of your day."

"You too, Angelo," Emily said as she climbed into her car. She watched as Angelo walked towards his car. She then cranked up her car and pulled out of the parking lot.

She drove home and tried to shake Angelo out of her mind, but she couldn't. *"I still don't know if he's in a relationship or not. He only said I should remain single. Does that mean he's going to pursue me? Maybe he'll ask me out after our business relationship is over? Or maybe he won't. I don't know. He's hard to read."* Emily thought about the condition of her life. Her dad, her job, Tony's offer, and now Angelo. She felt silly for including Angelo in the mix. But she had a feeling that Angelo just may turn out to be more than a client.

# MID-FEBRUARY 2020 CALIFORNIA

"Oh, girl. He's just playing mind games with you," Chelsea said while she sipped her third mimosa. Emily was swamped with work and had told Chelsea she did not have time to chit-chat and hang out with her, but Chelsea was convincing. "Don't you have to eat today? Come on! If you're going to eat, you may as well eat with me. I won't hold you after the meal is over, I promise. I just need to get out of this house. Please!"

Emily had rolled her eyes in reluctant agreement. They'd finished their brunch 45 minutes ago, yet Emily was still in deep girl talk with Chelsea. She told her about Angelo and Chelsea did not hold back her opinion. "Listen, if he was single and ready to mingle, he would have told you that," she said. "Telling you that you should stay single for now? What does that even mean? I don't like how vague he is ... probably lying about being married and having kids. I mean, seriously, who needs that much space if they don't have kids? These men think they're slick. Child, please. Next!"

Emily lightly tapped her feet on the bottom of her chair. She desperately needed to get back to work. She was also somewhat annoyed at how Chelsea dragged Angelo's name through the mud. Yet, she was concerned that Chelsea may be right. "Yeah, I guess you have a point there," Emily said.

"Girl, I *know* I have a point. You can do better," Chelsea said. "Well, I'm not going to hold you. I know you've got to get back to work. I got the bill, you go ahead."

Emily was relieved. She didn't want to be rude and cut Chelsea off. She was due to meet with Mr. and Mrs. Donahue in less than an hour and she really wanted to call Stacey back before the meeting. Stacey had sent her a text message 15 minutes ago that read: Call me ASAP! She was both worried and eager to find out what the urgency was about.

"Oh, you don't have to pay the bill," Emily said as she dug into her purse.

"No, I insist. I promised you I wasn't going to hold you up and I did," Chelsea said. "I'm sorry, let this be my treat."

*"She's got a point,"* Emily thought.

"Okay, but I'll cover the tip," Emily said, leaving cash on the table.

"Fair enough," Chelsea said.

Emily rose from her seat. "Gotta run, I'll talk to you later."

Chelsea said goodbye and Emily headed for the exit. She called Stacey as soon as she settled into her car. "Hey girl, what's up?" Emily asked.

"Girl, I need to facetime you for this, hold on."

Stacey hung up and called Emily back. When Stacey's face appeared on Emily's phone, she was grinning from ear to ear.

"Girl, what are you so happy about?" Emily asked, relieved that nothing was wrong.

Stacey held up her left hand and showed off a brilliant oval-cut diamond ring on her fourth finger. "I'm engaged!" Stacey shrieked. Emily gasped with shocked. This was completely unexpected. "Walter asked me to marry him on Valentine's Day! It was so romantic. There were rose petals, champagne, and chocolates. I mean he went all out," Stacey gushed. Emily wanted to be happy for Stacey, but she just didn't like Walter.

Stacey often told her that he was wonderful at buying her fancy things but was terrible at giving her time and affection. Stacey said that whenever she mentioned it to Walter, he would tell her that she was too clingy and other girls would be happy to receive the things she received from him. From what Emily understood, he never attempted to love Stacey in the manner that she needed. There were other isolated incidents that Stacey had told Emily about their relationship that bugged her. Any issues Stacey had with Walter always seemed to be Stacey's fault. So, Emily wasn't necessarily happy that Stacey was engaged to a man who seemed cold, unaffectionate, and egotistical.

"Oh, wow, Stace. That's crazy. Congrats!" Emily tried to exude happiness, but her friend saw right through her façade. "Thanks. You know I would love it if you were my maid of honor," Stacey said a little less enthusiastically.

"Of course, of course, you know I'll support you," Emily said.

There was a stint of silence before Stacey continued. "Emily, why don't I feel like you're really happy for me?"

*"Ugh, I thought I put on my happy face. She knows me too well,"* Emily thought.

"Why do you say that?" Emily asked.

"Because whenever you say 'that's crazy' to people, it means you aren't that interested in what they have to say, or you disagree with something they said. Plus, I know when you are faking, Emily. And you're faking right now." It was evident that Emily's lack of excitement displeased her.

"It's not that I'm not happy for you, Stace. I just want the best for you," Emily said apologetically.

"So, you don't think Walter is what's best for me?" Stacey asked.

"Do you?" Emily countered.

"Oh, so now you're getting smart," Stacey replied, now visibly upset.

"No, I mean, if you're happy, then I'm happy for you, girl. I just know that you've had some issues with him, and I don't know if getting married without those issues being resolved is the best thing to do. You even mentioned leaving him at one point, so this is a shock. Marriage is a huge commitment, and I don't want you to go into it lightly," Emily explained. Stacey looked as if she was about to explode.

"Well, you know what, Emily? When you're in a relationship, issues happen. No one is perfect. Or has it been so long since you've been in a relationship that you've forgotten how they work?"

*"Oh, no she didn't,"* Emily thought. "Wait a minute now, Stace. I'm honestly just concerned for you. Now it may've been a while since I've been in a relationship, but from what you've told me about Walter, he isn't exactly the best candidate for marriage. And deep down, you feel the same way too. You just wanted me to co-sign this engagement so you could feel better about it," Emily snapped.

"No, Emily. That's not it. I just wanted my friend to be a friend. I wanted some support, that's all. But you can't seem to manage that. In fact, you have a track record for not showing support and quite frankly, I'm sick and tired of it." Stacey's anger was now clearly evident. She was such a calm, peaceful person. Combativeness looked unusual on her.

"Stace, just chill, okay? I only want to see you happy, and if marrying Walter makes you happy, then fine. I'll be right there by your side," Emily said.

"But will you, Emily? Because it seems to me that every time it's time to celebrate me, you're absent."

Emily's face screwed up in confusion. "What are you talking about? I've always celebrated and supported you."

"No, you haven't Emily!" Stacey yelled. "You weren't there for my college graduation, but I was there for yours. When I told you that I was thinking about starting my cupcake business, you gave me more criticism than you did support. And on my grand opening, you weren't even there."

"Stacey, you know I had that big closing on your grand opening and—"

Stacey cut her off. "And now that I tell you that I'm engaged, you just can't be happy for me. I'm actually starting to wonder if you're really my friend."

Emily felt her face getting hot. "Stacey, you know good and doggone well I'm your friend! A real friend isn't going to stand by and watch their friend possibly fail. I only gave you criticism when you told me about your business because you have the tendency to procrastinate. I wanted you to be on your game. I didn't attend your graduation because I was showing a home to my biggest client at the time. As a matter of fact, *you* told me not to come to your graduation because you wanted me to have that major accomplishment under my belt. So, where is all this animosity coming from?" Emily stared at Stacey in confused anger.

"You don't get it Emily. It would have been nice if you had just once, chosen to support me instead of choosing your career," Stacey said. "You always pick your career over your family and loved ones and it's not right. There are things that you do that I don't think is right, but I don't call you out on it. I just let you do you and I remain *supportive* of your decisions. But you ... you can't do that. You always have to slide in your little negative commentary first and then say, 'Oh, but I support you' secondly." Stacey was fuming. Emily had no clue she felt like this.

"Stacey, it's never my intention to be negative. I'm just trying to be honest. I'm only real with you because I love you. C'mon, Stace. You know I support you! I'm sorry for not showing you support the way you needed it in the past, but you know I'll be right by your side at your wedding. So, let's just move on, okay?" Emily didn't like arguing with Stacey like this. They'd only had a handful of disagreements since grade school, but none of them had ever been this intense. Emily just wanted to diffuse the debate and make amends.

"Moving on sounds great, Emily. That's exactly what I think we should do," Stacey said, looking away from the phone.

"Good, okay. So, what's the first thing you want to do? Gown shopping, planning the bridal shower?" Emily asked.

Stacey turned her face back towards her phone. "No, I mean I think we should move on from each other," she said with a solemn expression.

*"Move on from each other? What in the world is Stacey talking about? She wants to stop being friends? Why is she being so dramatic?"* Emily thought.

"Stacey, chill. You're blowing this way out of proportion," she said.

"No, I'm not, Emily," Stacey said, close to tears. "You blow me off all the time. I can't count how many times you've canceled plans with me for work or to go support someone else. You just did it again at Christmas." Emily thought about how disappointed Stacey sounded when she cancelled their plans to go to her cousin Julianne's bachelorette party, but she hadn't thought it was that big of a deal. She'd thought Stacey understood.

"And to add insult to injury, you go and hang out with Chelsea with no problem at all." Stacey's eyes were on the brink of watering. "You claimed that you were so swamped with work and overwhelmed with your dad's illness, yet you made time to hang out with her. But you could never find time to hang out with me when you were swamped." Emily didn't know what to say. She felt terrible. "It's like you think I'm optional. Like you can blow me off and I'll just always be there for you."

"And this isn't coming out of nowhere," Stacey said, shaking back her emotions. "I've been thinking about it for a while now. I just didn't want it to come to this because you are my best friend. You are like my sister." Stacey's voice cracked at her last statement. "But I can't continue to be your friend because I finally see that I've been your friend, but you haven't been mine. So, as you said, let's move on. I can't be friends with someone who only half-heartedly supports my future marriage anyway. That's just not conducive or healthy for anyone involved. I'll be praying for your dad's health. Send your family my love. Bye, Emily," Stacey said.

"Stacey wait," Emily said, but she had already ended the call. Emily sat in her car, stunned. She couldn't believe it. Stacey had been her best friend since the 2nd grade. No way their friendship had ended via a FaceTime phone call. Emily looked at the time on the car clock. She needed to get going to show Mr. and Mrs. Donahue a few homes. She didn't have time to process what had just occurred. Duty called.

Emily pulled out of the parking lot of the restaurant and headed to the house showing. *"Maybe she's right,"* Emily thought. She had literally just had lunch with Chelsea in the midst of her being behind at work. *"If Stacey was in town and asked you to meet for lunch, would you have done it? Or would you have denied her and worked through lunch?"* she asked herself. Emily felt excessive guilt. She knew the answer. Stacey was right.

*"I'll make it right,"* Emily thought. But at the current moment, she had to put her game face on. Mrs. Donahue wasn't happy about Tony standing in for their first house showing, and she had made sure Emily knew about it. It was time to makeup for disappointing Mrs. Donahue. Emily didn't understand why everything seemed to be going wrong within the last three months. *"Why so much turmoil and uncertainty?"* she thought. *"It doesn't matter,"* she reasoned. *"Life goes on with or without you."* So, she decided to go on.

Emily pulled up at 2:08 p.m. for the 2:00 p.m. scheduled house showing. Mr. and Mrs. Donahue were already standing outside the house peeping through the windows. Emily beat herself up for not arriving five minutes earlier or at least on time. She always found tardiness to be unprofessional. Walking up the driveway at 2:09 p.m. was below her standard but the blow-up with Stacey had pushed her behind schedule. *"I need to tighten up. I'm slipping big time,"* Emily thought.

As if reading her mind, Mrs. Donahue expressed her earnest disappointment in Emily's late arrival. "Ms. Waters, I must say I didn't expect you to be late. Honey, are you sure we have one of Hassen's best? Because if so, I'd hate to see their worst," Mrs. Donahue said while looking Emily up and down.

"Don't start," Mr. Donahue said as he shot Mrs. Donahue a look.

"I'm sorry for keeping you guys waiting. My sincere apologies," Emily said.

"You didn't keep us waiting that long, Ms. Waters. We just arrived two minutes ago ourselves," Mr. Donahue assured Emily.

"You all are still due an apology, sir. I'm hopeful that this home will strike your interest." Emily fished for the house key in her purse but couldn't find it. *"Shoot, where is it? Think, Emily, Think."* She turned around to face a perturbed Mrs. Donahue and a patient Mr. Donahue. "It appears I left the keys in my glove compartment. Give me just one second," she said, embarrassed, as she shuffled past the couple.

Emily jogged to her car, grabbed the keys from the glove compartment, and hurried back to the front door. "Here we are. Let's take a look at what could possibly be your brand-new home," she said, forcing a friendly smile.

The couple stepped into the house and looked around. Emily crossed her fingers, hoping that they remained open to living quarters that were smaller than those they had requested. Truth be told, no matter how hard she tried, Emily could not find a house with their requested specification with their feeble loan. This had already been explained to the couple. Mr. Donahue seemed to understand, but Mrs. Donahue was a different story.

Emily showed the home with as much selling power as she possessed, but Mrs. Donahue was not having it. "Is this the best you could find? I'm not impressed at all," she said.

*"Impressed? Baby, you don't have the loan approval to be impressed!"* Emily thought. "I have a few other homes I can show you, Mrs. Donahue, but please bear in mind that your pre-approval amount will limit some of your expectations."

"Limit my expectation? Girl, listen here. I know the God that I serve. I know that our credit score and approval rate isn't great, but I also know that our God is limitless. I'm believing in Him for a miracle, regardless of what you or anyone else says."

Mr. Donahue went over to Mrs. Donahue and rubbed her back. "Baby, calm down. Ms. Waters is just doing her job." For a moment, it looked as if Mrs. Donahue was on the verge of tears but that quickly disappeared as she shook off her husband's arms.

"Can't you at least show us some better-looking homes?" Mrs. Donahue asked. "The only reason I even chose Hassen's is because I felt led there. I put it all in God's hands and figured that whoever He set us up with would be able to help us, but maybe I was wrong." Regardless of Mrs. Donahue's nasty attitude, Emily wished she could do more for the couple. Yet, it was out of her hands.

"It's not suggested that we show out-of-budget homes to clients, but I will be glad to show you a few other homes within your price range if you'd like," Emily said.

Mrs. Donahue breathed deeply. "Fine. I guess I'm asking for too much. Show us what else you have."

Emily nodded her head. "Yes, ma'am." She escorted them out of the home and showed them a few more selections. Although Mrs. Donahue wasn't satisfied with either of the houses, Mr. Donahue told Emily they would be in touch with her as soon as they made a decision. When he was out of earshot of his wife, Mr. Donahue asked Emily to excuse her behavior.

"I'm sorry about my wife, Ms. Waters. She's been stressed lately and tends to snap at everyone, myself included."

*"I'm stressed too but I'm not being nasty to people,"* Emily thought. "Thank you, Mr. Donahue. I will do my best to ensure that you guys are offered a great price for whichever home you decide."

Mr. Donahue nodded his head in appreciation. "Thank you," he said as he walked towards his vehicle.

Although she was emotionally drained, Emily headed back into the office to do some more work before calling it a day. It was the middle of February and based on her current progress, she wouldn't make her February numbers either. But she was determined to make everything work. She told herself she could carry the weight of her career and spend the extra time with her parents if she willed herself to do it. She could also mend her friendship with Stacey and figure out what to do about Tony. Then there was Angelo. She'd figure out what was going on with that situation too.

Emily had another flight home coming up in a few days. Her dad fussed about her stretching herself too thin by visiting home every two weeks, but Emily's mind was made up. She was going to be more present with her family. She thought maybe she'd ease up on the frequent trips when Benjamin's health was more stable. She fantasized about her dad's improved health. She was sure from her research and her own gut that the kidney transplant was her dad's best option.

So, during her next trip to Georgia, Emily planned to take the necessary first steps towards her radical plan. Emily knew the surgery would put her out of work for at least two weeks—maybe more—and her numbers would consequently take a hit, but she made peace with it. Her dad was worth it. Estella agreed with Emily's plan and said she would do it herself if she wasn't pregnant. She was glad to know she had Estella's support. Now, if only she could get her dad to support her plan too.

FEBRUARY 2020
SAVANNAH, GEORGIA

"Emily Waters," the front-desk clerk at the medical facility called, and Emily moved forward to fill out her donor paperwork. To say that she was nervous was an understatement. She was so focused on finding a solution to help Benjamin that she hadn't fully weighed the severity of surgery. Signing 'in the event of death' papers and reading up on the possible negative side effects of the donor and recipient surgeries made Emily apprehensive. *"What other options do I have? Dad's too stubborn to even consider the surgery. This is the only way to get his attention."*

Emily finished the paperwork and headed back toward the front desk. The woman in line ahead of her brushed passed her. She had on a powder-blue sweatshirt that read 'Beauty for Ashes' across the front. *"Umm, that's what Angelo said over burgers last month."* Emily thought while staring at the lady's shirt.

"Yes, ma'am, how may I help you?" the front-desk clerk asked as she called Emily forward.

"I'm just turning in my donor paperwork."

The woman looked over her papers. "I see that you wish to donate to your father, Benjamin Waters. Has he completed his paperwork as well?"

Emily adjusted her purse strap and thought of how to rationally explain her plan without feeling like a complete idiot. "No, he hasn't. I actually want it to be a surprise," Emily said.

"How sweet of you," the clerk replied. "So, is he currently on the waiting list?"

Emily racked her brain for an answer. *"You can sell water to a fish, Emily. C'mon, you got this."*

"No, he's on dialysis right now, and he's a little nervous about surgery. But if he sees his baby girl willing to go under the knife, he'll do it too. He's far too competitive to allow his little girl have more courage than him," Emily smiled.

The lady smiled kindly at Emily. "We appreciate your generosity. In the event that your father does not want to proceed with the surgery, will you still participate in the donor surgery?" Emily had toyed with that question for a while now. One minute she was okay with being a donor to a stranger and the next minute she wasn't.

"Can I think about that a little while longer?" Emily asked.

"Sure, that's no problem. For now, we will proceed with blood work. We already have your father's blood information. We will need a sample of your blood to test for kidney compatibility." The clerk studied her monitor. "Let's see. Our labs are closed on weekends, but we can fit you in Monday."

The lady looked at Emily for confirmation. "I have to fly back home tomorrow, and I won't be back for another two weeks," Emily said, disappointed.

"That's okay, we can go ahead and get you scheduled for blood work in two weeks. The results are normally available the same day so we can determine compatibility then as well."

"That's great, pencil me in. And please don't notify my father about any of this. Remember, it's a surprise." The lady dragged her fingers across her lips as if she were zipping her mouth shut.

"Your secret is safe with us."

Emily smiled at her and walked out of the facility. She looked up toward the bright afternoon sun and breathed in the cool air. *"Alright, God. I'm stepping out on faith. You do the rest. Change my father's heart. Thank you in advance."*

Benjamin sat in his recliner chair with his feet up, staring intently at the TV. "Pass the ball, man, pass the ball!" Emily walked in just in time to catch the next play. She sat down with two cold beverages and handed one to her dad while she tuned in. The NBA star dribbled the ball, drove towards the basket, and missed the shot.

"See, that's the problem right there. We got a ball hog on our hands." Benjamin shook his head while Emily nodded her head in agreement.

"Yeah, he's been hogging the ball all night," she said.

Emily loved to watch sports with her dad. Benjamin had played football and basketball in his younger years and always loved competitiveness. There was so much of Emily's personality that mirrored her dad's. She never backed down from someone challenging her courage.

The more she thought about how the surgery would be a challenge to her dad's fear, the more she believed her plan would work.

They finished watching the game and Elena called next on the TV. "Alright, y'all have watched enough sports. Now move over and let momma watch Lifetime while I eat my butter pecan ice cream." Elena settled in her seat and buried herself under her covers. Although frequent visits to Georgia had put a strain on her career, she loved every minute of it. She'd spent so much time away from her parents that she'd forgotten how vital being around them truly was. It filled a love void that she didn't know was missing. Her dad's sickness was a weird blessing in disguise.

"Mom, you know exactly how the movie is going to end before it even starts. All Lifetime movies are the same," Emily said.

"And I'm still going to watch it because I like it," Elena said with a comedic smug look. "Now hush up and let me watch my movie."

*"Just like old times,"* Emily thought. Every time Emily thought she was losing her career for the sake of family, she was reminded that family was more important.

*"I should slow down and smell the roses more often,"* she thought as the movie started. *"What's the point of being successful with no time to enjoy it with family?"* Emily began to rethink her sacrifices. The blow-up with Stacey was yet another reminder of how she'd put her loved ones on the back burner. She needed a change. She had to change. But she didn't know how to strike a work-life balance without being utterly overwhelmed. Moving back to Georgia wasn't something she wanted to do, but something had to give, and it needed to give sooner than later.

## MARCH 2020—CALIFORNIA

Emily was beginning to feel discouraged. She had just spoken with Ms. Rugsby about her February numbers. Emily had worked overtime to make up for lost time. She was giving her career the best she had, given her circumstances, but her best wasn't good enough. Emily's new mediocre work performances were taxing on her ego. Yet, Ms. Rugsby had faith in her. In fact, she gave Emily a redemptive responsibility.

"Emily, tough times happen," Ms. Rugsby said. "I know you're being hard on yourself but please know that your recent drop in numbers doesn't take away from how you have exemplified what it means to be a star realtor at this company." Ms. Rugsby stopped and looked her square in the eyes. "Emily, you are single-handedly the best realtor Hassen's has ever had ... which is why I want to place a dear friend of mine in your hands."

Ms. Rugsby smoothed down the lapel of her tailored gray pantsuit. "Not only is she a companion, but she runs in some pretty important political circles here in the city. She's searching for a home and wants to purchase one as soon as possible. That being said, if you are up to it, I am willing to personally refer you."

Emily lit up at the opportunity to redeem herself. She was both relieved and honored that Ms. Rugsby believed in her ability to take on a trusted assignment. Emily knew without a doubt that even if her March numbers were below average again, she would 100% knock this special assignment from Ms. Rugsby out of the park.

"But if you don't think you can handle it..."

Emily cut in. "Ms. Rugsby, I can handle it. I know I can. Refer her to me, and I will confirm to you why I am still one of the best here," she said as her eyes blazed.

Ms. Rugsby smiled. "Okay, I'm counting on you, Emily. Don't let me down." Emily stood up to shake Ms. Rugsby's hand. "I won't, Ms. Rugsby. You can count on me."

Ms. Rugsby nodded and made her exit, upon which Emily pranced around her office and gleamed at her new assignment. It was show time. Just then, Tony strolled past her office door and leaned on the post.

"Knock, knock. I didn't know there was a party going on in your office, Peach. What did I miss?" Embarrassed, Emily stopped dancing to the victory music playing in her head. She wondered how ridiculous she looked bopping around idiotically, but she was too excited to care.

"Hey, Tony. Nothing. I'm just umm … it's just a joyful day. Don't you think?"

She hadn't given Tony any more thought since he asked her to reconsider him. He hadn't mentioned it since then either, so she thought maybe he wasn't serious. *"If he was really interested in being with me, he would have put in the effort,"* she thought.

"May I pull up the door for a quick second?" Tony asked. Emily didn't want to be bothered, but she obliged. Tony pulled the door closed and sat in front of Emily. "Did you look over the folder?" he asked. He was once again wearing that lingering cologne that she knew would waft through her nostrils long after his departure.

"Yes, I looked it over," she said. She didn't plan on expounding, but she knew he would not likely leave without knowing what she thought.

Tony scanned Emily's face. "So, you understand that I never played with you, Emily. I was never dealing with you, my wife, or any other woman at the same time. I only wanted you, and I still only want you."

Emily wished she could just dismiss Tony, but truth be told, she liked him. She couldn't help that she was attracted to him. She also couldn't help how charming she found him. Yet, she wasn't sure about him.

"Tony, I … I don't really know what to tell you," Emily stammered.

"Tell me the truth, Peach. Tell me how you feel."

Butterflies gathered in Emily's stomach. She breathed deeply. "Even if I agreed to be with you, I don't think a relationship built on false pretenses will last. How can I ever place my confidence in you if I know that you are willing to withhold information from me to get what you want?" Tony leaned back in his chair. His eyes never left hers.

"I can't convince you to trust me, Peach. Putting your trust in me is something that you will have to decide to do … and I agree that if you believe this relationship or situation-ship started off on false pretenses then it won't last." Tony got up from his chair. "But to me, it didn't start off on false pretenses, it started off on a mutual attraction between two people. It started off with good times and better conversations. Peach, our chemistry and potential to have something great is there. You can't deny that. Just know that what you consider false pretenses, I consider a man willing to take a risk to get what he wanted."

Tony walked towards the door but stopped and turned around. "But I'll wait for you, Peach. I'll wait for you to make a decision. And I'll wait for you to build your trust in me. Whatever I can do to assure you, I'll do it. But I don't want to wait in vain. So, I'll need an answer eventually, Peach." With that, Tony walked out of the door, once again leaving behind his teasing cologne that muddied her emotions. Tony, just being Tony, tended to make a mess of her feelings.

Her mind told her a clear-cut no. *"He knowingly didn't tell you he was married and probably would have never told you about it. You had to find out from someone else. He can't be trusted."* But her emotions said, *"You like him, Emily, and he likes you too. You had great times together. And look at him! God took his time with that man. Plus, his wife left him first. So, was it really that bad?"* Emily needed some advice. Stacey would've been her go-to in an issue like this, but she wasn't an option right now. Emily texted Chelsea instead.

*"Are you free for dinner tonight? I need to vent."*

Emily waved at Chelsea from her seat. Chelsea spotted her and headed her way. Chelsea's walk could've easily been used on a runway. As she sashayed towards Emily, she caught a couple of eyes. Chelsea tossed her designer bag into the booth and slid into the seat across from Emily.

"Dish the tea, girl," Chelsea said.

Emily thought Chelsea was a bit unorthodox. 'Hey, how are you?' would've been her standard greeting before spilling the beans, but she supposed Chelsea didn't see the point of beating around the bush.

"Umm, well. I'm in a dilemma. I don't know what to do about this guy," Emily said. Chelsea rolled her eyes.

"Girl, I told you that man was lying to you. I'm more than sure that he's married with kids, and he wants you to be his little mistress. Don't give him another thought." Emily waited for Chelsea to finish degrading Angelo before she corrected her.

"I'm actually not talking about him. I'm talking about another guy." Chelsea smirked and crossed her legs.

"Oh, you have a *couple* of guys on your repertoire? No shame in that, honey. Okay, what's his name and what's the issue?"

"I don't have any guys on my repertoire. I'm not even currently dating," Emily said. Chelsea nodded her head as if she didn't believe Emily.

"Uh, huh, sure," Chelsea said.

Emily rolled her eyes and continued. "He's someone I was previously involved with, but I ended it based on what I believed to be a lie. And his name is Tony." Emily went on to explain the situation and waited for Chelsea's response.

"Honestly, Emily, I think it's romantic," Chelsea said as she stirred her sangria.

"Romantic? What's romantic about lying?" Emily asked.

"No, I mean it's romantic in the sense that he felt as if he couldn't risk losing you. That's the only reason he didn't tell you he was married, right? He just didn't want anyone else to move in on what he wanted. I find it romantic that he didn't want to risk that. Sounds like he really likes you to me."

If Emily wasn't confused before, she was definitely confused now. She'd thought Chelsea was going to tell her to ditch Tony. "So, you think withholding information, which I think is the equivalent to lying, is okay?" Emily asked.

"I don't think it's that black and white in this situation," Chelsea said. "The fact that he gave you an entire file to prove his innocence shows just how much he wants to clear his name with you. And then for him to say he's willing to wait on you?" Chelsea tilted her head back and shimmied her shoulders. "Oh, child. This Tony guy is giving me chills. I think you should give him a second chance."

Emily stared at Chelsea. She thought her advice was horrible. She'd wanted her to co-sign her thoughts but meeting up with Chelsea had only sent her into more obscurity.

"So, are you going to give Tony a second chance?" Chelsea asked. Emily took a deep breath and looked out of the window. She wasn't opposed to giving second chances. *"Everyone messes up sometimes, and even God says to forgive seventy times seven, right?"* she thought to herself.

"Earth to Emily," Chelsea said as she snapped her fingers. "Dang, can I have a moment to think?" Emily asked.

"Girl my bad. Get me together then," Chelsea said with a slight attitude. Emily looked down at her plate and back up to Chelsea.

"Maybe, I will. I need to think more about it."

Chelsea smiled. "Good, at least you're considering it." But Emily wasn't quite satisfied with Chelsea's reasoning.

"What if he has a habit of withholding information though? What if that's a red flag? I'm all for second chances but I just don't know," Emily said. She felt the urge to seek a second opinion on Chelsea's advice.

"Well, if you're all for second chances then give him another chance. You won't know if he's a habitual liar unless you catch him in another lie."

Chelsea's phone rang. Incoming call from Victoria showed on her screen.

"I'm sorry, girl, let me answer this," Chelsea said.

*"Victoria? Is that Ms. Prissy Vicky?"* Emily thought.

Chelsea chatted on her phone for a bit and then paused. "Wait a second, Vicky. You won't believe who I'm having dinner with ... Emily Waters ... Yes! Emily from high school," Chelsea continued. "Vicky said hello, Emily," Chelsea said. Before Emily could respond, Chelsea pulled her phone back and covered the mic.

"Hey, Emily. Let's ask Victoria what she thinks about Tony." Emily looked at Chelsea for a moment. She wasn't too keen on telling her business to other people, especially to two girls that were known to be gossipers in high school. But that was nearly 10 years ago. Chelsea seemed different, and Emily wanted advice.

"Go ahead," she said. Chelsea gave Victoria the details. *"I can't believe I'm seriously going to listen to what Ms. Prissy Vicky has to say,"* Emily thought.

Chelsea's face screwed up as she listened to Victoria's advice. Emily cocked her head to the side. "What'd she say?" she asked.

Chelsea looked at Emily. "I'll let her tell you." Chelsea handed Emily the phone. Emily awkwardly grabbed it. She didn't know what to expect.

"Hello?" Emily said.

"Hi, Emily how are you?" Victoria said.

"I'm good and you?" Emily replied.

"I'm good, thanks. So, I was just telling Chelsea that I think you should pray about it."

Emily paused. *"I know Ms. Prissy Vicky isn't advising prayer,"* Emily thought. "Pray about it?" she repeated like a parrot. Her shock at Victoria's response kept her from responding adequately.

"Yes, pray about it. Whether he didn't want to miss out on getting with you or not, he was still in a covenant marriage and should've had no dealings with you until he was a single man," Victoria said. "And I am with you, it could be a red flag. I'm not saying to dismiss him. But I think you should be cautious … and pray. I don't know if you believe in God or not but that's just my advice."

Emily was lost for words. She didn't know how to respond. Not only did Victoria give her what she considered sound advice, but even her tone of voice was different.

Ms. Prissy Vicky's voice always dripped with attitude, even if she didn't have an attitude, but the woman's voice on the phone didn't have a drop of nastiness in it. Emily's mind finally caught up to give a response.

"Yes, I'll do that. We actually have the same viewpoint on this." Chelsea gave a mocking face and beckoned for her phone. "Okay, well it was good talking to you and thanks for your input. Chelsea's asking for her phone." Emily handed Chelsea her phone.

"Alright, girl. I'll talk to you later," Chelsea said to Victoria and ended the call. Chelsea asked for the check and finished her drink. "Listen, I love Vicky and all, but lately she's been acting holier than thou," Chelsea said. "A couple of months ago she was basically unreachable and when we finally hung out again, we just didn't vibe the way we used to." Emily thought she had picked up on a little tension between Chelsea and Victoria, but she didn't want to assume. Now, she knew there was a bit of uneasiness between the two.

"She's still my homie but she doesn't seem to want to talk to me the way we used to." Emily thought about her recent fallout with Stacey and felt bad for Chelsea, yet she didn't want to speak on the ordeal. *"That's none of your business,"* Emily thought.

"Well, maybe y'all can talk it out," Emily said.

"Maybe," Chelsea replied. They sat and talked a little bit longer before they parted ways.

Emily thought about the difference in opinion between Chelsea and Victoria. Before bed that night, although she couldn't believe it, she took Victoria's advice. She prayed, *"God, I don't know what to do about Tony. Please guide my decision. Give me some sort of indication as to what I should do. In Jesus name. Amen."* Emily thought about Angelo right after she prayed. She had to meet him the next day to pick up his offer letter. He'd decided to make an offer on the first spacious home Emily showed him. She told him that the realtor normally writes the offer letter, but Angelo insisted that she at least take his letter and revise it as she saw fit.

Emily sent up one more prayer. *"And God, about this Angelo guy..."* Emily felt silly for praying about a guy who was just a client, but she knew God already knew what was in her heart. So, she continued to pray. *"I don't know what to make of him. If there's something there, let that be revealed too."* More prayer requests came to her mind. *"In every area of my life, God, give me clarity. Please restore my dad's health and if Stacey is meant to be in my life, restore that relationship as well. In Jesus' name. Amen."* Then she climbed into bed and fell asleep.

Emily arrived at Angelo's place bright and early. She followed the directions to his home and assumed she was in the wrong neighborhood. She double checked her GPS, but it showed she was in the correct area. The apartment complex he lived in wasn't in the best shape. She was confused. *"How did he get approved for that home? Surely, he doesn't willingly live here with the income he must have."* Emily rang the doorbell and waited. She heard what sounded to be live music coming from his apartment.

"Coming!" Emily heard Angelo yell as he approached the door. He opened the door and smiled. "Good morning, Ms. Waters." Emily looked down and saw Angelo's dog, Guardian, standing at attention next to him.

Emily gasped. "Oh, my goodness, he's so pretty! And big! Can I pet him? —I'm sorry, I'm so rude. Good morning, Angelo."

Angelo laughed, "That's okay. He tends to grab attention and yes, you can pet him."

Emily bent down to pet Guardian. His fluffy black fur was smooth under her hands. "Aw, he seems so sweet. I can't imagine him hurting a fly," Emily cooed.

"He wouldn't ... unless I asked him to. He's excellent at taking commands. That's why he's such a good guard dog. Do you want to come in while I grab the letter for you?" Emily didn't want to be rude.

"Sure, thank you." She stepped into the apartment and looked around.

It wasn't a shabby place. In fact, it was very clean. Minimalistic. It appeared to be a one-bedroom apartment and it didn't look as if Angelo had a lot of belongings. There was no sign of anyone else living there besides Guardian. His doggy bed was nuzzled in a corner. It was a humble abode, but there was a golden trumpet on the sofa that caught

Emily's eye. "I thought I heard live music coming from in here. So, you're a musician?"

Angelo walked over to a drawer and pulled out his offer letter. He handed it to Emily and walked over to the trumpet. "Ugh, I don't really classify myself as a musician. Musicians tend to share their talents with the world. I kind of just play here by myself." Emily watched him as he fiddled with the horned instrument.

"I don't mean to impose, but are you any good?"

Angelo grinned at her. "I think that's a subjective question. How about I play a little tune and you judge for yourself?" Emily nodded in agreement.

"Okay, let's see what you've got."

Angelo stood up and placed his fingers on the trumpet. He breathed into the instrument and intricately moved his fingers back and forth across the valves. The music he produced sounded like a slice of heaven. Emily lost herself in the notes. She closed her eyes and savored every key and riff change. She opened her eyes only when Angelo finished playing. She looked at him as he placed the instrument down.

"So, what'd you think?" Angelo asked.

Emily put her hands on her hips. "What do I think? Are you kidding me? That was the best live music I've heard in my entire life. I mean it was terrific! I don't have the words to express how terrific that was." Angelo sat down and blushed. "Where did you learn to play like that?"

Angelo motioned for her to sit down. "You can have a seat if you'd like." Emily walked over and sat next to him on the couch. "It's a gift," he said.

Emily stared at him. "You mean to tell me you naturally play that well? Stop lying," she teased.

Angelo smiled. "Yeah, I was just blessed with the gift. What gifts do you have?" Emily wanted to ask him more about his musical talent, but his question gave her pause.

"Umm, I don't think I have any gifts per se," she said as she glanced towards the ceiling, thinking.

"You don't think you have any gifts or talents? Well, what are you good at? What do you do well?" Angelo asked. Although Emily was accomplished, she never considered herself gifted or talented—just a hard worker. She didn't know how to answer his question.

"I've always been competitive. I have grit as my dad would say," Emily said using air quotes. "I was into gymnastics as a child, and then ran track as a high schooler... I was always the best at sports because I was more determined than everyone else." Emily thought about her career at Hassen's. "I'm also usually the best at my job, but that's slacked off a bit lately." Angelo listened as Emily talked.

"Well, if I had to guess, I'd say that your grit and competitiveness is a gift. And if I were you, I wouldn't stress too much about your job. I'm sure it'll get better."

"You think my personality traits are a gift?" Emily asked. She's never thought of her characteristics as a gift.

"I think personality traits can be used as gifts, yes," Angelo said. "Think of it this way. If someone is naturally optimistic, they can use their optimism to influence others to be hopeful. Whether it's a kind word to a stranger or shifting the environment for those around them with their cheerfulness, their personality becomes a gift to others. I think everyone has a talent or gift. Some people just don't realize they have it. Or they do know they have it and aren't using it correctly."

*"Am I using my gifts correctly?"* Emily thought. She pondered the question for a second before she put her attention back on Angelo. "And how does one know that they are using their gift correctly?" she asked. She was trying to ignore the pestering questions that floated through her mind about Angelo. She could hear Chelsea's voice ringing in her ears along with her own critical thoughts of him. But whenever she was around him, she felt oddly comfortable. Her conscious told her that he wasn't a liar. Yet, she still had so many unanswered questions about him.

"A good indicator is to look at the fruit you are bearing. Does it help anyone? Encourage anyone? Bless anyone? But most importantly, is it what God wants you to do?" Emily was curious as to whether Angelo believed he had it all together.

"Do you think you are using your gifts correctly?" Emily asked.

"Yes, I do," Angelo said.

"Well, you sure aren't sharing your musical gift with the world—" Emily hoped she hadn't offended Angelo, but for someone to be so preachy, she didn't understand why he opted to withhold his talent.

Angelo smiled at her. "I'll tell you what. I'll one day share my talent with the world if you agree to use your grit and competitiveness in the way God wants you to. Deal?" Angelo had his hand reached out for Emily to shake. Emily lifted her chin.

"And how do you know I'm not already using it correctly?" she asked. "Because you asked me how someone knows if they are using it correctly. If you were using it correctly, you wouldn't have to ask.

You'll know when you're walking in your purpose. A knowing comes with it," Angelo said with confidence.

Emily's inquisitiveness kicked in. "Well, why are you so confident that you are walking in your purpose and have yet to play the trumpet for anyone else?" Angelo still had his hand stuck out for Emily to shake.

"Because right now isn't the time for me to share that particular gift. I know it isn't. God will point me in the right direction when it is time. For right now, I know I'm on the right track because I talked to God about it," he said. "Now, are you going to shake my hand or not, Ms. Waters?"

Emily playfully rolled her eyes. She grabbed Angelo's hand and shook it. "Deal," she said, glancing down at the healed wound on his forearm. She wanted to ask about it but decided against it. Guardian walked up to Emily and sat next to her feet.

"I think he likes you," Angelo said. Emily smiled and petted the dog once more. She wanted to stay and talk with Angelo more, but she needed to get going.

"Well, Angelo I appreciate your hospitality, but I need to get going," she said as she stood.

"Of course, of course. Let me see you out." Angelo rose from the couch and walked her to the door.

"I'll review your offer and tweak it if necessary. Hopefully there won't be any back and forth with the seller. But if so, I'm convincing. I'm sure we can talk them down if needed."

Angelo nodded. "You're not one of Hassen's best by chance. I'm sure you will."

Emily gazed at him. *"Goodness, this man is beautiful ... and he's spiritually sound. Why exactly is he single? Or is he single? I don't know. Make your exit, Emily. You're drooling."*

"Why, thank you. I'll be in touch," Emily said.

"Yes, ma'am. Talk to you soon," Angelo said as he waved goodbye. He watched Emily get into her car and didn't close the door until she'd pulled off. There was so much chaos going on in her life, but Angelo had the uncanny ability to make her forget about all her troubles. His spirit was calm, yet his presence was demanding.

Emily was captivated. Yet, she was frustrated because she still didn't know much about him. She was hoping God would answer her prayers about him and everything else soon. In the meantime, she had to go forth with what she could handle on her own. She was scheduled to fly back to Georgia in a few days for her donor blood work. With the plan to save her dad in mind, a redemptive assignment at Hassen's, and the possibility of getting to know Angelo better, things were starting to look up. She drove away from his house with a hopeful smile.

# SAVANNAH, GEORGIA — MARCH 2020

Emily arrived at the medical clinic for donor compatibility testing. She rolled up her sleeve and the nurse stuck her arm with the needle to retrieve a sample. "Alright, that does it," the nurse said as she slid the needle back into its casing "We'll call you later today with the results. In the event that your blood is incompatible with your dad, we do have advanced technology to possibly make the transplant successful. So, don't fret if the results show incompatibility." The nurse handed Emily a compatibility chart as a reference.

"We will be in touch soon. Have a great day Ms. Waters." Emily thanked the nurse, rolled down her sleeve, and exited the building. She was beaming from ear to ear. She knew she would be compatible, based on the chart. She recalled her parents' blood types from memory. She remembered taking a sneak peek at their medical records years ago, and Emily was a shoo-in. *"Now, all I need you to do is change my dad's mind, God. Please do it for me. Do it for him. Do it for all of us."*

As Emily prayed, she headed to her parents' house for a surprise visit. She knew the clinic would likely call in just a few hours. She needed to test her dad's temperate to see if she would reveal her plan to him today or if she would wait. She didn't want to wait until after the donor surgery to tell him, but she was willing to have her kidney sitting on ice before she broke the news if his attitude didn't shift.

"Hey, baby! What are you doing here a day early?" Elena said as she opened the door upon Emily's arrival.

"Just wanted to start the weekend early. I needed the break. You know I've been swamped at work." Emily hated lying to her mom, but she couldn't risk Elena finding out about her plan prematurely. She learned long ago that her mom wasn't the best at keeping secrets.

"Oh well, baby, come on in," Elena said. Emily walked in and saw her dad glued to the TV.

"Well, look who done decided to show up early! How you doing, Emi baby?" Benjamin asked as he got up to hug Emily.

"I'm doing fine, Dad. How are you?"

Benjamin seemed to be in a pleasant mood. "I'm doing better," he said. "What are you doing here today? Thought you were flying in tomorrow. You're not rushing home because of that coronavirus, are you?"

Elena answered before Emily could. "No, she's not running from that virus. She needed a break from work, so she came on home where life is more comfortable. Ain't that right, Emi?"

Emily smiled at her mom. "That's right, Momma."

Benjamin grunted. "Well, if you were running from that virus, I wouldn't blame you. That thing is spreading like wildfire. You know, they have a couple of cases in your state now," Benjamin said. Emily nodded her head. The U.S. had declared a public health emergency last month and the rising cases across the globe was alarming. San Francisco had gone as far as banning public gatherings for a certain number of people. But so far, despite a few changes, life was going on as scheduled.

"Yeah, I know. But work is going on as usual, so I just needed a break," Emily said.

"You wouldn't be overwhelmed with work if you'd stop hot-tailing it down here every two weeks. How are you going to be the best if you can't put your best foot forward? I told you, I want you to take over California. You ain't going to do that from Georgia," Benjamin said as he plopped down on the couch. Emily decided to use one of her old tricks. She knew how to soften her dad's heart when she needed to. Both she and Estella had learned that sometimes Benjamin's hard exterior could melt away like butter with the right words.

Emily curled up by Benjamin, laid her head on his shoulder, and wrapped her arms around his bicep. "I hear you, Dad, and just as soon as you are well, I'll stop making the sacrifice to come down here so often." Benjamin sighed. Emily grinned. She knew her play was working.

"What if I never get off dialysis? You just going to keep risking your career and burning yourself out? Are you going to keep flying back and forth like this?" Benjamin asked. Emily could hear the concern in Benjamin's voice.

"Yes, Daddy. I'm going to risk it all for you because you would do it for me. I can always rebuild my career or get another one. But I only get one dad."

Benjamin argued, "Emi, I'm supposed to risk it all for you. That's how it's supposed to be. I risked it all so that you could have it all. You have so much success in the palm of your hands. I didn't risk it all for you to turn around and throw it away for me." Elena sat quietly in her chair and listened to their banter.

Emily glanced up into her dad's eyes. "Daddy, if you stay on dialysis then I will continue to risk my career, but if you—"

Benjamin cut in. "If I have this surgery, you wouldn't have to travel so much and you'll get back to your career."

Emily sat up and examined her dad's face. Elena's eyes also studied Benjamin. He continued, "And if I have this surgery, I won't be a burden to your momma anymore. She won't have to drag me back and forth to dialysis three times a week to care for me the way she does now."

"It's not a burden, Benjamin," Elena said. Benjamin tossed his hand up, dismissing Elena's statement.

"Yes, it is. I know it is. You don't have to lie about it to spare my feelings. It's interrupting your life. My dialysis is a burden to everyone around me. It's ruining Emi's career, it's making you bend over backwards caring for me, and honestly, it's draining the life out of me," Benjamin confessed. Emily and Elena remained silent as they waited for him to finish.

"And in a couple of months, Estella will birth my first grandchild. I want to be well for him. I thought I could make it just fine on the treatments. I thought I would be okay ... but I'm not." Emily teared up as Benjamin continued. She knew it must've taken a lot out of her dad to swallow his pride and admit the hard reality. Elena continued to study her husband with her hands tightly clasped in her lap. She held her breath as he continued.

Benjamin took a deep breath in and out. "I'll carry any burden for my family, but I refuse to be one to them. God knows I don't want to, but if having the surgery means removing the burden from my family, and if it means I can live a better life than the one I have right now, then I'll have the surgery."

Emily's insides bubbled over with delight. She tossed her head back as tears of joy slid down her cheeks. She threw her arms around her dad and squeezed tightly. "Oh, thank God!" The lump in her throat prevented her from saying anything more.

She glanced over at Elena who also had tears streaming down her face. She got up from her seat and wrapped her arms around both Emily and Benjamin. After they'd hugged for a few more seconds, Elena broke the embrace and wiped the tears from her face. Emily did the same. Benjamin also had a lone tear on his face.

"Oh Jesus!" Elena yelled out, "You're so faithful. I know there's a God in heaven because only God can move a heart as stubborn as yours." Emily laughed out loud in ecstasy.

"Yes! I know right mom! God is so good."

Benjamin smiled. He felt good knowing that his change of heart brought his family great joy and relief.

"I need to call Estella," Emily said as she hopped up from her seat.

"Yes, you call her, and I'll call the doctor and let him know we need to be added to the waiting list. I pray we can get a donor sooner than later." Emily grinned at her mom like a Cheshire cat. "Why are you grinning like that, Emily?" Elena asked.

"I'd hold off on putting Dad on that waiting list, Mom," Emily said still grinning.

"And why is that?" Benjamin asked. Emily turned to face both her parents.

"Because I am your donor," Emily said, with her head lifted in confidence.

"Now, wait a minute, Emi," Benjamin interjected. "I don't want you to give me your kidney. I can wait on the waiting list. I can hold off."

Emily bit her bottom lip. "Daddy, with all due respect, it's not your decision to make. If I give you my kidney you won't have to wait for one. Besides, it's far better to receive a kidney from a living donor than from someone who has passed away. My mind's made up. I've already gone through with the first steps. In fact, the clinic should be calling me today to confirm our compatibility."

Elena's face grew pale. Benjamin looked frantic. "Don't worry, y'all. It'll be fine. It's all aligning exactly how it's supposed to." Emily squeezed her mom's shoulder on the way up the stairs to call Estella. "I promise, Mom. It'll be okay."

Emily FaceTimed Estella when she made it to her old bedroom. "Hey, Emily," Estella answered. "What are you doing back home?"

"Dad's getting the surgery!" Emily blurted out.

"What?" Estella's face lit up. "Did he tell you that?" Emily bobbed her head up and down like a little schoolgirl.

"Yes, he said he didn't want to be a burden on me or Mom anymore and that he wanted to be present for his soon-to-be grandson. So, he'll have the surgery," Emily gleamed.

"Babe," Estella yelled into the other room. Emily saw Reggie enter the room in the background.

"What's going on baby?" Reggie asked.

"Dad's having the surgery!"

"Yo! Are you serious?" Reggie asked with widened eyes.

"Yes, look here's Emily. She just told me."

Reggie hovered over Estella and looked down into the phone. "What up, Emily? Man, are you for real? Pops going to have the surgery?"

Emily's cheeks hurt from smiling so much. "Yep, I'm dead serious Reg. Dad's going through with the surgery ... and I'm going to be his donor." Emily grinned even more.

"Oh wow, Emily. That's what's up. That's love right there," Reggie said. "Hey, I'm going to catch you later. I got some breakfast cooking for your hungry little sister. I don't want it to burn."

Emily shooed Reggie away. "Go ahead bro. Thanks for taking care of my sis." Reggie threw up a piece sign before he left.

"Always," Reggie said as he exited. Estella turned her attention back to Emily.

"So, is everything set? Did you receive the green light for the donor surgery?" Estella asked excitedly. Emily plopped down on the bed.

"I haven't received official word yet. I'm waiting to receive the confirmation call."

Estella let out a sigh. "If I wasn't pregnant, I would've offered my kidney. And I know if Mom didn't have fluctuating blood pressure, she might've tried giving hers too. We don't need you to take the credit for giving Dad a kidney. You already like to gloat too much," Estella teased.

"Hey, what can I say? The G.O.A.T. must gloat," Emily laughed while Estella smirked at her insinuation at being the greatest of all time. "Y'all don't have to sacrifice your feeble organs. Emily will save the day with her well-strengthen kidney," Emily said as she flexed her arms and kissed her muscle.

"Whatever Emily," Estella said snickering at her sister. "Listen, I'll talk to you later. Reggie's calling me to come eat."

Emily watched Estella and her protruding belly as she hobbled towards her kitchen. "Alright, sis. Take it easy. Love you." Emily hung up the phone and laid across the bed. She was floating on cloud nine.

*"Lord, I can't thank you enough for turning my dad's heart. I know that was nobody but you. Thank you."* It wasn't quite noon, but Emily felt a surge of tiredness sweep over her. She stretched and yawned. *"Must be the jet lag and adrenaline,"* she thought. She laid

across her bed and closed her eyes. Within minutes, she slipped into a trance-like sleep. A paralyzing sleep.

She had slipped just beneath the surface of sleep because she heard her phone ring. She tried to snap out of her slumber to answer it, but she couldn't. Her limbs felt locked in place and her mind was stuck in a realm between consciousness and unconsciousness. Emily fought hard to shake herself awake from the dense fog of lethargy that encapsulated her to no avail. Eventually, she stopped fighting the tight grip of oblivion and allowed it to drag her into a deep sleep.

*The weathered grass stands about three feet high. It sways gently in the wind. I'm alone in an open hilly field. In my peripheral vision, I see the grass on top of a hill move. I turn to see what caused the disturbance. I can't see anything, but I feel it. An entity. Moving slowly but deliberately. Then, it appears. A snake. Slick and black, slithering silently down the hill. It is beautiful despite its menacing approach. It drops down from the hill into the grass in the open field where I am standing. Then, it disappears.*

*I put one foot behind the other, slowly inching away from where the snake landed. As I move backwards, the serpent pops its head up from the grass. It gradually rises on its belly displaying its full length. It hovers several feet above the sun-scorched grass flicking its tongue in and out of its mouth. Venomous hisses escape its mouth. Then without warning, the snake decomposes into the grass.*

*I stand still. Too timid to move. "Emily ... Hey, Emily." I whip around. A woman standing in the grass waves from the distance. Her presence is warm and inviting. She's radiant, glowing. Her hair is long and black ... slick and shiny ... just like the snake. I peer at her, but I can't make out her face. She drops down into the grass and disappears.*

*I stand still. My ears are ringing. My eyes dart back and forth. Chills creep up my spine and sweat drops off my brow. It's deathly quiet. The silence is interrupted by a caw. I look up and see a bird. A raven flying over the grass. A folded piece of paper is lodged between its claws. It drops the paper in the grass and flies away.*

*Steadily, I walk forward. I kneel in the grass to locate the note. But I can't find it. I maneuver my hands through grass and dirt desperately. I hear shuffling in the distance. "Emily ... Emily." The woman's voice hisses. I keep shuffling through dirt. More sweat beads form and run down my face. I catch a glimpse of white peeking through the dirt.*

*The note. I hurry to grab the paper. "Emily ..." I can feel the heat of breath on my neck. I unfold the paper.*
Matthew 26:21

Buzz. Buzz. Emily jumped awake at the sound of her phone vibrating on the nightstand. *"Matthew 26:21,"* Emily thought. She immediately grabbed her phone and searched for the verse.

*... Truly I tell you, one of you will betray me."*

Emily read the verse in silence a few times before she put her phone back down. She had never believed in superstition, but she did believe in warnings. If it wasn't for the note left in the grass, she wouldn't have given the dream much thought. But a snake dream paired with a Bible verse was alarming.

Emily grabbed her phone to read the verse once more. She noticed a missed call from the medical center and a social media message notification. The medical center had left a voicemail. She played back the message.

"Ms. Waters, this is Nurse Smith calling to update you on your blood compatibility. Please give us a call at your earliest convenience. Thank you." Emily called back immediately.

"Hello, yes, this is Emily Waters. I missed a call from you all. It was in regards to my blood compatibility results."

"Yes Ms. Waters. This is Nurse Smith. Thank you for calling us back. We were calling to inform you that the results are incompatible. However, this may not be a cause for concern. With today's advanced technology, it is possible that your kidney may still be donated to Mr. Waters. We would like to schedule a consultation with both you and your father to further discuss details." Emily waited for the nurse to finish before she inquired about the obvious error.

"I'm not opposed to a consultation. However, there must be some sort of mistake. There isn't any reason why I shouldn't be compatible with my dad. Can you double-check for accuracy?"

The nurse paused a beat before answering. "Yes, we can do that Ms. Waters. However, considering the sensitive nature of our job, we double check compatibility before we contact any of our clients. If you are available today, feel free to swing by before noon so that we can retrieve another blood sample. We can have your results by the end of business today."

"Yes ma'am. I'm on my way now," Emily said getting up from her bed.

"Great, we will see you shortly. I'll ask the front desk to send you straight back upon your arrival," Nurse Smith said.

"Okay, thank you," Emily said. She ended the call and looked at her social media notification. Victoria Brown sent you a message.

Emily opened the message and read it.

Hey Emily, I know this is completely random ... But can you call me? I need to talk to you.

Victoria listed her number in the message. *"What could she possibly want?"* Emily thought. She pulled on her shoes, grabbed her purse, and headed downstairs.

"Emily, we need to talk to you about you being a donor," Benjamin said when he saw her jogging down the stairs.

"I already told you, it's not your decision, Dad," Emily said as she grabbed the handle to the front door. "But I'll be back in a bit. You can try to talk me out of it later ... though you won't succeed." She winked at Benjamin and locked the door behind her. She jumped in her car and headed toward the medical clinic. She decided to give Victoria a call on the way there.

"Hey, is this Victoria?" she asked.

"Yes, it is. This is Emily, right?"

Emily nodded her head. "Yes, so, what's up?"

Emily couldn't help but remember that Victoria had always had long, shiny black hair. Her profile picture revealed that she still had her dark tresses. Gorgeous flowing hair ... just like the woman from her dream. The woman who hissed her name like a snake. Emily's guard was up.

"Umm, there's no easy way to say this ... but I think you should be cautious of Chelsea," said Victoria.

Emily grabbed her chin with one hand while gripping the steering wheel with the other.

"Why do you say that?" she asked.

"I just think you should be careful," Victoria said.

Emily shifted in her seat. She didn't like the idea of someone who was supposed to be Chelsea's friend talking about her behind her back. She began to think that Ms. Prissy Vicki hadn't changed at all. *"She always had snake-like tendencies,"* Emily thought.

"Isn't she your friend? Why are you advising me to be careful of your own friend?" Emily didn't hold back her cynicism. She didn't like gossip or backstabbers and she didn't have a problem confronting them if they came to her with any mess.

"I know you and I don't have the best history, and I know my past doesn't paint me as a trustworthy person," Victoria said, "but I really think you should stay clear of her."

"Listen, Victoria. I don't mean to be rude, but if you can't tell me why you're saying this about your own friend, then how else am I supposed to view you? Why would I count anything you say as credible?" Emily waited for Victoria's response.

"If I was to be honest, Emily, Chelsea and I aren't on the best of terms. Ever since I got saved, she and I have been distant ... I don't think she's meant to be a part of my life anymore," Victoria said.

Emily dodged in and out of traffic to get to the clinic by noon. "Okay. That explains why *you* may want to distance from her, but why are you suggesting that *I* distance from her?" she asked.

"Because she doesn't really like you, Emily," Victoria said plainly. Emily mulled over Victoria's explanation.

"And how do you know that? Did she tell you that? Or is it just a hunch? Better yet, maybe you know this because you've been gossiping about me to her?" Emily stated matter-of-factly.

"No, I haven't gossiped about you, but Chelsea has said some things about you that didn't sit well with me. I used to engage in gossip with her but lately when she tries to talk to me, I get off the phone with her. I can't live like that anymore," Victoria said.

"You can't? But isn't that what you're doing now? Gossiping about Chelsea to me?" Emily asked.

"No, what I am doing is warning you," Victoria said.

"I won't go into detail, but she seems to be jealous of you. But you do as you please. Continue to hang out with her if you want. I just thought you ought to know. Oh, and I know I said this to you before, but pray about it. Ask God to show you the truth."

Emily didn't know if she should believe Victoria or not. *"Just because she mentioned God and prayer doesn't mean she's being honest. Even demons knew who Jesus was and Satan quoted scripture."* Emily thought. "Okay, then. Thank you," she said as she hung up.

Then it hit her. *"Wait, Chelsea has long flowing black hair too. What if Victoria is right? Or what if they are both snakes? They were always two gossiping peas in a pod."* Emily climbed out of her car and headed into the clinic to give her blood sample again. *"I don't have time for either one of them. I have more important things to do,"* she thought, but as she walked towards the clinic she once again took Victoria's advice.

Emily prayed, *"Lord, I don't want any Judas Iscariots in my life. Show me my enemies and remove them. In Jesus' name, Amen."* She walked through the front door just as she finished praying.

"I'm here for my blood sample. I'm Emily Waters," she told the front desk.

"Yes ma'am, Ms. Waters. The nurse is waiting for you. You can head back straight through those double doors." Emily proceeded to the back, gave her sample, and tried to relax as she thought about how Benjamin would have a better-quality life soon with her kidney donation. She smiled, breathed in, breathed out, and exited the facility with another spurt of hopefulness.

Emily chomped on her mom's chicken salad sandwich and wiped her mouth. "Why are y'all looking like that? It's going to be okay." She had just told Benjamin and Elena, for the one hundredth time, that there was no way they could talk her out of being her dad's donor. Elena looked uncomfortable, as did Benjamin. "What is wrong with y'all?" Emily chuckled. "Everything will work out. We already know God is in this. I asked God to turn your heart Dad, and He did. You didn't want to have this surgery… everybody knows that. God turned your heart towards this surgery because this is His plan."

Sipping on her lemonade, she continued, "Don't y'all fight me on this. God approves of this. I know He does. I'm just waiting on the clinic to call me back so we can get the ball rolling. So, just let this happen, okay?" Emily adored how concerned her parents were about her wellbeing. They had sacrificed so much for her throughout the years. Emily found honor in making this sacrifice for her dad's health. Benjamin sat up in his chair. "Emily, I—"

Ding dong. "I'll get it." Emily jumped up and rushed to the door to greet her sister.

"Hey, Stella." Estella had texted Emily earlier and told her she and Reggie were on the way to celebrate Benjamin's change of heart. They only lived 20 minutes away, so they were there in no time.

"Hey girl," Estella said as she hugged Emily. "I can't thank you enough for doing this for Dad." Emily squeezed her sister while being careful of her bulging belly.

"Girl, of course. I love him too much not to do it."

Reggie stepped in behind Estella. "What's up, Em?" he said as he hugged Emily.

"Nothing much bro-in-law."

"Shoot, I don't know about that. You giving up a kidney. That sounds like a bit much to me. You're always trying to one-up somebody. How can I ever top a kidney donation?" Reggie joked.

"I don't know, bro," Emily laughed. "You just need to step your game up is all I can suggest."

They all laughed and headed toward the dining room where Benjamin and Estella were.

"Hey, hey, hey!" Estella said as she hurried over to hug Benjamin. "I'm so happy for you, Dad." She and Reggie both hugged and greeted Elena as well.

"What brings y'all over?" Benjamin asked.

"Umm, hello, Dad? A celebration brings us over." Estella reached down into her oversized purse and pulled out a bottle of sparkling cider. "We simply must celebrate the move of God. Him changing your mind is reason to pop a bottle," she grinned.

"Yeah Pops," Reggie chimed in. "It's a little cool outside, but I'll throw something on the grill if you don't mind."

"And I'll whip up the side dishes," Estella said as she looked at Elena. "Mom, you just rest for once. You look like you need it. Relax. Emily will be okay with one kidney. You and Dad need to stop stressing."

Emily wrapped her arms around her mom. "Yes, Mom for goodness' sake, I'll be fine. I'll help you with those sides, Estella," she said. She smiled as she washed her hands to prep the food. A celebratory BBQ was just what the family needed.

Emily's phone rang just as she dried her hands. It was the medical clinic.

"Hello," Emily answered. She put the phone on speaker so that everyone could hear and celebrate the good news.

"Yes, may I speak to Emily Waters?" the woman asked.

"Speaking," Emily replied.

"This is Nurse Smith calling you with your blood compatibility results."

Emily grinned. "Yes, ma'am."

The nurse continued, "Unfortunately, Ms. Waters, the blood test is once again reading as incompatible." Emily frowned and cocked her head to the side.

"No ma'am, that can't be right," Emily refuted.

"Ms. Waters, do you know your blood type?" Nurse Smith asked.

Emily shifted her feet before she answered. "I know both my parents are *B* blood type. So, I assumed I was an *O* or *B*."

The rummaging of Nurse Smith shoveling through papers caused static over the line before she spoke. "Well, Ms. Waters, your blood type is *AB*. I only asked if you were aware of your blood type because the compatibility chart given to you would have shown you that *AB* blood type is incompatible with *B* blood type."

Emily looked up at her mom. Elena looked panicked. She looked over at her dad. He had a stony facial expression. Estella and Reggie looked just as confused as she did.

"Both *O* and *B* blood types would have been compatible, correct?" Emily asked, glaring at her parents.

"That is correct," Nurse Smith answered. Emily's eyes darted between Benjamin and Elena. They both refused to look at her.

"Can you give me one second?" Emily asked Nurse Smith.

"Yes, ma'am. Take your time."

Emily paced up the stairs into her room. She unzipped her suitcase and grabbed her donor research folder.

Emily had explored the ins and outs of donor surgery, compatibility, risks, and the likes. Her radical plan was perfect. She knew she hadn't mistaken her blood type. She was too meticulous to make such a blatant error. She flipped through the papers until she saw the paternity-determination blood-type chart. Emily read over the results of *B* and *B* blood type parents. The chart read: O or B.

No AB blood type in sight. "Nurse Smith," Emily said.

"Yes ma'am, Ms. Waters?"

Emily felt winded. Her chest heaved in and out as if she'd climbed Mount Everest. It felt as if her heart was going to give out.

"You said I'm *AB* blood type?" Emily's hands shook as she held her phone in one hand and the paternity blood chart in the other.

"Yes ma'am. You are *AB* blood type, but as previously discussed, a successful kidney transplant is still feasible. There may be a greater risk involved, which is why we will need to consult both you and your father. How would you like to proceed?" Emily's heart pounded in her chest. Her ears were ringing. Her palms sweated profusely.

"That's a good question Nurse Smith. I'll have to call you back."

Emily slowly walked back down the stairs. She silently returned to the dining room where everyone was waiting. Elena was sitting at the table with her head bowed down. Benjamin stood over her rubbing her back with downcast eyes. Estella and Reggie were still standing studying Benjamin and Elena as if they were foreign entities. Emily walked over, stood in front of her parents, and leered at them. Words were swirling around in her head, but they wouldn't come out of her mouth.

"I was trying to tell you Emily ... I just didn't know how," Benjamin said. He still hadn't looked up.

"Tell me what, Dad?" Emily asked. Tears pooled in her eyes. She could feel her throat tightening with each passing second.

"I'll tell her," Elena croaked. Emily looked at her mom as she lifted her head. Elena's face was muddied with tears. Stress lines had appeared in unusual places throughout her face. She squeezed Benjamin's hand and cleared her throat.

"Emily ... Emily, baby." Elena's voice cracked as more tears poured down her face. "I'm so sorry." She looked over at Estella. "Estella, I'm sorry ... I'm sorry for keeping this from you two for all these years." Elena set her eyes back on Emily. "Emi, baby ... Benjamin isn't your biological father."

Emily stared at her mother. The ringing in her ears turned into white noise. She felt as if she had stepped into a portal. A portal that distorted truths and broke hearts.

Benjamin finally looked up at Emily. His eyes were red and swollen from bitter tears. He looked as if he wished the floor would swallow him alive. "Emily, you know this doesn't change anything. You *are* my daughter. In every sense of the word, you are *my* daughter!" Benjamin pointed to himself and sniffed back the mucus that had accumulated in his nostrils. Estella stood back, looking on in horror. She was in just as much shock as her sister.

"No ... no, Daddy... that's not right though, is it?" Emily asked. Tears dropped down from her chin like water. She wiped snot from her face with the back of her hand. "Because Mom just told me that you aren't my dad. You aren't my dad!" Emily broke down into excessive tears. She couldn't catch her breath. Benjamin left Elena's side to console Emily.

"No!" Emily said as she pushed Benjamin off. "Don't touch me. Please don't touch me!"

Emily's chest hurt from her heavy breathing. Her head was floating and pounding at the same time. She looked over at Estella who was also in tears. Reggie looked on solemnly.

"Did you know about this?" Emily asked Estella.

"No! Of course not," Estella exclaimed in bewildered agony.

"She didn't know," Elena said gravely. "No one knows but your dad and I." Elena tried to explain. "Early on in our marriage, your dad and I briefly separated."

"You mean Benjamin, right? We've already established that he isn't my dad," Emily sarcastically said. Anger was building inside her. She was convinced she had fallen into an illusionary purgatory.

Elena continued, "We thought our marriage was over. We were young and stupid, and we let insignificant things get in the way." She grabbed a napkin and wiped her face. "In the midst of our break, your dad met this other woman ... and when I found out about it, I was furious."

Elena stopped to blow her nose. Benjamin was back at her side holding her hand. "I wanted to have someone else too. So, I started seeing this guy I never truly cared about. He was just a fill-in for what I really wanted. But then your dad found out I was with him and decided he wanted me back. He wanted our marriage to work." Elena rapped her fingers on the dining room table. "That's all I ever wanted, so we got back together. We got serious about God and our marriage and decided to make it work no matter what."

"Little did I know that I was pregnant when we vowed to stick it out. We knew there was a possibility that you weren't Benjamin's, but it didn't matter to us. We wanted to be together. We vowed to be together. So, we stayed together." Elena looked up at Benjamin and cracked a half smile. "We told each other that there was no need for a DNA test because you were going to be Benjamin's either way, but when you were born and opened your eyes ... when I saw those pretty amber eyes ... I knew you weren't his." Elena lowered her head again.

"But none of that mattered," Benjamin said, "because from the time I saw those amber eyes, from the time I held you in my arms, you were mine. Emily, nothing will ever change that."

Emily broke down again. "So, I have eyes like my real dad? Does he even know that I exist?"

Elena replied without lifting her head. "Yes, you have eyes like him, and no, he doesn't know. We never told him, and he never asked."

Emily was beside herself. "So, all my life you looked into my eyes and said I had eyes like ambers ... knowing that these were the eyes of my real father? And you never thought to tell me the truth?" she asked, targeting her question at Benjamin. "What happened to having integrity? What happened to doing what was right? How could you teach us to live honestly when you let me ... let us live in a lie? Emily screamed.

"And y'all had no intention of telling us, did you? This only came up because it came out..." Emily felt her face getting hot. Her gaze stayed on Benjamin. Although both parents had lied to her, she felt most betrayed by him. She was daddy's little girl. They had so much in common. Her smile. Her humor. Her grit. She had thought all of it was inherited. They had allowed her to believe all of it was inherited.

"Honestly, Emily ... no, we didn't plan on telling you or anyone else. We didn't think it mattered," Benjamin said calmly. "It never mattered to me or your mother. You and your sister are everything to me."

Emily crossed her arms tightly across her chest.

"Are you Estella's father?" Emily looked over at Estella. Estella looked as if she was holding her breath for Benjamin's response.

"Yes, I am Estella's father, and I am your father too, Emily."

Emily guffawed in frustration. "Are you her *biological* father?"

Benjamin folded his hands together, "Yes, I am Estella's biological father."

Emily tightened her mouth. "Perfect. So, Estella is my half-sister and you're not my dad." She turned around to walk out of the room and gather her things. She couldn't stomach either one of her parents any longer.

"Emily, please don't leave," Elena begged. Emily ignored her and walked out of the room. Estella followed her.

Once they were in Emily's old bedroom, Estella closed the door.

"Emily, I am so sorry about all of this." Emily remained silent. She marched around the room gathering her things and tossing them in her suitcase. "Emily, I don't think you should leave right now. You're upset and I don't think you should drive." Emily kept packing. She packed all her things, including some of her belongings that she normally left there. She had no intention of coming back any time soon.

She zipped up her suitcase and brushed passed Estella.

"Emily, please just wait a minute or at least talk to me."

Emily stopped and looked at her sister. She extended her arm towards Estella with her car keys dangling in her hand.

"You can drive me to the airport and have Reggie trail us to bring you back here, but it'll be a cold day in hell if you think I'm staying another second in this house." Estella knew Emily was past the point of conversing so, she grabbed the car keys and followed her sister back downstairs.

Benjamin and Elena were at the foot of the stairs, waiting for them to come down. When Emily reached the bottom step, Benjamin stood in her path.

"Emi, please forgive us. We love you more than you'll ever know. I love you past myself. Please don't leave like this. Just stay the night with us. We can sit and pray about it."

Emily twisted her face in disgust.

"Pray about it? I'll tell you what. You and Mom can stay here and pray about it. And while you're praying, pray for forgiveness for allowing your 'daughter' to believe in a lie. Pray that God will show you how out of line you were for thinking it was okay to never tell your 'daughter' the truth. And pray to God that He'll work on me to forgive you because, right now, I'm leaning towards never seeing either one of you for a very long time ..."

"Now, can you please move?" she asked.

Elena pleaded once more. "Emily, please don't leave. I'm so sorry. Everything will be okay. Let's just let this blow over and start fresh tomorrow so we can think more clearly."

Emily was getting agitated. "I don't need a fresh start to think clearly about anything. It's clear that you lied, and it's clear that you thought it was okay to lie. Please move." Benjamin parted his lips to speak again but she interrupted.

"Please move! You are holding me here against my will. Please move!" her eyes burned into Benjamin's. The pain reflected in her eyes was enough to suck an ocean dry. Realizing that he placed the agony into the eyes of his beloved, Benjamin reluctantly moved. Emily slipped passed him and walked out of the door. She walked briskly to her car and slammed the passenger door shut. In the house, Elena melted to the floor while Benjamin held her tightly.

Estella slid her seatbelt below her stomach and put her sister's sports car into drive. They drove in silence all the way to the airport as Emily gazed out of the window watching the blur of trees, cars, and buildings pass by. She thought about how her day was just as blurred as the images in front of her. How was it that in the morning she had been thanking God for changing her dad's heart, and by late afternoon she'd discovered he wasn't her dad at all? Bitterness hovered over her soul. Bitterness towards Benjamin, bitterness towards her mom, but in that moment, primarily bitterness towards God.

*"You let me get excited for nothing,"* she thought. *"You let me praise you just to turn around and throw it back in my face."*

Estella parked the car and unbuckled her seatbelt. "Emily, are you sure you want to fly back today? You can stay with me and Reggie if you want. Just to clear your head."

Emily unfastened her seatbelt and adjusted her seat to recline. "No, I don't want to stay here. I need to get back to work anyway," she said as she watched an airplane take off from the landing strip.

"Do you think they'll tell me who my real dad is?" Emily asked. Estella reclined her seat as well. Parked-car therapy appeared to be the only immediate medicine for their pain. So, they took it by the mouthful.

"I don't know …" Estella said as she also watched the plane ascend into the clouds.

"Momma always said, 'you're just like your dad' … I wonder who she was referring to?" Emily asked. Estella looked at Emily.

"I know you don't want to hear this … but you are a lot like Dad. Blood or not, you picked up on a lot of his ways." Emily thought about all the ways she prided herself on being like Benjamin.

"Maybe you just think that because that's what we were taught to think. Maybe they made up all the ways we were alike just to cover up the fact that we weren't alike at all." Emily wanted a drink. A stiff one.

"I beg to differ," Estella said. "It's natural to pick up on the habits and thought processes of others if you're around them long enough."

Emily didn't want to be anything like Benjamin at that moment—a thought she would have never imagined to think.

"Yeah, well I sure hope I didn't pick up on his or Mom's habit of allowing the people they claim to love to live in a delusion." Estella was hurt by this new revelation too, but she didn't have the same logic as Emily. She knew her parents only did what they thought was best, even if it wasn't the best thing to do. Yet, she thought it best to allow Emily to sort out her feelings without judgement just as she was sorting out hers.

"Are you really not coming back to visit them?" Estella asked. Emily's mind floated to the great moments she had had with her parents over the past few months. It was all bittersweet.

"I don't see myself dealing with them at all right now, but I'll come down in the next month or so to visit you and Reggie." Emily thought about her newest work assignment. She could go back to pouring herself into her job and nail the task Ms. Rugsby had given her. She saw a small silver lining in her dark clouds, but she needed to get back to Cali to make sure that lining didn't turn dismal black.

Estella kept Emily company until it was time for her to board the plane. They embraced and felt each other's heaviness before Emily walked towards the terminal.

"I love you, Emily. Take it easy, okay? Call me when you land," Estella said, making stern eye contact with her sister.

"I love you too, sis. I'll call you." Emily walked away feeling as if she was walking away from all that she knew. She had built her entire identity on the premise of being much like her father. *"Who am I if not Benjamin Water's daughter?"* she thought. She didn't know. She'd always been so sure of who she was, but now, she wasn't so convinced.

## MARCH 2020—CALIFORNIA

Breaking News: Shelter in place has been ordered for San Francisco County effective March 17th

Emily read the headline of the news article on her phone while leaving the office. *"What? I can't stay home ... I need to work! I can't miss out on this sale!"*

When Emily returned to California, she had one mission—get back to being Hassen's #1 realtor. Ms. Fletcher, the trusted client given to Emily by Ms. Rugsby, was her top priority. When Emily received the loan approval for Ms. Fletcher, her jaw dropped. If Emily sold a home to her, it would be the biggest catch of her career. Her commission check would be enough to make some realtors retire for the year—which was why the shelter-in-place order couldn't have come at a worse time.

She zoomed home to catch up on the news. A thousand other questions ran through her mind. *"Is it really that bad? Is it that contagious? Is it airborne? How long will they demand that we stay home? What in the world is going on?"* Emily pulled into the driveway of her home, rushed through the door, and clicked on the evening news.

"A stay-at-home order has been mandated for the following counties in the Bay Area." The news reporter listed several counties, including San Francisco. *"You've got to be kiddin' me,"* Emily mumbled under her breath.

"Essential workers may resume duties as usual," the reported continued.

*"What makes a person 'essential'?"* Emily thought. *"Don't we all make the economy function?"* She sat down to listen to the reporter list a few occupations that were deemed essential. "Healthcare operations, grocery stores, gas stations, government assistance agencies ..." the reporter continued but made no mention of real estate agents.

Emily imagined staying home alone for an extended period of time. It made her stomach turn. If she had too much time alone, she would have to face herself. Her identity crisis. Her pain. Her demons.

She couldn't afford to stay at home, in more ways than one. She needed work to keep her busy, and she wanted that six-figure check. Emily texted Ms. Rugsby for more details.

Hey Ms. Rugsby. I'm sorry to disturb you. I'm sure you are abreast of our county's current state of affairs. What does shelter in place mean for us? Are we considered essential workers?

Three dots appeared on Emily's screen as Ms. Rugsby typed. The dots disappeared and reappeared for what seemed to be an eternity as Emily waited on her response.

I am verifying now, but it appears we are not considered essential workers. I'm trying to get more information as we speak. In the meantime, contact your clients via electronic services. I can't in good conscience keep Hassen's open right now. I will update all staff via email as soon as possible, so be on stand-by for these updates. Please shelter in place and do not report to the office until further notice.

*"This can't be real,"* Emily thought. She paced the floor, thinking. There was only so much she could do from home. Working from home meant no open houses, no house showing, and no walk-throughs. Not going to the office meant no human interactions, except for possibly through the phone or laptop. She couldn't function like that. Emily needed the rush of life to keep her going. She'd never had to, nor wanted to, sit still.

Emily's phone buzzed. Incoming call from Mom. She stared at the phone until it stopped ringing. It buzzed again. Incoming call from Mom. Emily was past annoyed with Elena's constant phone calls. She had already sent her mom and Benjamin a text message requesting that they back off. She needed to sort out her feelings, but admittedly, she had not sorted out anything besides her tasks and assignments at work. She had put the betrayal and pain on layaway until her heart could afford to take it.

Incoming call from Dad. Emily rolled her eyes and exhaled deeply. "Y'all just don't get it do you?" she said aloud. She once more stared at her phone until the ringing stopped. Then her phone binged. New voicemail received. Emily chose not to listen to it. They were always the same. *"Hey Emi. I just wanted to hear your voice. I know you need space but please don't shut us out. We love you."* Yada, yada, blah, blah. Emily was sick of it. First, there was the biggest lie of all time, and now the blatant disregard of her request for distance. Unbeknownst to them, they were only pushing her farther away.

Emily's phone binged again. New text message from Estella.

Hey sis, are you okay? We heard about the shelter in place order.

Emily loved her sister and wanted to maintain a relationship with her, but sometimes she felt betrayed by her too. She knew Elena and Benjamin asked Estella to contact her. If Estella was going to be their secret agent, then maybe she needed to pull back from her as well. Emily opened the text and replied.

Mom and Benjamin put you up to this, huh? I'm okay, I'll just have to work from home.

Yes and no. I was going to reach out to you a little later tonight, but they were worried about you and asked me to reach out now. I hate that you're going to be locked up in the house by yourself, Estella texted.

I'll be fine, Emily responded.

She didn't have much else to say to Estella. She didn't like how she seemed to be okay with her parents' treachery. Estella made excuses for them and iced over the seriousness of the ordeal. It was as if Estella wasn't as hurt as her. *"Yeah, I'm going to pull back a little from you too, sis,"* Emily thought.

*"Maybe it's because she knows who her father is, and you don't. She gets to claim Benjamin as her own, and you don't,"* Emily's mind said. She tried to shake off her negative thoughts. She knew Estella was a victim just like her, but the thoughts floated in her head, nonetheless.

Okay, I'll check on you later. Take care. Love you, Estella texted.

Love you too, Emily replied.

She flopped down on the sofa, still fully dressed, and hopped on social media. Everyone expressed their opinions of the Bay Area's state of emergency. One follower said, *"This is crazy! It feels like we're in a movie."* Another follower said, *"We should be thankful that government officials finally got something right! Have you guys seen how other countries were affected by this?! People in China and Italy are dropping like flies! Stay home and be glad about it!"* Another follower said, *"FYI: If you need toilet paper, good luck... just left 3 different stores and they're all out."*

*"This is madness,"* Emily thought. She got up from the couch, went into her kitchen, and surveyed her food inventory. She had shopped for a few things when threats of a shut-down had loomed in early March,

but she was unable to get everything on her list. Shutting out the world to get back into excellent career standing had left her somewhat uninformed with how hectic things had become. She had fallen into the habit of eating take-outs and working late.

She was thankful that she purchased toilet paper and paper towels in bulk, but she needed more food. She had enough to make it for the next week but not much more than that. Emily grabbed her keys and headed out the door to stock up. The last thing she needed was to be stuck at home creating horrible new dishes from random food items over the next few weeks.

"Oh ... my ... goodness," Emily said as she pulled into the parking lot of a grocery store. She had never seen so many people shopping at one time. It was complete chaos. She thought about leaving and going to another store, but she figured all grocery stores were likely brimming over with customers. It was like Black Friday on steroids – Pandemic Edition. Emily found a parking space a good distance away from the store. She hustled towards the entrance on alert clutching the pepper spray attached to her keys. People can get crazy when panicked.

Once inside, she seized a cart and headed towards the poultry and produce section. There was barely any food left. Nothing but beat up vegetables, unwanted fruits, and unappetizing meats. She wasn't the only late scavenger searching for food, and she didn't want to leave empty handed. She sighed and grabbed what she could salvage. "Something is better than nothing, right?"

Emily whirled around at the sound of a familiar voice and was greeted with the tranquil face of Angelo.

"Oh. Hi, Angelo. How are you?" Seeing Angelo amid this firestorm was like seeing a mirage in a dessert. He seemed out of place. Emily thought he was too poised for this type of insanity.

"I'm great. How are you holding up?" Emily asked as she picked up an unsightly rutabaga and tossed it between her hands.

"I'm doing great given the county's current state. Just thought I'd grab a few things before the bunker down," Angelo replied.

Emily glanced at Angelo's basket. "Doesn't look like you've had any luck shopping either," she said, eyeing his saltine crackers, canned tuna, and applesauce.

Angelo glanced down at his basket and frowned. "Yeah, I've had better. My stash at home isn't too bad, but I thought I'd come in and grab a few more things. I guess I thought wrong," Angelo flashed a smile.

"Excuse me, ma'am," a lady rudely said as she reached across Emily to get to the last vine of tomatoes that Emily had had her eyes on.

"Oh, actually, I was going to snag those," Emily said.

"*Was* being the operative word," the lady said as she snatched the tomatoes and walked away.

"Oh, no she didn't ... I'll be right back, Angelo," Emily said as she turned to retrieve the tomatoes and to give the lady a piece of her mind. But Angelo grabbed her shoulder.

"I have some tomatoes back home if you need some. Don't confront her. It's not worth it."

Emily gazed up at him and offered a smile. "You're right. No need in entertaining foolishness. You can keep your tomatoes though. I'll make do." Angelo nodded his head.

"Well Ms. Waters, I'm headed to check out. Since tonight is the last night before isolation, how about we enjoy each other's company? My treat? I'll whip up a decent meal if you'd like?" A last hurrah with Angelo before what felt like an oncoming apocalypse sounded nice.

"Sure, that sounds great," Emily said.

"Cool, I'll meet you back at my place shortly," Angelo said as he walked away.

Emily thought about her previous prayer request. God had yet to answer her prayer concerning Angelo. She didn't know what to make of him. God had also yet to answer her prayer about Tony or reveal to her who her enemy or enemies might be. Then, there was the rift between her and Stacey. Now, this maddening pandemic that was forcing her into solitude and away from a healthy check. The one prayer God had answered concerning her dad had resulted in a fiasco.

Emily grabbed a few more items and headed to check out. She stood in line and waited impatiently with everyone else. Eventually, she checked out and left. She walked towards her car, tossed in her items, and headed home. She called Angelo en route.

"Hey, just letting you know I'm dropping these pitiful groceries off first and I'll be over."

Angelo laughed. "Okay, that's fine. No rush. I'll see you when you get here."

After putting the groceries away, showering, and throwing on something that said, 'I'm comfortable but also cute', it was 8:00 p.m. Emily mulled things over on her trip there. *"What are the chances of him spending time with me on the city's last free night if he was with someone else?"* She knew there was still a chance that he was spoken for, but she was beginning to seriously doubt it. She knocked on the door and waited.

Angelo came to the door with a dish towel in his hand and his loyal dog, Guardian, at his side. "Hey, glad you made it. Come on in."

Emily stepped into the apartment and smelled fresh bread in the air. "Mmm, it smells good in here. What'd you make?"

Angelo closed the door behind her. "Nothing major," he said with a shrug. "You can join me at the table. Food's ready. I hope you enjoy it."

Emily walked into the small dining room area where the table was set for two. Smothered chicken, rice, and vegetables lay on both plates. A loaf of bread was placed in the middle of the table.

"Did you bake that bread from scratch?" The aroma reminded her of a bakery Benjamin used to take her to back home when she was small. She shook off the memory. She didn't want to become angry or sad in Angelo's company.

"Yes, it's not that difficult. A little dough, a little kneading, and hey presto! You have bread," Angelo said, kissing his hands like a chef. Emily smiled and took a seat at the table. "What do you want to drink?"

"The strongest thing you have," she said with a light laugh. "I'm kidding, I'll take whatever you're offering." Angelo poured her a glass of tea.

"Are you kidding, Emily? Or are you stressed?" Angelo asked with a stern facial expression. She waited for him to sit down in his seat across from her to answer.

"Are you not stressed? We're in a global pandemic. I think this is a stressful situation," Emily said as she forked her chicken.

"I think there's reason for precaution ... not necessarily stress. May I bless the food first?" Angelo asked while Emily chewed the delectable chicken. She swallowed and smiled wryly.

"Yes, I'm sorry. Go ahead." She bowed her head and Angelo quickly offered thanksgiving for their meal.

"Do you want some bread?" he asked as she opened her eyes from prayer.

"Yes, please. It smells delicious," Emily said. He plated a healthy slice of bread on her plate and showed her where the butter was on the table.

"Are you nervous that you'll catch the virus?" Angelo asked.

"I haven't given that much thought. I'm more concerned about being in isolation and my career," Emily admitted.

"What's so scary about being alone?" he asked.

"I'd just rather be at work, that's all," she said. She didn't want to tire him with her problems.

"You can do some work from home though, right?" Angelo asked.

Emily chewed her food and wiped her mouth. "This food is delicious by the way," she said. She was stalling, attempting to get Angelo off the subject of working from home. She didn't want to think about it.

"Who taught you how to cook?" she asked.

"Thank you," Angelo said. "Cooking shows and cookbooks, believe it or not," he grinned. "So, is isolation your only concern?" Angelo asked.

Emily groaned inwardly. It was clear that he was not going to stop talking about the impeding stay-at-home order. "I've just never had to stay put. I prefer keeping busy," she replied.

"It's good to work," Angelo said, "but maybe sitting still for awhile isn't a bad thing."

"I suppose it'll be okay," Emily said.

They both paused from conversing while they ate. Emily knew her demeanor was probably of a killjoy. She tried not to think about being in isolation and facing herself. She tried to block the memories of eating fresh bread with whom she thought was her biological father too, but she couldn't help it. She thought coming over to Angelo's would make her feel better, but now she wasn't so sure.

"Is everything okay?" he asked.

*"Goodness, I'm being so rude. Pep up, Emily!"*

"Yes, yes, I'm fine. I'm sorry if I'm aloof. I've been a little off lately." Emily instantly regretted her confession. Now Angelo was sure to dig for more info.

But he didn't inquire about her statement. He simply nodded. Emily attempted to change the subject again. *"No time like the present to get unanswered questions answered,"* she thought.

"Angelo, can I ask you a personal question?" she asked.

"I've invited you into my personal space, why not ask a personal question?" Angelo said.

"Are you seeing anyone?" Emily blurted out. She stammered as she continued, "I know you said you weren't married, and you had no children ... I was just wondering if you were with someone and if you were buying your home for you and your significant other."

Angelo gave a friendly smile. "If I was with someone, wouldn't it be weird to spend this evening with you instead of them?"

Emily blushed bashfully. "That did cross my mind, but I wanted to know for sure. I wanted to hear you confirm or deny it, so I won't keep guessing."

Angelo finished his last bite of food. "No, Emily. I am not seeing anyone. Nor am I dating anyone, nor am I married or soon to be married." Emily's heart smiled. It was nice to hear some good news.

"Can I ask you another personal question?" she asked. Angelo sipped his drink and gave her his full attention.

"Ask as many questions as you'd like ... just as long as you are willing to answer mine."

*"Ugh, an ultimatum,"* Emily thought. *"Whatever, go for it."* Emily buttered her last piece of bread and asked, "So, why do you need that big ol' house to yourself?"

"I have plans for it," he said. Emily eyed Angelo as she bit into her bread.

"So, you plan to live in it until you move a family of your own into it?"

"Something like that," he said. Emily leaned in to take advantage of his willingness to answer her questions.

"Do you work another job in addition to being in the army? I mean, your approval rate was crazy good ... especially for the Bay Area. Are you an undercover millionaire? A prince in disguise like Prince Akeem in *Coming to America*? I mean, what gives?" Angelo laughed and revealed that brilliant smile that made Emily's heart skip.

"No, Ms. Waters, I'm not a prince. But my father is well off."

*"Oh, that makes sense,"* Emily thought.

"Then why are you living here?" she asked. Cringe. *"Why did you say that? That's so insulting!"* she thought.

Angelo looked around his home. "What? You don't like my place? I thought it was alright."

Emily shook her head. "No, I'm sorry ... it's fine. I just—"

Angelo cut-in with laughter. "Don't apologize. It's okay. I try not to rely on wealth that's all. I like to discipline myself. Stay humble. That's why I drive Ol' Faithful, my 1969 Chevy. I've witnessed worldly possessions consume people one too many times. So, I just don't relish it."

Everything was making sense now. Either he was a masterful liar, or he was being truthful. Emily opted to believe the latter. "One more question and I'm done," she said.

"Shoot," Angelo replied.

"It's hard to tell if you're just being a gentleman or if you have other intentions ..." Emily stared at Angelo from across the table.

"That's not a question, Emily," he said. Emily didn't want to flat out ask if he was pursuing her. Because what if he wasn't? Rejection in the middle of her chaos would be crushing.

"You're right, it's not ... Can I use your bathroom?" Angelo leaned back in his seat.

"Yes, it's straight down the hallway. You can't miss it. This is a matchbox of a house after all," he joked while pointing toward the hallway.

Emily playfully winced at his comment and walked down the hall. She had a little pep talk with herself in the bathroom mirror. *"Just be easy. Enjoy the evening. No pressure. If he wants you, he'll make it known."* She breathed deeply, gave her appearance one last glance over, and made her way back into the dining room.

Angelo was clearing the table and placing dishes in soapy water. "Let me help you with that," Emily said as she grabbed glasses from the table.

"Thanks," Angelo said as he began washing utensils. Guardian brushed Emily's leg as he bowed down to lay at her feet.

"Hey there, buddy! How are you? I can't believe he didn't mosey around the table while we were eating," she said.

"I've got him trained pretty well. You're a good boy, aren't you, Guardian?" Guardian wagged his tail and pounced in circles.

"He's adorable," Emily said.

"So, Emily I do believe it's my turn to ask you a few questions," Angelo said.

"I guess that's fair," Emily said while rinsing and drying a dish Angelo handed her.

"Why are you dreading isolation?"

Emily shrugged her shoulders. "I told you ... I just don't want to work from home. I prefer human interactions." Angelo's eyes burned into the side of Emily's face. She knew he wasn't buying her answer.

"That's not fair, Emily," he said.

She looked up at him, "What's not fair?"

"I was honest with you, but I think you're holding out on me. You said you've been a little off lately. Care to explain?"

Emily wiped the water off a casserole dish. She had been holding in all her emotions. She didn't have her dad, mom, sister, or any friends to confide in. She felt alone. Isolation would only amplify those feelings. Emily didn't want to enter into tomorrow's seclusion without at least attempting to unpack some of her feelings. And here was Angelo with a listening ear. *"Why not?"* she thought.

"It started with my dad's health. His diabetes took a turn for the worse, and he ended up on dialysis." Emily took a deep breath. "I was worried—scared that I might lose him—so, I decided to travel back and forth from California to Georgia every two weeks just to check on him."

"That's commendable," Angelo said, "That couldn't have been easy." He drained the water and proceeded to clean the sink and countertops. Emily leaned against the cupboards and crossed her arms.

"No, it wasn't. I started to fall behind at work. I became irritable and tired all the time from the jetlag. I was frustrated with work and with my dad for being stubborn. We wanted him to consider a kidney transplant, but he refused for a while." Angelo washed his hands and leaned on the counter to listen. "Finally, he changed his mind—which was nothing but God—or so I thought." Emily took another breath. "Long story short, turns out my 'dad' isn't my real dad. I've been lied to my entire life, and I don't know how to process it. Oh, yeah and I lost my best friend of over 20 years … Oh, and I may have an enemy posing as an ally."

Emily didn't want to mention her problems with Tony for obvious reasons. "And now, the world is flipped upside down with this pandemic. How will I pay my bills if I can't work? It's just way too much on my plate right now." She felt relieved at spilling out her story.

Angelo remained stationary. Analytical. "Have you talked to your parents since you found out?"

Emily uncrossed her arms. "No. Why would I do that?" she asked with furrowed brows. "So, they can lie about why they lied?"

"No," Angelo said. "I'm sure they won't lie to you again, knowing the pain they've caused. Did they explain why they never told you?"

Emily told Angelo the back story her mother had given her.

"That's tough," he said.

"Tell me about it," she replied.

"But I don't think they meant to hurt you."

Emily tilted her head back. "I know they didn't. My mind knows that. But my heart won't budge. I just can't deal with them right now."

Angelo leaned up from the counter. "You want to go sit down?" he asked.

"Sure," Emily said.

They made their way over to the sofa. Guardian followed and curled up in his doggy bed.

"About this potential enemy, what makes you think you have one?"

Emily didn't want to divulge her dream. He might assume she was a weirdo for believing her dream had meaning. "I had someone warn me about someone else I hang around occasionally. But I don't know whether to believe them or not."

"Enemies can be tricky," Angelo said, "Sometimes they are obvious, other times it takes discernment. God'll show you. Just pay attention to them—their words, their actions. Sometimes enemies end up telling on themselves."

"And about your friend of over 20 years. If they're meant to be in your life, they will be," Angelo said.

Emily reclined back in the couch. "Yeah, I know."

Angelo turned to face her. "I don't have any more questions, but can I be honest with you?" Emily turned to look directly at him and nodded her head, trying her best to listen to his words instead of becoming lost in his appeal. Sitting so close to him, feeling his strength exuding through the room, was distracting.

"I think you should make peace with your mom and dad. I know they weren't right for what they did, but everyone involved will be better off if you forgive them."

Emily snapped out of her sappy daze and sat up. His words weren't as appealing as his looks. "Well, I just found out not even a month ago, so I need a little more time to get past this. I'm literally in an identity crisis right now." Angelo could hear the offense in Emily's voice.

"I get that. I'm not saying it'll be easy, but I know from experience that it's best to forgive quickly. Harboring ill feelings only hurts everyone ... including you."

Emily was a tad perturbed at Angelo's forgive-and-let-go advice. "I know that ... and I will forgive them, just as soon as I get past my anger, hurt, and confusion of who I may possibly be," she said, trying not to sound snippy.

Angelo glanced her over. Unintimidated, he continued, "Why are you confused about who you are? You know your strengths and weaknesses. You know your personality. Your likes and dislikes. Maybe you don't know everything about yourself, but you have a general idea. Knowing who your biological parents are doesn't determine who you are. God defines who we are, not your DNA." Emily knew Angelo meant well, but she didn't want to hear a sermon about her identity in Christ.

She didn't want to hear about forgiveness in the midst of betrayal, and she didn't want to hear about the pandemic not being a stress activator. She just wanted to vent without being preached to. But it appeared Angelo was incapable of being a silent listening ear—one that listened only and held their two cents for later.

"Yeah, I know," she faked a yawn. She didn't want to sit around for more of Angelo's preachy banter. As alluring as he was, it wasn't enough to tempt her to stay. She was ready to go.

"I think I'm going to call it a night," she said as she got up from the couch.

"Ah! So, you're the dine and dash type?" he said, getting up with her.

Emily's cheeks flushed hot from embarrassment. "Oh, I'm not! I promise I'm not. That's what it looks like though, huh? I'm sorry …"

Angelo stretched before stepping into his slippers. "Don't apologize. Go get your rest … Oh, but one more thing. Have the sellers contacted you yet?"

*"You blew it, Emily. Now he'll think you're not interested in him because you're running off. Now, you're just his realtor, and he's just your client. Congratulations,"* she thought.

"No, not yet. But I'll let you know as soon as they do," she said, changing her casual tone to a professional one.

"Great. I'll walk you out," Angelo said. Guardian hopped up and walked out of the door with them. Emily climbed into her car, regretting that she'd made an impulse decision to leave. Angelo closed the car door for her as she rolled down the window.

"I'm sorry to leave so soon. I really enjoyed myself. Maybe we can do it again one day if we survive coronavirus and this quarantine," she said as she gazed into his eyes, hoping her own eyes exposed just how much she really like him.

"Maybe. You take care, Emily. Drive safely." With that, Angelo backed away from the car and walked toward his home, with Guardian loyally walking by his side.

Emily sat transfixed in the car. *"No text me when you get home? Is he even going to watch me drive away?"* Angelo turned back around when he made it to the door and tossed his hand up, signaling a sendoff. *"Was that a dismissive wave?"* Unsure of what to make of the gesture, Emily waved back and pulled out of the driveway.

The noise in her head clashed with the sound of the radio. She cut off the music and drove home in silence. *"Maybe ... that's all he said ... maybe. It should've been a 'sure' or 'looking forward to it' if he wanted to pursue me. Not a 'maybe'. And what was up with that hand toss?"*

Emily let all her thoughts run together. Benjamin's health, the lies, the breakup with Stacey, Tony's proposition, the ambiguity of Chelsea's and Victoria's sincerity, where she stood with Angelo, her job, the looming isolation, the present state of the world. The closer she got to her home, the more depressed she became. *"Talk to me ..."*

Emily felt a nudge in her spirit to talk to God about the cyclone that was whirling in her head, but she refused. *"You already know what's going on,"* she thought. *"Nothing's changed. It's only getting worse. I've talked to you, but you aren't answering."* She made her way home, consciously ensuring to cease speaking in what she felt was a one-way conversation with God. She arrived at home, showered, and sat in front of the TV with a large bowl of chocolate ice cream. Perhaps the cold treat could soothe her. Her phone buzzed. Emily quickly picked up the phone wishing it was Angelo. Text Message from Tony.

Disappointed, Emily opened the message.

Peach. How you holdin' up? This shutdown is crazy, huh?

Emily shifted on the couch to reply.

"I'm good, Tony. Yeah, it's a mess.

Three dots quickly appear.

Any plans on how you're going to keep business going while locked down?

I guess virtual showings and electronic paperwork. This sucks! **Emily replied with an exasperated emoji.**

Yeah, I know. **Tony replied.** I don't know what I'm going to do with myself locked down in this house for too long.

Ditto. **Emily replied.**

Maybe we can keep each other company, virtually of course. **Tony replied with an inquisitive emoji.**

**Emily paused a beat.** Company during isolation sounded good.

No harm in virtual connection, **she replied.** Sounds good to me.
Three dots.
And when the time is right, maybe we can connect in person ... outside of work. Dinner or lunch? Laser tag or a theme park? Your choice, my treat? **Tony asked.**

Emily thought about it for a brief second.

One thing she knew for sure was that Tony wanted her. He pursued her. It was obvious. Angelo came with too much haziness. If he wanted her, he would have said so. Besides, a date with Tony wouldn't hurt. *"It's a date, not a commitment,"* she reasoned.

I suppose that'll work, **she replied.**

Tony responded with a grinning smiley face.

Cool, I'll hit you up later, Peach. Good night.

Good night. Emily replied.

She watched half a season of a TV show before drowsiness kicked in. She headed for bed and glanced at her phone one more time before turning off the light. No message or call from Angelo. She placed her phone on the nightstand and closed her eyes. She tossed and turned for a while, irritated that she was beyond sleepy a moment ago but couldn't find rest presently. But eventually, sleep took over and Emily rested.

*Floating over the water. Sunlight breaking though ominous clouds. Suspended in the air as it circles around me. The multi-colored winged bird loops around slowly. Stalking me. Every jewel engrained in its wings illuminates with each passing turn. And with each passing turn it gets closer and closer.*

*The power building behind its wings causes the water below to ripple. It circles. Faster and faster. My clothes wave in the wind like a flag. The whooshing sound in my ear is deafening. Glimpses of gold, turquoise, purple, coral, yellow, and green flash by. Its massive wings and sharp talons threaten me. I panic.*

*It keeps circling. It keeps getting closer. It picks up speed. Its swiftness is inconceivable. The eagle moves like lightening. It's fast. Too fast. Dangerously fast. A spark ignites behind it. Fire follows the eagle as it speeds around me. The heat is felt on my face and body. I scream for it to stop. It circles all the more. Closer, closer. Then it slows.*

*An inferno typhoon dances about us. The eagle continues to circle at a considerably slower rate. The ignited fire dies out. It's incredibly close. Seven or eight feet out. I examine every feather and stone as it glides around me. My heart rate slows. In the midst of the fire, the eagle is calm. It hasn't devoured me, though it has had every opportunity.*

*I continue to watch. It slows even more. It comes within arm's reach. I hold my breath but it doesn't attack, nor do I feel threatened. It circles once more, brushing its wings against my bare leg. What does it want? I succumb to curiosity and extend my arm to touch it. Its feathers are soft and warm. It allows me to gently glide my hand across its wings.*

*It inches just a tad closer as it circles once more. My hands run down the dark brown feathers of its face. Beautiful shimmers of gold pop out like stars from its coating. It lifts its head to look at me. Those eyes ... those eyes are ... familiar. They are full of power. Full of strength. Full of fire. Those eyes. They burn into my soul. They beckon me. Call me. Those eyes ...*

Emily's eyes popped opened. She blinked a few times before she rubbed the crud from her tear ducts. Small rays of sunlight peeped through her curtains. She reached for her phone 6:00 a.m.

"Great," she grumbled. She had intended on sleeping in but her internal alarm clock said otherwise. Her wild dream could also take credit for her early rising. *"These dreams are getting weirder and weirder,"* she thought.

Emily sat up and stretched. If she was in the office, she would've reached out to Ms. Fletcher and Mr. and Mrs. Donahue. The last time she spoke to Mr. Donahue, he said he would decide on a home and reach out. He had yet to call, so Emily decided to reach out to him and Ms. Fletcher at 8:00 a.m. sharp. She figured she'd whip up a decent breakfast, set up her laptop, and watch the news until then.

Emily had enjoyed a hot cup of coffee, waffles, eggs, and sausage by 6:45. *"Still over an hour left to kill,"* she thought. She hopped in the shower, brushed her teeth, took off her satin bonnet, and changed from one set of pajamas into a different set. She didn't need the extra time to doll-up or beat traffic. She looked at the clock. "Only 7:15? Guess I'll watch the news." She clicked on the TV.

News of the most current Covid-19 cases and deaths were reported. Emily still couldn't believe how drastically things had changed within a few months. She recalled reading about an alarming virus in China back in January, but she hadn't thought much about it. China was a couple of continents away. She saw no need to worry. Even when the first few cases hit the States, she didn't think it would get this bad. She scrolled through social media. All she saw were more opinions about the lockdown.

"I'm not making light of the situation, but I needed this mini vacation," one of her friends said. "I'm a single mother but my job says I'm essential. I can't go to work because my children have nowhere to go. I don't have any paid leave and I don't know if I'll still have a job if this shutdown last too long. What exactly am I supposed to do? Did they even consider people like me?" another friend said. Emily shook her head at her friend's plight.

"This is crazy," she thought. She kept scrolling. Her cousin Melinda made a post. "Listen, don't nobody, and I do mean NOBODY, come anywhere near me! I got Lysol, rubbing alcohol, and hand sanitizer on deck! If you come anywhere near me, I'm spraying you with one of the three! Maybe all three! FAIR WARNING!" Emily smirked as she read Melinda's post in Melinda's voice. Melinda had quite a few comments under her post. People mostly commented with laughing faces as Melinda was one of social media's many comedians.

Emily mindlessly scrolled until 8:00 a.m.

"Time to work," she said as she cracked open her laptop. She pulled her file for The Donahue's. "*Might be too early to call*," she thought.

"On to Ms. Fletcher," she said. Whether she was up or not, Emily made sure to at least send her an email. Her email address appeared to be affiliated with a government agency. Emily was sure a businesswoman like her was awake regardless of the shutdown. She figured she was likely working from home just like her.

She hit send on a perfectly composed email to Ms. Fletcher, then she sat for a few minutes in silence. She had a house showing scheduled with a young woman for tomorrow and wondered if she was still interested in a virtual tour. Emily sent her an email as well. Bing. Her email went off. It was Ms. Fletcher.

"*Hi, Emily. Yes, I am still interested in purchasing a home. A virtual tour sounds great, but I highly doubt I will get a true feel of the homes though a monitor. I am available to tour whenever you are. Thanks for reaching out.*"

Emily smiled. She was ecstatic to show a home or two to Ms. Fletcher. A few years ago, she had almost sold a home virtually to a contract worker stationed in Europe. He was looking for a home for his wife who was still in California. She didn't think her sales tactics would carry through electronic services, but her skills had nearly landed the sale that day. She was hopeful she could pull it off this time with Ms. Fletcher.

Emily needed time to research a few homes, so she scheduled the tour for the following day. *"Can't wait,"* Ms. Fletcher replied. Bing. Her email went off again. The young woman had replied. *"Hi, Mrs. Waters. No, I don't want a virtual tour. I'll hold off on purchasing a home until this lockdown blows over."* Emily typed a professional response to the woman regardless of her ill-feelings about missing out on the sale.

She emailed her remaining leads about virtual tours. She had a few house closings to handle, all of which were waiting for inspections, appraisals, and final walkthroughs. She didn't know if house inspectors or appraisers were considered essential, but she figured they weren't. *"Nobody is going to close on a home without appraisals. Nobody is going to accept a virtual walkthrough. If I can't close, what's the point of selling?"* Emily thought.

She sighed and decided to call Mr. Donahue.

"Hello?" a woman's voice answered. It was Mrs. Donahue.

*"Ugh,"* Emily thought.

"Hi, this is Emily Waters. How are you today, Mrs. Donahue?"

"I'm doing well. What can I do for you?"

Emily went into realtor autopilot. When she finished, there was silence on the line.

"… Mrs. Donahue? Are you there?" A drained sigh emerged from the line.

"Ms. Waters, we are in the middle of a global pandemic and you're calling me about a house? I doubt you are considered essential, so why are you calling us?"

Emily rolled her eyes and started to reply but Mrs. Donahue continued, "It doesn't matter, honey. You don't have to explain. Even if we weren't lockdown, we wouldn't be buying a house right now."

Emily's face screwed up in confusion.

"Oh, I apologize. The last time I spoke to Mr. Donahue, he said he would let me know when a decision was made on which home you all wanted."

Emily heard Mrs. Donahue pop her lips. "Yeah, well. Things have changed since the last time we saw you. Is there anything else, Ms. Waters?" Emily wanted to inquire about the change to convince her that she could work things out for them—but decided to leave well enough alone.

"No ma'am. That's it. If I can be of service to you in the future, please don't hesitate to call." Mrs. Donahue gave an uninterested farewell before ending the call. Emily wished she could've reached Mr. Donahue. Maybe she could've kept them hooked. She brushed off the second loss of the day and decided to research homes for Ms. Fletcher.

"Whatever, if I can land Fletcher, she'll make up for all my lost clients one hundred times over," she reasoned.

She was done searching for homes with Ms. Fletchers' requirements by 10:00 a.m. In between searching for Ms. Fletcher's home, Emily received at least seven more emails opting out of virtual house showing. *"No biggie. Let me find out about these home inspections and appraisals,"* Emily thought. Just as the thought crossed her mind an email from Ms. Rugsby appeared across her screen.

*Good morning, Realtors! Many of you have reached out inquiring about virtual showings, walkthroughs, inspections, and the likes. I appreciate each of your dedication to your careers. At this time, our only option is to offer virtual tours and walkthroughs. Home inspectors and appraisers are not essential workers, and neither are we. However, just as we can visit a home for a virtual showing, the home inspectors and/or appraisers can inspect the home if they are willing. Of course, closings can be performed through virtual services and email. Please stay safe you guys and shelter in place as often as possible. – Sincerely, Ms. Rugsby."*

Emily grinned. There was hope. She fiddled on her laptop for the next two hours looking at homes to visit for virtual tours. Losing leads didn't mean she couldn't gain new ones.

"Pandemic ain't going to stop me," she said as she sipped her coffee with a smirk. "As a matter of fact, I'm videoing today." Emily jumped up from her couch and headed to the bathroom to do her makeup. She took her time to ensure she put on a perfect face. "Cute," she said to herself as she waltzed away from the bathroom mirror.

Emily picked out a vibrant dress and a comfortable pair of high heels. She intended to record a virtual tour in at least three separate homes. She grabbed her keys, set her alarm, and made her way to her car. Emily put on some upbeat music to pep herself up. *"You got this, Emily. Throw out the bait. You'll hook somebody."* She backed out of the driveway and made her way towards her selected location.

As she cruised, she felt as if she had driven into a zombie apocalypse movie. The usual blustering streets of San Francisco were empty. It was eerily quiet. No horn honking. No traffic. No pedestrians. Nothing. She made her way towards the Golden Gate Bridge and drove right over it. No switching lanes to beat slower traffic. It was a straight shot. *"Now that's a first,"* Emily muttered. She almost felt as if she should go back home. It felt illegal driving around while no one else was.

*"Wait ... is this illegal?"* she thought. She was only five minutes out from her first selection, so she decided to keep driving and investigate that when she reached the house. She pulled into the driveway of the home and researched the legality of her actions.

"Blah, blah ... is it legal or not? All I need is a yes or no," Emily said as she read through articles that didn't offer much of an answer. One article said it was predicted that the San Francisco stay-at-home order might be contested in court by a few rebels like herself.

"I'm not a rebel, I just need my money," Emily said. She kept reading. " ... breaking a federal quarantine is punishable by a fine or imprisonment ..." Emily continued. "Okay, but that's if I have the virus. What if I don't?" She searched a few more articles but didn't find a concrete answer. "Whatever, I'm here now. If I can go for a walk, I can record in an empty home." She proceeded into the house to film.

She put on her best smile and sales pitch. She made her way around the house showcasing the home's fixtures and amenities. After recording quality content, Emily hopped in her car to repeat the same steps at the next two locations. Afterwards, she scurried back home. The empty city made her feel like a criminal at risk of being arrested on a misdemeanor charge. Once at home, Emily edited her videos and uploaded them to her social media platforms.

Satisfied with her first day of working from home, Emily made a sandwich and sat on the couch. Her mind floated to the inevitable. She thought about Benjamin. She wondered if he was okay and how his dialysis treatments would fair under the pandemic. Yet, she also pondered about her real dad. *"Who is he? What's he like? Is he even still alive? Besides our eyes, do I look like him? Do I act like him?"* she thought.

"Oh, my goodness... what if he has other children?" Emily said out loud. The thought had never crossed her mind. *"What if I have more sisters? A brother? Brothers? What if they all know each other? Love each other?"* Emily's heart broke as she thought about the possibility of having an unknown close-knit family somewhere in the world, another source of love that she had missed out on because of her parents' divisive lie. Emily was completely torn. Though angry, she considered checking in with her mom and dad to see if Benjamin's dialysis was going well or if the pandemic had affected his treatment schedule. But she dug in her heels on the idea.

*"I'm not calling him,"* Emily thought. She thought about her real dad again. *"Did he even know mom was pregnant with me? Did they give him the opportunity to know the truth? Or did they lie to him just like they lied to me?"* Emily bitterly chewed her food. *"50%".* She rolled the percentage around in her mind like a rolodex. *"I only know 50% of who I am... of what I'm composed of."* Tears glossed over her eyes. They dropped down her cheeks and tickled her chin. She rubbed them away. *"I'm not whole if I only know half of me."*

Her sadness quickly gave way to anger. Emily tried to swallow down her resentment like her BLT. It wasn't working. She finished her sandwich and rose from the couch. She needed to get up. Move around. Do something to release what remained bottled in her core. Though she didn't have much to clean, she settled on housework.

Emily rummaged through the closet for cleaning supplies. She vacuumed and swept every room of the house. She sat down to take a breather, but her anger bubbled up again. She resumed cleaning with dusting and mopping. She wiped down all counter tops, took out the trash, and folded a load of clothes. Emily cleaned every inch of her home until her anger finally subsided.

It was 5:00 p.m. before she stopped. Exhausted from cleaning or her anger or both, she flopped down on the sofa and rechecked her business email and other platforms for leads. Zero messages across the board. Emily sighed, *"Give it time,"* she said to herself although she didn't think time would result in leads during a lockdown. She didn't have the energy or mental capacity to dwell on the pandemic's effect on her leads or how long the pandemic would threaten her career. After the waves of sadness and anger she had just suffered, she only desired to escape into the welcoming arms of entertainment.

Curled up on the couch, she watched a couple of movies as she hopped back and forth on social media. The amusement kept her mind idle well enough to suppress her triggers. By nightfall, she headed for the kitchen once more to make a quick dinner before she settled back down on the couch for more entertainment. Aside from the noise coming from her flatscreen, her home was deadly silent. Normally, the quietness offered her an oasis away from her demanding life. But today, that same stillness enticed her mind to drift to unpleasant places.

Around 11:00 p.m. Emily decided to call it a night. She was tired of watching movies and TV shows. She'd also had enough of fighting off her feelings which occasionally interrupted her entertainment. As she prepared for bed, she replayed her last talk with God in her head. The one where she refused to talk to Him. *"He doesn't care,"* an invasive thought said to her, *"If God cared, He would've answered your prayers by now."* Emily shook back the thought. Although she questioned why God hadn't answered her prayers, she felt as if He still cared in some capacity. *"But does He? Does He really care?"* the invasive thought continued.

Emily repressed the thoughts and lay down. She spoke out loud. "I know He cares. I may not understand everything, but I know God cares." Closing her eyes, she pushed the thoughts away. She shoved the restlessness towards the back of her mind. She forced the uncertainty of maintaining a steady income away. She was determined to persevere. *"It's in my DNA to make it ... Wait, that's what Benjamin used to say. Is it really in my DNA?"* Emily pushed that thought away as well. After fighting with her thoughts for over an hour, she finally met Mr. Sandman and drifted off to sleep.

Emily's eyes popped open. It was around 6:00 a.m. She closed her eyes again to see if she could fall back to sleep. *"Useless,"* she thought. She picked up her phone and unconsciously clicked on a social media app. Before she realized it, 7:00 a.m. had arrived. She rolled out of bed, showered, and poured cereal and milk into a bowl. Settled on the couch with her laptop, she logged back onto social media to finish watching an engaging video.

In no time, 8:00 a.m. came. Emily was amazed at how much time social media took off her hands. She was grateful for the distraction, but now, it was time to work. First thing on her list was to email Ms. Fletcher. While she waited for her response, she reposted one of her virtual house tours online. She kept checking her posts for likes, comments, or shares but no one responded. *"Give it time,"* she told herself again. Bing. Her email flashed. It was Ms. Fletcher. "Yes, I can do the tour today. Is 10:00 a.m. fine with you?"

Emily immediately responded. "Yes, that's perfect. I'll see you then!" Excitement bubbled in her core. She picked out the perfect outfit to showcase the three homes she had selected for Ms. Fletcher. She wanted to arrive 15 minutes before the showing so she could scope out the big selling points. Emily replayed how she had run late for the

Donahue's appointment in her head. *"That won't happen today,"* she thought. She headed to her vanity to apply her makeup. "8:30," she said as she finished dolling up. "I'll leave in an hour."

She took off her head wrap and proceeded to style her hair to her liking. "Good enough," she said. Emily frowned when she realized the lockdown meant she couldn't get her hair or nails done anymore. *"Back to the basics I guess,"* she thought. She tried on her outfit to make sure it looked decent. Satisfied with her appearance, she returned to the couch. New text message.

How's it going Peach?

It's going. **Emily replied.** How are you?

She waited for Tony's reply.

I'm alright, I guess. So far, isolation isn't too bad. I binged watch a couple of shows. Reached out to a couple clients, then pretty much chilled the whole day. What about you?

Emily looked at the clock. 9:00 a.m. She couldn't afford to lose touch of time.

I recorded a couple of virtual tours and contacted a few clients. I ended up binging on TV too **she responded.**

You did more than I did. Honestly, I may kick back and enjoy this solitude... just wish I had a little company **Tony texted.**

Emily reminisced about the times she and Tony had hung out. They always had a good time together. Always. He was attentive and romantic. Once he had planned a simple, yet picture-perfect picnic date with a charcuterie board filled with fine cheeses and delicacies. He arranged flowers and lit lanterns all about them in the warmth of a sandy beach. They watched the late afternoon turn into twilight as they relaxed on a plush blanket. When night fell, they gazed at the stars while discussing everything under the sun from God to aliens.

Emily snapped back to present day and replied.

Yeah, company would be nice ... I'm redeeming my good work standing with a client Rugsby gave me today. Apparently, they're buddies. Doing a little virtual tour for her at 10.

Three dots appeared.

You got this, Peach! I'm going to go ahead and say congratulations now because all you do is win! Congrats! **Tony typed with accompanying confetti-filled emojis.**

Emily smiled.

Thanks Tony **she replied with smiley faces.**

I'm going to let you go. I know you like to be early, and I don't want to hold you up. Be easy. I'll hit you up later, Tony replied.

Okay, talk to you soon, Emily texted.

She rose from her sofa to take one more look in the mirror. *"Looking like a winner,"* she said to herself. Emily was ready to get her tour started. She looked at the clock. It was a little after nine. Restlessness settled in as she waited around. *"I could use the extra time to sell certain points of the house,"* she thought.

Emily grabbed her things and headed out the door. Once again, she drove her car through the vacant streets of San Francisco. She zoomed down the Golden Gate bridge and made her way to the beautiful property she had selected for Ms. Fletcher. She inserted the key in the door and walked inside. "Well, I'll be ..." Emily said as she glanced around. "This'll sell itself." She imagined only the most affluent people in San Francisco would live in a house of its caliber. It was the type of house she aspired to have one day. The type of home that would prove to her dad that she had finally taken over California.

She mentally muted Benjamin's voice in her head. Though his voice confirmed that she could have a dream house one day, she didn't want to hear it from him. Perhaps from her real father. Emily perused the house to examine the details. She made mental notes of the granite, floorings, and modern flare. As she rehearsed her selling points, her phone rang. Incoming call from Chelsea. Emily accepted the call.

"Hey, Chelsea. I'm going to have to call you back ... Hello? Hello?" Emily could hear Chelsea talking but she sounded distant, muffled. "Chelsea, I can't hear you ... Do you have me on speaker?" Emily waited and listened. It dawned on her that Chelsea had unknowingly dialed her number. She went to end the call but paused when she heard Chelsea yelling. Worried that something terrible had transpired, Emily stayed on the line.

"You don't love me! I don't think you ever loved me! You'd love her if she was your wife though, wouldn't you?!" Silence. Emily knew she should hang up. The nature of the call reverberated a domestic matter. Yet, she couldn't bring herself to terminate the call. A male's voice—likely Henry—sounded off in the background and was met with Chelsea's rebuttal.

"I'm sick of this! All I've ever done was take care of you and these kids and what do I get in return? A confession from you that I was never your first choice," she screamed.

*"You're invading their privacy, Emily. Hang up,"* she told herself.

"Yes, you did! You meant it. You were drunk when you said it and you always let your nasty skeletons and secrets fall out the closet when you're drunk!" Emily kept listening. "And wouldn't you know? She grows up to be a successful businesswoman. Just your type, right? I could've been that! I could've been successful in a career if I hadn't given up my life for you!"

Emily stopped in her tracks. She placed her index finger over the volume at the bottom and pressed down hard. "There's nothing about her that's better than me! Never was, never will be! I was prettier than her in high school and I look better than her now. She doesn't have kids or anything else stopping her, so of course she's one of the best realtors out here! I only befriended her to try and see what you saw in her. Her personality is as dry as Death Valley!"

Images of the black slinky snake from her dream popped in Emily's head. The beautiful woman with the long black hair and radiant appearance flashed across her mind like a kaleidoscope. "No, I remember exactly what you said. You said you were going to ask Emily to be your girl but never got a chance because I made a move on you before you could do it." More silence. "I asked you if you regretted not pursuing her and you said the way I act sometimes, yes."

Emily could hear Henry now. "Chelsea, just stop ... You're drunk. You always bring this back up when you're drunk. I don't know what else you want me to do. I told you I'm sorry a thousand times, but you won't let it go."

Chelsea hurled a slew of insults at Henry, laced with heavy profanity. "I'm tired! I'm tired of it all. I don't want to be with you anymore and I'm tired of raising these kids by myself. You never help! I'm leaving and you can keep the kids for once. I'm going to be the career woman I always wanted to be ... You know, like your beloved Emily. Sign the papers when I send them." Emily heard Chelsea's expletives draw closer to the phone, so she quickly ended the call.

Flames shot from Emily's head as she grappled with this new revelation. *"That deceitful, lowdown heifer,"* she thought. She thought about the first time she ran into Chelsea in California. She remembered how Chelsea had looked her over with a skillful eye. How she seemed different. Odd even. How there was something about her that she couldn't quite put her finger on. Naively, Emily had never concerned herself with what that difference may have been.

Stacey had told her to feel Chelsea out—see what the oddity was all about. She could hear Stacey's voice now. *"Girl, I told you to be careful."* She missed her. Wished she could call her. To hear her voice. Get her opinion. See if she supported her gumption to knock Chelsea's head off her shoulders. Emily recollected the whipping she'd put on Chelsea in the 5th grade. She coveted a modern-day replay.

She looked at the time. Ms. Fletcher would be there shortly. Emily chewed her bottom lip and jutted out her chin. "Heifer ain't going to mess this up for me. I'll deal with her later," she said out loud. She postponed rehearsing in her head how she would confront Chelsea and focused on her selling points. After she calmed down, Emily thought that maybe, just maybe, God had given her that inkling about Chelsea to warn her. Maybe God had also put it in Stacey's heart to caution her about Chelsea too. Maybe she'd just missed the messages.

Emily deserved an Academy Award for the performance she enacted for Ms. Fletcher. She exceeded her own expectations. Ms. Fletcher graciously expressed her appreciation of Emily's presentation. "Oh wow, Emily," Ms. Fletcher said, "I know I said I wouldn't likely buy a home that I hadn't been in… but my goodness, I just may be sold! You're as amazing as Cathy said. Let me give it some thought, and I'll get back to you." Emily's heart leaped. "Thank you so much Ms. Fletcher. I aim to please. You can reach me by phone or email, whichever works for you."

She wrapped up the virtual call with Ms. Fletcher and walked toward the windows that overlooked the city. Transparent streaks of sunlight filled the void streets below. Emily wrestled with how to handle Chelsea. The idea of cursing her out or petitioning her for an old-fashioned beat down, or both, bounced off the walls in her brain. She looked down at her phone. Apparently, she hadn't read her Bible verse of the day. It was still listed in her notifications. She wanted to ignore it. She didn't want God to stop her retaliation. Yet, her gut nudged her to read it. She clicked on the app: *The Lord will fight for you; you need only to be still - Exodus 14:14*

A cynical laughed erupted from Emily's diaphragm. The irony was incredible. "Are you serious right now? I didn't even ask you about this." Emily crossed her arms tightly across her chest. She paced the floor not knowing what to make of God responding to an issue she hadn't asked of Him. The timing was too impressive to be a coincidence, she could admit that. But she struggled with God replying to this unasked issue, yet not responding to issues she had inquired about.

Emily was quite frankly disappointed that God had given directives in this ordeal. "You could've at least let me slap her one good time." She sucked her teeth and rocked back on her heels. Her tastebuds hungered for revenge. She sighed. Again, she could hear her dad in her ear *"Vengeance is mine says—"* Emily interrupted the thought.

"Yeah, yeah, I know". She stared out of the window, absorbing the scenery, the Bible verse, and her dad's annoying advice. "Okay, God. I'll let you handle it." She breathed in the picturesque view one more time before she turned and exited the home.

Back home, cozy in her pajamas, Emily rechecked her email. No messages.

*"That's okay,"* she thought. *"I received two messages today. My enemy was revealed, and my goal of being #1 at Hassen's again is in full effect. God, I know you love me. I know you care. I'm sorry for my back-and-forth ways with you. I'm just frustrated ... overwhelmed ..."*

*"You still lost your best friend. You still don't know who your real dad is. Your entire childhood was a lie. It shouldn't take Him that long to answer prayers. I mean, He is God, isn't He? If He could answer the way He did today, He could've answered those other prayers."* The invasive thoughts returned. Emily laid back on her sofa and pulled the quilt over her legs. She fervently shook her head in disagreement. "No. Not today, Satan. Not today," she said as she flicked on the TV.

A sluggish two weeks passed. Emily supposed it was either Friday or Saturday. The days were melting into each other. Her internal alarm clock had died. It was a quarter till 9:00 a.m. and she was still in bed. As the days whiled away, so did her enthusiasm for work. Emily didn't think the isolation would kill her career motivation—and it hadn't up until a few days ago. In fact, she was doing pretty well career wise. Angelo's sellers had agreed to his offer, but the real highlight of her week was after she had shown Ms. Fletcher two more homes.

"Emily, you have made home buying so exciting. I want to purchase the first home you showed me. I really do, but I can't commit without viewing it in person. I need to make sure I'm making the right decision." Ms. Rugsby's follow-up email, warning the agents to perform virtual showings *only,* darted across Emily's memory. Ms. Rugsby had made sure to bold and italicize the word 'only' in the message. Yet, Emily refused to miss out on this type of commission. *"Either you improvise, or you rebel,"* Emily thought.

"Ms. Fletcher, for you, I will make an exception. I'll leave the door unlocked for you tomorrow morning. Take your time and get a feel of the house. Call me when you leave, and I'll come after you and lock it up. Deal?" Emily knew Ms. Rugsby may scold her. *"She'll get over it,"* she thought. *You told me not to let you down ... This is me not letting you down."* Emily rehearsed excuses to give Ms. Rugsby in her head.

Ms. Fletcher agreed to view the home alone. Fifteen minutes after she walked into the house, she promptly called Emily.

"Oh, Emily! I am one thousand percent sold. How soon can we get the ball rolling on this?"

Cha-ching. *"Jackpot!"* Emily thought as a smile wider than the Amazon River stretched across her face. For the first time since she left Savannah earlier that month, Emily was starting to feel like her old self again—the top competitor at any game she played. She had officially hooked the biggest catch of her career in the middle of a global pandemic. Now, it was time to reel it in.

Emily immediately notified Ms. Fletcher on the next steps of the buying process, just as she had notified Angelo. She was disappointed that her phone call with Angelo remained strictly professional and less than five minutes long. She'd left enough space in the conversation for him to interject any other interest or concerns about the weather or how she was doing in isolation, or how he was holding up being home alone with Guardian ... but she was met with static. She concluded that all hope of a future or a friendship or possible relationship with him was ruined. Apart from that one awkward phone conversation, she hadn't heard from him since the night before the pandemic.

Her dad always told her she wouldn't have to question whether a man wanted her or not.

"You'll know it," he always said. She was downright sick of hearing his voice in her head motivating her, encouraging her, as it always did. Yet, Emily knew her distaste for his voice didn't mean he was wrong. In this instance, she admitted Benjamin's advice was right. After she advised Angelo to reach out to his lender for appraisals, she hadn't heard word of any appraisers being sent to his home. She figured the lenders had stopped the process due to covid. Ms. Fletcher confirmed her suspicion.

"Emily, I was able to get a personal inspector, but the lenders are halting the appraisals for safety concerns. I understand their stance, but this is frustrating," Ms. Fletcher said.

"For you and me both," Emily agreed. Her unsuccessful attempts to draw new clientele, in conjunction with the lenders halt on closing her sales, put a sour taste in Emily's once motivated mouth. Contrary to her previous beliefs, the pandemic had indeed stopped the show.

Her days were filled with tedium. Watching TV, strolling through social media, sporadic workouts, reading, short walks up and down the sidewalk, cooking, cleaning. Wash, rinse, repeat. She was miserably bored. In addition to her boredom was her internal turmoil. No matter which room she lounged in, the scratches on her soul bled.

Bouts of depression rocked her back in forth. Up and down, she went. Day in and day out Emily fought within herself. She fought to forgive her parents. She fought to discover the Emily whose dad wasn't Benjamin Waters. She fought the anxiety of feeling as if she was losing her career. She fought the invasive thoughts tempting her to lose her faith. She fought against her need for human interaction, her need to dump her mind on a trustworthy source. Who could she talk to? Who would understand her plight?

Tony had faithfully checked in with her every day. Even if he only texted, she appreciated his company, but it wasn't enough to keep her from feeling lonely. Estella checked in a few times. Emily kept their conversations brief. Her heart remained guarded against her. Benjamin and Elena had finally ceased their persistent calls. Emily considered texting Stacey a time or two but decided to respect her request to end their friendship, no matter how much it hurt.

Saturday, March 28. Emily read the date on the screensaver of her phone as she lounged back on her pillows. *"Yeah, I thought it was Saturday."* Her phone dinged. New Message from Tony.

To us clinking wine glass emojis accompanied the text.

What are we celebrating? Emily replied.

I take it you didn't check your email this morning **Tony** responded. We're essential.

Emily opened her email and clicked on her unread message from Ms. Rugsby.

She read it aloud. "I'm pleased to inform you that the California Organization of Realtors are officially deemed essential workers … Appraisers were also listed as essential."

Emily sat up and texted Tony.

Yes! I'll toast to that.

Emily clicked her proverbial wine glass to Tony's by sending the same emoji.

Yeah, there are still restrictions on face-to-face contact of course Tony replied. I still want to play it safe as possible. These covid cases and deaths are rising like crazy.

Emily nodded in agreement before she texted back. She was excited to possibly close on a few homes, but venturing out onto the bare streets of California, unless absolutely necessary, wasn't an activity Emily desired to indulge in anymore. Reports of people dying in her own county from the strange disease that was coronavirus was unsettling.

Yeah, the numbers are skyrocketing all over the state. It's getting bad she replied.

Three dots appeared and disappeared.

Can I FaceTime you? I'd rather talk than text. It'll be nice to see your face.

Emily frowned. She had FaceTimed Tony a few times while quarantined, and every time she felt the need to rip off her bonnet, quickly style her hair, and slide into something more presentable than her overworn bathrobe.

Yeah, give me a second she responded.

Emily's phone buzzed. Tony was FaceTiming her. She answered with the front-facing camera turned away from her.

"Dang, Tony. I didn't mean a literal second."

Tony laughed while Emily hurried to the bathroom. She laid her phone face down on the counter.

"Aw, come on, Peach. I just wanted to see you in your natural element."

Emily turned on the faucet and splashed her face with cool water, then blotted it with a towel. "No sir, I think not," she said as she tried to bring life into her ginger coils.

"I know a natural beauty when I see one. I'm sure whatever you're doing is unnecessary," Tony said. Emily slathered a moisturizer on her face and spread a clear gloss on her lips. She exchanged her bathrobe for a pink tank top and picked up her phone.

"There she is! You look beautiful as always," Tony said. His nicely groomed beard cupped around his ebony chin perfectly. He too donned a tank top, his well-formed arms protruded outwardly, catching Emily's eyes.

"I didn't know you had tattoos, Tony." Intricate wings spread out across his chest onto the tops of his shoulder blades. Tony rubbed his chest and gave a faint smile.

"Yeah, it's just this one. Got it a few years ago."

"Are they eagle wings?" Emily asked, her mind floating to her persistent dream.

"No, they're angel wings."

Tony pulled down his shirt, displaying the full tattoo. Emily became flustered at his exposure. She shook it off to focus on the tattoo. A name etched in cursive was the focal point of the artwork. A woman's name. "Oh, is that your wife—ex-wife's—name?" Emily didn't recall that name being on Tony's divorce papers, but perhaps she was wrong.

"No, it's my daughter's name. We had a baby five years ago, most perfect thing I've ever seen." Tony averted his eyes. "She was premature. Born at 23 weeks ... she fought hard. My little champion," Tony smiled a little wider. "But I guess she was too perfect for us to keep. She gained her wings, and I engraved them over my heart." Emily was speechless. She had no clue Tony had suffered in such a way.

"I'm so sorry," was all Emily could invoke.

"Don't be sorry, Peach. I never experienced a love quite like being a father. Best thing that ever happened to me. I wanted us to try again. Shoot, after that experience of love, I wanted a whole football team." Tony chuckled. "But she didn't want to try anymore. She said she couldn't go through that pain again." Tony exhaled.

"We argued about it on and off for years. Until finally she completely disengaged from me. She said I pushed her away... that I ignored her pain and never comforted her. So, she found comfort in someone else. Or at least that was her excuse ..."

Emily stared at Tony as he bared his soul. She didn't think he could be much more attractive than he already was, but currently that theory was being tested. A man that wasn't ashamed to express his sensitivity always appealed to her.

"There's never an excuse to cheat," Emily said.

"Yeah, I know," Tony replied, "but I could've been more present to her pain. I was so busy trying to move on from it, I didn't understand why she wanted to wallow in it. I guess we just grieved differently."

There was a brief stretch of silence before Tony continued. "So, when she admitted that she was having an affair, I told her I could do better. That I could be more present. But she said she would never give me what I wanted. She would never have children, and that we should just end it. She moved out within two months and served me papers shortly after." Emily rested her head on her hands as she listened. "So then, I started noticing you. Well, I'd always noticed you—you're hard not to notice—but it didn't matter because I was trying to make my marriage work," Tony said as he reclined in his seat.

He continued, "I wasn't going to approach you, but I heard a few other guys in the office saying they were going to make a move on you… and I couldn't have that."

Emily twisted her face. "What other guys?"

Tony smiled. "I ain't telling you."

Emily persisted. "C'mon, Tony tell me, please," she cheesed like a kindergartener into her phone.

"Nope," Tony said. "You might like them, and I'll be a sore loser if you decided to be with one of them."

Emily smiled. "Tony, trust me. I'm not attracted to anybody in that office, okay?"

Tony scratched his beard and smoothed it down. "Except me, right?"

Emily rolled her eyes and smirked. "You're alright I guess."

Tony laughed. "Just alright, huh? I'll take that."

They talked until Emily's stomach groaned from hunger. She headed downstairs and pulled out some eggs from the refrigerator.

"Oh snap, Chef Peach! What you about to whip up? I know you got some good southern recipes in your repertoire."

"I have a couple dishes," she smiled, batting her lashes, "but right now I'm just doing scrambled eggs and toast."

Tony and Emily chatted until their phone batteries dwindled to the single digits.

"Dang, Peach. My phone's about to die. It's burning hot in my hand too."

Emily laughed. "Mine too. We've been talking for about three hours."

Tony sighed. "Yeah, it's always good talking to you. You don't have to wait until I call before we speak Peach. The phone works both ways. Call me, okay?"

Emily nodded her head with an insubordinate smile. "I'll call you, Tony. I promise."

Tony smiled back. "Alright then, I'll talk to you later."

Serotonin permeated throughout Emily's body as she hung up the phone. She felt downright good. She sent out an email to Angelo and Ms. Fletcher's lenders and emphasized the fact that appraisers were now essential. By evening, she received a reply from both lenders who agreed to send appraisers to the selected properties. The combined commission checks from the sale of Angelo's and Ms. Fletcher's homes would undoubtably make Emily the highest paid realtor at Hassen's. And she was just getting started. So, Emily ended the day on a high note. An astronomically high note.

## APRIL 2020—CALIFORNIA

Emily sat by the phone waiting for his call. She had left the door unlocked for Angelo to do his final walkthrough alone. He seemed joyful enough that his home buying process was coming to a gradual end. Emily couldn't help but wonder if he was also happy that their interactions with one another were also soon ending. Her phone buzzed. "Hi, Angelo. Is everything fine with the house?" Emily asked.

"It's perfect. Exactly how it should be," Angelo said as he stepped into his apartment. Emily heard Guardian barking excitedly in the background.

"Great," she replied. "Well, you're one step away from being a homeowner. Congratulations!" Emily smiled brightly to convey positivity despite her awkward feelings.

"Thank you, Emily … May I ask you a question? Non-business related?"

Emily's breath left her throat. "Umm, sure. What is it?" Emily asked.

"If you don't mind, may I FaceTime you?"

Emily groaned. *"What is it with these men and FaceTiming?"* She rose from her couch to become presentable. "Yes, give me a couple of minutes, okay?" Angelo agreed. Emily spruced herself up and was settled back on the couch when Angelo FaceTimed her.

"Hey, Emily. Are you okay?"

Emily remained reserved. "I'm fine, and you?"

Angelo searched her face and read her body language. "I'm well … I think we somehow got off on the wrong foot. Did I offend you the night before the pandemic?"

Emily shifted her weight on the couch. "No, you didn't offend me," she lied.

Angelo's deep eyes were fixated on Emily. "Yes, I did. That wasn't my intention. I was only trying to help. I know I can be relentless at times." Emily remained silent. Angelo continued, "I wanted to give you space. I didn't want to annoy you. Plus, I wanted to give you time to think about what I said."

Emily cocked her head to the side. "What did you say?"

Angelo fiddled with an Express Envoy package on his coffee table. He opened the box and tossed Guardian the squeeze toy that was inside. "I talked about your identity and forgiving your family."

Emily couldn't believe her ears. Was he crazy? He had just admitted to offending her with this same topic, and now he was bringing it up again. She smiled, remembering that Angelo was still her client and not a potential man in her life that she could feistily combat with.

"Angelo, I'd rather not talk about my personal life right now if that's okay with you." Emily maintained a phony smile plastered across her face.

Angelo petted Guardian's head and tossed the toy across the room again before he replied. "Okay ... would you like our interactions to remain business-focused only?"

Emily paused before she responded. She appreciated his straightforwardness—they had that in common. But what else did they have in common? Emily didn't know. Angelo had annoyed her to no end, yet her aggravation hadn't canceled her intrigue. She was undecided.

"I don't know..." Emily answered truthfully.

"That's fair," Angelo responded. "I won't hold you up. You have my number if you want to talk. Thank you for helping me purchase this house."

Emily nodded curtly. "You're welcome."

Angelo ended the call leaving Emily feeling conflicted. *"He's an odd one,"* Emily thought. *"So why am I still drawn to him? And why hasn't God advised me of what to do about him? Or Tony?"*

Emily could feel the invasive thoughts' attempt to return—to adamantly tell her God didn't care about her feeble petitions. She was getting tired of this faith battle. One minute she was convinced God cared about her and her problems, regardless of how big or small they were. She was convinced God had cared the day she learned of Chelsea's betrayal. She knew God was for her when He blessed her career wise. Then the next minute, she wasn't so sure of her convictions. She was, after all, still battling the same struggles, every day despite her prayers.

Her phone buzzed. Incoming call from Mom. Emily ignored the call. Seconds later, Elena called again. Emily watched the call go to voicemail. New text message from Estella. "Back to this little shindig, huh?" she said as she ignored her family and flicked through the channels in search of a good show to watch. Her phone buzzed again. Incoming call from Estella. *"What do you want?"* Emily thought irritated, but she answered the phone nicely.

"Hey, Stella."

"Hey, Emily."

Something was wrong. Emily knew it. Estella's voice dripped with hidden apprehension.

"What's wrong, Stella?" Emily asked alarmed.

"Don't panic, Emily. But Dad hasn't been feeling well. He has a low-grade fever." Emily's heart fell into her stomach. A low-grade fever. A phrase that wouldn't have meant much prior to March 2020. But in this pandemic, a low-grade fever could mean the worse. Emily struggled for words.

"Does he have it?"

"We don't know yet. He and Mom are going to get tested today. He was being stubborn as usual and refused to test at first. Mom said he's had a cough for about a week now." Emily's intestines balled into clusters. Her chest tightened.

"What about Mom? Is she okay?" Emily rose from the couch and paced the floor.

"She said she feels fine." Estella said. Guilt fell over Emily for ignoring their calls.

*"But I had a right to be angry. They lied. I just needed my space ..."*

Estella broke through her thoughts. "Emily, I know everything has been hard. It's been hard on you. It's been hard on me. It's been hard on all of us. I understand you shutting them out, but you didn't have to shut me out too."

Emily bobbed her head, "I know, I know, Estella. I'm sorry. I've just been so mad. I keep trying to get past this, especially with what's happening in the world right now. But this is *hard*."

"It is. God knows it is," Estella reassured her. "I've been struggling with the betrayal, too. It's not easy talking to them, but it's helped me process the pain. Plus, at the end of the day, I know they never meant to hurt us."

Emily settled on her dining room chair as silent tears dropped from her chin onto the floor. The lump in her throat kept her from speaking. Estella understood Emily's silence.

"I'll let them know you're thinking about them," she said. "I'll keep you posted. You're not in this alone, Emily. Call me when you feel heavy."

Emily forced an "okay" from her mouth and hung up the phone.

She crumbled to the floor and allowed herself to feel the gravity of her inner tumult. Her broken spirit scattered across the chilly floor like lost marbles. She lay there, in the middle of the floor, tucked into a fetal position and cried dreadfully. Her soul bled dry as her body shook from the harsh sobs. When she didn't think she could cry any more, she uncurled her body and rolled over. She allowed her mind to float as she gazed at the ceiling's textured pattern. *"How did I get here?"* She consented to the stillness of the room. She permitted it to rush over her. For weeks she had been alone, but this was the first time she had been still.

Emily deliberately altered her breathing. She sucked air into her lungs and allowed it to seep out slowly. She breathed. For the first time since leaving Georgia, Emily finally breathed. After breathing, though she thought they had dissipated, more tears slid down her temples and into her hair. She calmed herself and breathed again. She thought about Benjamin, her sweet superhero dad, not being her dad. More tears rolled across her temples and into her hairline. She breathed again. She thought about her loneliness and the continuous invasive thoughts that punished her, sifted her every day.

"God ... God ..." The words wouldn't arrange. Emily hoped that God understood the dialect of tears since language refused to form on her lips. Words couldn't adequately express her ache even if they chose to form. She lay there and cried out the extra tears she swore she didn't have left. When she was sure she'd depleted the very last bit of her tear supply, she sat up. She was surprised at her disposition. She felt mysteriously replenished. The air felt cleaner. Her heart felt lighter. She supposed she was experiencing what some may consider the peace of God.

A resilient tranquility hovered over Emily all day. The ecstatic state followed her into the afternoon and evening. Indeed, it appeared God did understand the linguistic of tears. For her pain had dried up for the day and her rest was discovered in the sweet arms of heaven. The invasive thoughts came. They told her that her peace would be short-lived. Emily neither agreed nor disagreed. She simply smiled and enjoyed the gift of peace that she had been allotted for the day.

Emily stared at the zeros and commas. Her mind attempted to absorb the dollar amount shown in her checking account, but she was having a hard time processing the numbers. She'd accumulated a six-figure amount the year before, but she had never received that amount from one sale. Ms. Fletcher's appraisal, final walk-through, and closing had happened swiftly. Emily hadn't had time to take in the fact that she was steps away from being in another tax bracket until she found herself in it.

"Emily, you have been a joy. Best realtor I've ever had. Cathy has a jewel in you. Thanks for all your help," Ms. Fletcher said to Emily after the closing paperwork was signed. Ms. Rugsby also called Emily to congratulate her.

"I knew you wouldn't disappoint me. Your tenacity never ceases to amaze me."

Emily had officially stepped into a new career realm. A realm she'd always dreamt of. Closing with Ms. Fletcher opened the door for more big-ticket clientele, which meant even bigger doors for career advancement and financial opportunities.

*"So, this is how it feels..."* Emily thought. *"But how do I feel?"* She didn't rightfully know. Accomplished? Yes. Successful? Yes. Happy? Should be. Yet, happy wasn't an accurate description. If she could celebrate with her family, if she hadn't have been lied to, if she had someone to share it with, maybe happy would be a precise adjective. But as it stood, she remained remote, quarantined from celebrating the greatest accomplishment of her life.

Two more weeks had passed since Emily had learned that Benjamin and Elena were being tested for covid. The day after Emily learned that her parents may have covid, Estella informed her that they both tested negative. Relief encompassed Emily. She was grateful that her parents were okay.

"Do you want to speak to them? I have them on the line now," Estella had asked. The serenity of her 'peace of God' breakthrough had managed to float into that next day. Emily, against her natural stubbornness, listened to her conscious request to speak with them.

"Emily ... hey, baby. It's nice to hear your voice. Are you okay?" her mother had asked. Emily gave short yes and no answers to all of Elena's questions. Eventually, Benjamin's voice emerged on the line.

"Hey, Emi. I imagine you can still take California by the throat from home, right?" he teased. Emily remained silent at his usual easy-going demeanor. Nothing was easy about this conversation, and Emily refused to pretend that it was.

"Well, your old man is doing fine," Benjamin said in response to Emily's silence. "Thank you for checking up on me. I love you." Emily never opened her mouth while on the phone with him. Her tongue remained still between her teeth. Estella broke the tension by ending the call.

"We love you. Emily. I'll talk to you later."

Emily hadn't talked to her family since. Not for their lack of trying, but for Emily's unwillingness. She was aware of Benjamin's health status from Estella's text updates. *Dad's treatments went well today. He's a little drained, but he's in decent spirits* were usually Estella's reports of his dialysis treatments. One day Estella texted her about Dad's plan to retrieve a new kidney.

Dad's going to go forward with the surgery. He joined the donor's list today. Emily didn't respond to that message. She didn't know how to.

*"You were supposed to give him your kidney. You gave him your word,"* guilt told her. "I'm not a match anyway," Emily reasoned. "Even with the so-called advanced technology, his body could reject it. Plus, we're in lockdown. Nothing I can do about it now." She had a few other get-out-of kidney-donor-jail-free cards to play if guilt persisted. "He probably wouldn't even take a kidney from me since he held the truth from me for so many years. His guilt wouldn't let him. No one gives a kidney to someone they're in a quarrel with."

*I died for you while you were yet a sinner ...*

Emily had heard the inner voice but ignored it. God couldn't expect her to do what Jesus would have done, at least not so soon after disloyalty. She couldn't even open her mouth to talk to Benjamin, let alone lie on an operating table to give him a kidney. That was too much to process. Everything swirling in her life was too much to process. Even the fulfillment of her financial dream and career status was too much to unpack. She needed a distraction.

Something to take her mind off things. But there wasn't a thing to do. Her house was clean, and she was tired of mindless entertainment. Working out only stimulated her for an hour or so, and reading was just the same. With nothing to distract her, maybe someone could... and she knew of just the handsome someone. Emily closed her banking app and phoned Tony.

"Peach, what's up girl?"

Emily straightened up on the couch. "Same old thing, different day," Emily replied.

"Yeah, I think that applies to most of us," Tony said with a sigh. "I was finally able to close on a home yesterday, so I guess I have a little something to celebrate."

Emily perked up. "Well, that makes two of us. I closed with Ms. Fletcher."

"Peach! Man, what? That's amazing, congrats! I'm not shocked though. I called it beforehand."

Emily smiled into the phone. "Yeah, you did. Thank you. I wish I could properly celebrate it. I guess I'll pour myself a glass of champagne and toast to myself."

Tony laughed. "You don't have to do that, I'll toast with you. FaceTime?" Emily ripped off her headwrap and robe.

"Sure, let me pour a glass and I'll call in a minute."

Emily dashed to the bathroom mirror to spruce herself up before she poured herself a celebratory drink. Then, she FaceTimed Tony. He had a shot glass filled with a clear liquid. "Umm, sir, I thought we were toasting, not turning up."

Tony chuckled. "I don't have any champagne. Vodka is all I have so it'll have to do." Emily tilted her head to the side. A quick thought raced across her mind. "What? What's that look for?" Tony asked.

"Nothing, it's a bad idea," she, said shaking her head.

"What's a bad idea? Tell me," Tony said, setting down the shot glass on his kitchen counter.

"I was just thinking that it's highly unlikely that either one of us has the virus—since we've both been in quarantine with no real human interaction. So, maybe I could share a glass with you ... in person ..." Tony gazed at Emily as he rolled the concept around in his head.

"I actually don't think that's a bad idea. We've been in lockdown going on a month now and it's driving me up the wall. I think I may go stir crazy," he said.

Emily nodded, "Same here."

Tony grabbed his shot glass and poured the liquid back inside the bottle. "I don't like liquor this early anyway, but champagne, I can do that," he said as he smiled into the camera, his white teeth brilliantly contrasting his dark skin.

"Okay, well then ... I'll see you in a bit?" Emily asked.

"Yes ma'am, you will," Tony confirmed.

The call ended and Emily's stomach filled with butterflies. She hadn't fully thought her 'great idea' through. *"Tony in my home? In my personal space?"* In times past, they always gathered in public spaces.

The one time they were in private led to a hard fight with temptation. She came out victorious then, but she wasn't so sure she could do it again. *"Lord, help me,"* she thought. *"Just help me."*

Emily jumped up at the sound of her doorbell chime. She made her way to the front door and stopped at the mirror in her foyer to check her appearance one last time. Her mind raced with excitement and apprehension. *"It's cool, be cool. Relax."* Emily turned the doorknob and pulled the door back, a bit too eager to finally engage in face-to-face contact for the first time in weeks.

"Peach! What's up, girl?" Tony greeted her with his usual charisma.

"Hey Tony," Emily grinned. "Come on in. Is that food in your hands?" Tony stepped inside the doorway. His signature scent wafted in her nostrils. Memories of Tony's last visit to her home flooded her mind. *"That won't happen,"* Emily told herself.

"Yeah, Pippin' Pizza is taking curb-side orders, so I grabbed us a little something. I remembered how much you liked their calzones." Emily's stomach rumbled as if on cue. "And from the sound of it, I made a perfect choice."

She blushed. "Thank you. That's so sweet of you." Tony let Emily led him to the kitchen. "You can set it on the counter. Let me grab us some plates." She turned to the cabinets, sensing Tony's eyes on her back. She grabbed the plates, then whirled towards another cabinet for wine glasses. She then moseyed over to the refrigerator to grab the champagne. Tony's eyes tracked her every movement. She threw her hand on her hip and bugged out her eyes at Tony.

"Have I grown an extra arm or something? I'm trying my best to ignore your gawking but goodness!" Tony smiled and stood to plate the food.

"You know, it's hard for me to keep my eyes off you. It's so easy to let them wander." Emily huffed and poured the champagne while she walked towards the couch.

"Well, I'd appreciate it if your eyes could wander to plating that food. Didn't you hear my stomach growling?" Tony made a face, plated the food, and followed her to the couch.

Emily strategically found a wholesome movie to watch before Tony's arrival. *"Nothing sexually explicit. Don't want that to lead to any ideas. Nothing lovey-dovey. Don't want to stir any emotions.*

*Nothing scary. Don't want him to hold me and keep me safe from the bogey man ... Dang, what can we watch?"* she asked herself. She settled on old cartoons.

Tony sat down next to Emily on the couch and placed their food on the tray tables. He glanced at the TV and turned into a ten-year-old child.

"Oh, snap! They got *Hey Arnold!* on here? *Rugrats*? *As Told by Ginger*?"

Emily laughed at Tony's kid-like expression. "Yeah, they even have some old throwbacks on here. She flipped through the streaming service to show Tony classic children's shows including *The Jetson's*, *Pink Panther*, and *Looney Tunes*. Tony's face lit up even more.

"Oh, man, that's crazy. I need to buy this service ASAP. You got all the good shows. I don't know why you're bored. I'd be in cartoon heaven if I were you."

Emily smiled and handed him the remote. "Well, I'll let you do the honors."

Tony grinned. "I don't know where to start ... so, let's start with this." He raised his wine glass. Emily followed suit. "To you, Emily, for being the baddest ... in more ways than one. He playfully looked her up and down, admiring her beauty and figure. "To the baddest, most extraordinary realtor California has ever seen. Congratulations, Emily."

Tony went to clank his glass against hers, but she pulled her glass back. "And to you Tony," she said, glass still raised. "Congratulations on your recent closure. And thank you for your continued support. I appreciate it." Emily brought in her glass to clink against Tony's. They locked eyes for a spell before she dropped her gaze to her bubbly beverage. Tony picked up the remote while she dived into her food. She closed her eyes as she pulled steamy cheese away from the breaded meal with her teeth.

"Mmm, oh my goodness," Emily said as she closed her eyes, savoring the taste. "I'm so glad you thought to buy this." As Tony chewed his food, he casually shed the light jacket he was sporting. Emily turned her gaze away from his sculpted arms.

"No problem, Peach," he said, completely oblivious to how he had raised Emily's temperature. *Or was he?*

*"He knows what he's doing. Taking off his clothes and whatnot. Well, it doesn't matter because after this meal and a few episodes of this show, I'll make sure to signal his need to leave."*

The signal to leave was never given. Tony and Emily watched cartoons and talked about silly childhood memories until late in the evening. After laughing at one of his adolescent stories, Emily looked down at her phone to check the time.

"Wow, it's going on 7 o'clock. I've worked up an appetite again."

Tony sat up from his reclined position. "Really? That time flew by. I'll see myself out if you need me to get out of your hair." Emily had thoroughly enjoyed his presence in her home. She didn't necessarily want him to leave. Besides, they only had a couple more episodes to see to complete the full season of the series they were watching.

"No, you're fine. We can at least finish the show before you leave. I'll whip us up something really quick."

Tony stared incredulously at Emily. "You would cook for me?" he asked, dramatically placing his hand over his heart.

Emily smirked at him. "Slow your roll player. Technically, I'm cooking for myself. But it would be rude to not offer you a plate. Southern hospitality is a real thing just so you know." She arose from her seat and stretched. Tony gawked at her again.

Emily sucked her teeth, cocked her head to the side, and stared back at him.

"I'm sorry," chuckled Tony. "You're distracting. It's honestly, your fault that I keep staring. Shouldn't look the way you look." Emily rolled her eyes and walked toward the kitchen.

"Blame God for that, not me," she yelled from over her shoulder.

"I won't blame Him, but I'll sure thank Him. May even shout because goodness me! The Lord has been good, Emily. He's blessed you exceedingly." She looked back to see Tony waving his hand in the air as if he was in worship.

Emily laughed at Tony and rummaged through her cabinets and refrigerator for a quick meal. She settled on shrimp and grits. After cooking, she handed him a bowl of the timeless creole dish. He scooped up a thick helping, gobbled it down, and stared solemnly at her.

"Now, see, Peach. If you wanted me to move in all you had to do was ask. Because if your cooking is *this* good, I need to go ahead and take up residence here." Flattered, Emily smiled. She'd been doing a lot of that since Tony's arrival.

"I'm glad you like it. You can take up residence here if you pay the bills," Emily joked. But Tony's face remained grave.

"I'd do way more than that if I was your man, Emily." Emily looked into Tony's eyes. The look on his face said he meant every word. His actions said he meant every word. A part of her wanted to take him up on his offer. But the other part hung on to the lie of the past —or his hidden truth—same difference in Emily's eyes.

*"Why did he mislead me about his shambled marriage? His then estranged, now ex-wife? Things could've been so simple if he would've just been honest ..."*

Emily grabbed the remote and pressed play. She wasn't ready to face that issue. Not tonight anyway. She just needed carefree company. Yet, she knew she couldn't keep stringing him along. Eventually, he would demand an answer. She couldn't decide if she should put the past behind her and move forward with a relationship or if she should take Tony's past deception as a red flag. She supposed the decision was up to her being that God hadn't answered her yet. She'd decide soon enough. But for now, more TV.

As the theme song to the TV series ended Tony stood up and stretched out his legs. "Well, Peach, I know you're tired. Your head started nodding toward the end. I'm heading on home so you can rest." Emily removed the blanket from across her legs. He was right. She was fighting off sleep, but she didn't want to ask Tony to leave. In fact, she wouldn't have opposed him sleeping on the couch.

Emily looked at the time. It was close to 12 a.m. "Yeah, I am pretty tired." She joined Tony in stretching. He pulled on his light jacket and headed toward the door with Emily on his heels.

"Thank you for this. It was nice having company today. I enjoyed it," Emily said.

Tony nodded. "The feeling's mutual. I always enjoy your company. But you know that already."

Emily smiled and opened the door. A few stars shone in the midnight sky along with a vivid crescent moon.

"Good night, Tony," she said.

Tony didn't immediately respond. His eyes lingered on her face. First on her eyes, then up to her coils, and finally down to her lips. He leaned forward and swooped in for what Emily thought was a kiss. Yet, Tony opted for a sweet embrace. When he let go, he held her hand for a moment before releasing it. "Good night, Peach."

Emily stood in the doorway for a minute longer, watching Tony climb into his Jeep. She closed the door and strolled to the couch to turn off the TV. As she made ready for bed, she was somewhat disappointed. She'd purposely avoided watching certain shows with Tony to circumvent any potential mishaps. So, why was she dissatisfied with Tony's hug? It was clean and wholesome just like the cartoons they'd watched. She considered that if they hung out again, perhaps she'd set the TV on a PG-13 show.

Emily yanked back the glass door to the shower and strained her ears. *"Was that my doorbell?"* she thought. She waited. Listened for the chime again. Ding dong. Emily screwed up her face in confusion. It was a little past 9:00 a.m. Who would be ringing her doorbell this early? Who would be ringing her doorbell at all during this state-wide lockdown? Emily rushed out of the shower and patted herself dry with a towel. She threw on her robe and made her way to her security camera. It was Tony.

Emily hesitantly made her way to the door. *"What could he possibly want? And why didn't he call first?"* She cracked open the door, not wanting to completely open it. She felt exposed in only her robe.

"Hey, Tony. Is everything okay?"

He backed up a little, attempting to show respect.

"Yes, everything is fine. I'm so sorry to disturb you Peach, but I think I left my phone over here. I can't find it anywhere." Emily opened the door a little more.

"Oh, okay. The couch probably ate it. I'm a little indecent so let me check for you. I'll be right back." Tony nodded while Emily stepped away. She tossed pillows back and forth and dug her hands between the cushions. She located the phone and headed towards the door. "Here it is," she said, sliding Tony the phone through the door.

"Thank you," he said. "Again, I'm sorry to have bothered you ... Have you eaten breakfast yet?"

Emily tightened her bathrobe. "No, not yet. I was just showering before you rang."

"Let me bring you some breakfast for this early morning disturbance," he suggested. Emily wanted more time to think about her and Tony. To decide which one was leading her correctly—her head or her heart? She needed to think without being in his presence. His appeal would only distract her from making a sound decision. But she wanted the distraction, didn't she? And she was hungry.

"Okay, that sounds good," she agreed. Tony smiled, exposing the one dimple that appeared occasionally in his chocolatey skin.

"Cool, I'll grab us something. I'll be back shortly ... by the way, Peach. You're the natural beauty I always knew you were. Glad I could see you in your raw element." With that Tony winked and walked toward his Jeep.

Emily inhaled and shut the door, her knees weakened by his sensational eyewink. *"Mercy me. Mercy me,"* she thought. *"Mercy me."*

Once again, what was meant to be a short visit extended well into the evening. Tony and Emily played spades, charades, and even went for a short walk up the street and back. He had divulged more information about his life than Emily expected, including more details about his marriage and divorce. She had, in turn, opened up about her tumultuous circumstances and hardship in coping with it. She even admitted her reasoning for inviting him into her home.

"I feel bad, honestly," she said, relaxed on her couch with Tony inches away. "I invited you over yesterday because I needed to escape. I didn't want to fight with myself or this solitude anymore. I used you in a sense. I'm sorry."

Tony looked over at her with a serious face. "Emily, use me, girl. Use me 'til you can't use me no more," he said, holding his serious expression before erupting into hilarity. Emily joined him.

"No, seriously, Peach," he said, switching to a more solemn tone, "this solitude isn't good for some. It's driving some people to suicide, you know? When you're locked inside with your demons, your problems, with no way to escape, either you face them and overcome them... or they overcome you. I'm glad to be a distraction for you, but eventually, you'll have to deal with it before it deals with you." Emily remained silent, taking in Tony's words.

"But you're such a handsome distraction," Emily teased. She didn't know if it was another distraction, a sincere confession, or that blasted tantalizing cologne, but she felt flirtatious.

Tony smiled coyly. "Oh, am I?"

Emily nodded. "But don't let that boost your ego too much."

Tony inched a bit closer to her. "I won't. I promise."

He leaned in. Emily sat up.

"Emily, I know I asked you, and I told you I would wait on you to give me an answer, but that's becoming difficult to do." Emily searched Tony's face. The face of a man who needed an answer. And needed it sooner rather than later.

"If you can't forgive me, if you can't get past it, I understand. But I need to know. Emily, I don't want to waste your time or mine. I'm a relationship kind of guy. I loved being married, and I hate that it didn't work ... I don't want to just hang out with you. I want to date you and see if this can lead to something good, something solid. So, what's it going to be?"

Emily probed her heart. She investigated her mind. What did they have to say? What did God have to say?

Nothing as far as she knew. He hadn't answered. *"All love is a gamble, isn't it? If I walk away, I'll always wonder what if. If I say yes, I won't have to wonder. I'll know."*

Emily breathed deeply and stared into Tony's determined eyes. Fear and exhilaration flooded her. "I forgive you, but I'm nervous, Tony."

Tony cupped her chin towards his, his manly hands gentle on her apple-shaped face.

"We'll be nervous together." His eyes smoldered as his lips touched hers. Such a sweet, yet passionate kiss. Emily caught her breath as he pulled away. She stared into his eyes, hoping they would give her an indication that she was making the right decision. Instead, he leaned in for one more kiss and she obliged. He held her in his arms as they turned their attention to the television set. Emily flipped to a scary movie. Safe in Tony's strong arms, she doubted the thriller would scare her one bit.

*The Golden Gate Bridge. It lies bare. Void of vehicles and souls. There I stand. Head up, eyes towards the sky. Watching it fly. The gold flickering from its feathers. Its multi-colored wings spread wide, soaring high in the clear horizon, sun beaming. The majestic eagle with the familiar eyes dances around the sky. The crimson blood-stained wound still right above the beryl stone, taking nothing away from its captivating essence. Simply beautiful.*
*Then, footsteps.*
*Footsteps on the bridge toward the left. I turn toward the sound. Tony. Walking in a steady, confident stride. His charm is detected yards away. My heart beats a pace faster with each step he takes. I*

*face him. Waiting for his approach. Anticipating his touch. His warmth.*
*Then, more footsteps. From the right this time.*
*I toss a glance over my shoulder. Angelo. Walking, no, running toward me. I furrow my brows. He raises his hand upward, in a stopping motion, mouthing something. He gets closer. Stop? Yes, stop he says with mounting authority. His allurement, his strength also detected yards away. Militant. Determined. Steadfast. He keeps running toward me.*
*I turn back to face Tony. His smile glinting. His appeal stronger than ever. I glance once more back at Angelo. Except he's no longer running. He's fighting. Battling something. His back blocks his opponent from view. I turn back towards Tony. He extends his hand. I walk towards him and take it. I glance up toward the clear sky. The eagle circles and soars away. I glance back at Angelo once more witnessing his battle with an unseen enemy. Tony tightens his arms around me.*
*We walk away ... and I don't look back.*

Emily awoke, initially confused as to where she was or what day it was. The dead weight of Tony's arms lay over her torso, constricting her movement. Her head was tucked just beneath his chin. They had fallen asleep on the couch wrapped in each other's embrace. She stirred reaching for her phone to check the time. 1:00 a.m. Emily delicately wriggled free from Tony's grip. She stood to drape her blanket over him just as his eyes popped open.

Groggily, he asked, "What time is it?"

Emily proceeded to place the blanket over him. "It's late, but you can crash here until the morning. I'm heading to bed."

Tony tossed the blanket aside. "I would, but I don't have a change of clothes, a toothbrush, or anything. I'd hate to greet you with bad B.O. in the morning."

Emily shrugged. "You can leave before I even notice ..."

Tony yawned and laid back into the couch. "Yeah, I'll do that. Thanks, Peach."

"You're welcome," she said as she made her way to her bedroom. She threw herself into bed, momentarily thinking about her dream. She felt slightly repentant dreaming of Angelo while lying in Tony's arms. But there wasn't a choice between Tony and Angelo. Angelo had never rightfully presented himself as an option. So, there was nothing to consider. Or at least that's what Emily told herself.

Morning presented itself with sunshine and questions. Lost in the presence of Tony, Emily hadn't considered what she had committed herself to last night. Were they a couple? Or were they just dating to explore if being a couple was a possibility? *"Oh goodness,"* she thought while she showered. *What about my celibacy?"* Surely Tony wouldn't agree to celibacy before … what? Marriage? Was that the goal? *"Why am I even using Tony's name in the same sentence as marriage?"*

More thoughts rushed in. Thoughts of Angelo. She would have to see him one last time—to hand him the keys to his brand-new home after the closing. *"I could just leave them in the bushes,"* she considered. She didn't want to, nor could she possibly, face him after agreeing to whatever she had agreed to with Tony. Seeing him would only cause confusion. Her natural allurement to Angelo would make her second-guess being with Tony.

How would he take her moving forward with Tony if he knew? Would he care? Emily was due to conduct his final closing paperwork in a few days. She planned on dropping off the keys the same day. *"Even if I drop the keys in bushes, I should at least FaceTime him one last time to congratulate him. That's just professionalism."* She shook her head to free her mind of Angelo. "Should've stepped up when you had a chance," Emily said aloud. "Tony knew not to miss out on a good thing."

The buzz of her phone startled her. It vibrated louder than usual on the surface of her porcelain throne. She stuck her head of out the shower to peep at the caller ID. Incoming call from Estella. Emily was in a relatively great mood, courtesy of Tony. She'd call Estella back after she finished her shower, but before Emily could complete her thought, her phone buzzed again. Incoming call from Estella. Emily made her way out of the shower to dry off and moisturize her skin. Her phone buzzed again from Estella's incoming call.

"Ma'am, shouldn't you be watching virtual Sunday service or something? Why are you blowing up my phone?" Emily asked jokingly.

"Hey, Emily," Stella said. "… Dad's in the hospital."

Emily's enthusiasm fled. "What's wrong with him?" her heart raced a mile a minute.

"We don't know," Estella replied. "Mom called me right before I called you. She said he wasn't feeling well last night so they went to the emergency room. From there, they admitted him to the hospital. That's all I know."

For a brief moment, Emily questioned why neither her mom nor her dad had called her to tell her the news. *"Why would they?"* she reasoned. *"Time and seclusion from them is what I requested."* She fought for words. "... Okay, uh ... how did Mom sound?" Estella breathed.

"Normal, I guess? You know Mom is hard to read sometimes." Indeed, she was Emily thought.

"His last treatment went fine though, right?" Emily recalled Estella texting the usual 'Dad's fine' message.

"Yeah, everything went as usual ... hold on, Emily. That's Mom calling me now. I'll call you back."

Estella ended the call, leaving Emily slightly, though not completely worried. Illness came with the kidney failure territory she supposed. She completed her beauty rituals and headed to her living room. Her phone buzzed again, this time from Tony.

"Good morning, Peach." Emily pondered how long Tony had slept on her couch. It had felt good knowing a man was in her home. She felt secure, protected.

"Hey, Tony. Did the couch allow you a decent rest?"

"I would've preferred my bed honestly, but it worked. What are you—"

Vibrations cut into Tony's question. Estella was calling back.

"Hey, let me call you back. My sister's calling me." Emily clicked over. "Hey, what's up?"

Estella sighed into the phone, "So, apparently Dad has covid ..." Emily froze. "He was having a hard time breathing. He has pneumo— ugh, Emily hold on. That's Mom calling again. I'll hit you right back."

Emily waited silently on the edge of her couch. Pneumonia? Dad has pneumonia? And kidney disease? And covid? If there was ever a time to pray ... *"God, please spare him. Please heal him. I know I haven't forgiven—"* Her phone buzzed again. It was her mother this time.

"Hello? Hey, Mom."

Elena spoke calmly. "Hey, Emi baby."

Emily waited for her mom to continue, but she didn't. "Hey Mom, Estella told me about dad. How is he?"

Elena was slow to answer. Too slow in fact. "Hello? Mom, did you hear me?" Emily pulled the phone back from her ear ensuring the mute button wasn't inadvertently pressed. "Hello?" Emily repeated.

"Yes, I'm here, Emily," was all Elena said.

"How's Dad?" Emily asked again.

Elena wasn't the type to search for words. They normally rolled effortlessly out of her mouth. This was so even when Benjamin had the heart attack. But today, it appeared Elena was struggling for the right thing to say.

"Emily ... you know ...Benjamin loved you."

Emily's heart picked up its pace again. Considerably faster than the last time. "Yes, Mom. I know Dad *loves* me." Emily emphasized the present tense form of the word. Because no other tense—especially past—could possibly be applicable to describe Benjamin Water's current state.

"Emily, he wanted me to tell you that he was sorry. That he never wanted to hurt you." Elena's voice quieted to a whisper. Emily knew her mom was straining back tears.

"Well then, put him on the phone, Mom. Put him on the phone so he can tell me," she said, her voice rising and cracking.

"Emily ..."

"Put him on the phone, Mom!" Emily sobbed. "Momma, please ... please put Daddy on the phone!" Emily dropped down to the floor. Her heart felt as it was being squeezed in a vice grip.

"Emily, I'm so sorry, baby. I didn't want to tell you over the phone," Elena said, now softly crying, distraught both from losing a part of herself and from hearing her daughter breakdown without a mother's consolation. "Is there anybody I can call, Emily? Anybody that can come check on you? I don't want you there by yourself."

A panic attack. Emily had never had one before, but she was sure she was having a massive panic attack. Her chest felt tight. She struggled to catch her breath. Nausea flooded over her. Elena gripped the phone in fear for her daughter's mental state.

"Emily, baby, please calm down. Listen to me, okay? You've got to breathe." Emily heard her mother's words but couldn't seem to complete the simple task of inhaling and exhaling at a normal rate. Elena's attempts to coach her out of her frenzy proved futile. Before long, Emily heard her mother do what she'd always done best.

"Jehovah God, I come to you asking that you send peace over my baby right now in the mighty name of Jesus. Ease her breathing, Lord. Settle her heart and mind. Help her, please. She's not alone if you stand with her, God. Please, Jesus, have mercy ..." Emily heard her mother continue in prayer. Her words rang out, distorted yet powerful.

Eventually, the panic subsided, and Emily recalled how to control her breathing. She took big, exaggerated gasps in and out.

"That's it, Emi, that's it. In and out." Elena coached her daughter into a state of calm. Emily sat on the floor stunned. Lost. "Okay, Emily. I'm going to hang up and FaceTime you, okay?" Emily absentmindedly nodded her head. In seconds, Elena beheld her daughter's face. She wanted to cry at the sight of Emily's visible agony.

"Hey, baby. It's going to be alright. Everything's going to be alright," Elena said praying Emily would view her words as true instead of a cliché.

Emily looked past the camera in a daze. Elena didn't offer any more words. Neither did Emily. Elena sat in silence with her daughter over FaceTime for what seemed to be endless hours, though it couldn't have been more than 20 minutes. Emily eventually broke from her hazed trance and cleared her throat to speak.

"I'm going to go lie down ... I'm tired," she said.

Elena nodded her head, "Okay, call me back when you wake up."

Emily offered a curt nod and ended the call. She stood up from where she sat, walked into her bedroom, covered her body and head with her sheets and went to sleep.

The annoyance of her cellphone vibrating on her nightstand interrupted her sleep. She removed the covers from her head. *"Did I dream it all?"* Emily thought. She reached over to check her phone. Three missed calls from Mom. Two text messages from Estella.

Hey, Emi. Please call me or Mom as soon as possible. She's gonna need us now more than ever.

Tears fell as Emily now grieved for her mom. *"How will she cope without Dad? He was her everything ..."*

It wasn't a dream. A cloud of disillusion hovered over her, insinuating that the events of the morning were false. But the missed calls and text messages said otherwise. Emily remained in bed. Her mind couldn't process it. Her mind wouldn't process it. Sleep. Sleep would make it all go away. She didn't feel her heavy heart before the buzzing of her phone woke her up. If she could just go back to sleep, into unconscious oblivion, all would be well. So, Emily slept.

Persistent buzzing and doorbell chimes disturbed Emily's rest once more. She grimaced at the pain she encountered from waking up. She rolled over to check her phone. More missed calls and text messages. This time from her mom, Estella, Ms. Rugsby, and Tony. She looked at the time. A quarter past 5:00 p.m. *"I slept that long?"* Emily thought. Her doorbell rang once more.

Emily sat up to return her mother's call. "Hello? Hey, Mom. I'm sorry. I ended up sleeping the day away."

Elena released a breath of thankfulness. "I'm sorry, Emily. I was worried. Part of me thought that maybe you were just sleeping, but I had to be sure ... so, I called your boss and asked if she could check on you. She mentioned a man named Tony might be able to drop by and check on you. Something about you guys being friends ... anyway that's him at your door now. I have him on the other line. Please let him in. You need to be with someone right now."

Emily sighed. "Mom, please. I don't want any company. I just want to sleep."

Elena answered in a firm tone. "Emily, get out of that bed and open the door right now."

Emily didn't want to be seen grieving by anyone who wasn't immediate family. She and Tony had just begun to be whatever it was that they'd agreed to be. It wasn't his place to comfort her in *this* matter. Losing a client, sure. Divorce talk and other matters of the heart, why not? But *this*? This was too personal and too soon. Emotional exposure and vulnerability at this altitude wasn't something shared lightly.

"This is private, and I don't want him involved in this. Just let me grieve alone today. Mom, please."

"Emily, I understand that. In normal circumstances, I wouldn't have involved anyone in this. But I can't be there for you, and neither can your sister. You need someone with you right now. It's not good to grieve alone like that. Please just do it for me. This day has been hard enough. Please just open the door for me."

Emily could hear the worry and anguish in her mother's voice. She didn't want to cause her anymore undue stress. She got out of the bed, splashed cold water on her face, and headed for the front door.

Tony was now banging on the door like a mad man. Emily swung it open but avoided eye contact. She turned her back to him and dragged her feet to the couch where she plopped down. Tony closed the door.

"Yes ma'am, Mrs. Waters. She opened the door ... Oh, no problem. Yes, I'll call you back after a while."

Tony wrapped up his call with Elena and walked cautiously towards Emily. He didn't know what to say. He thought about how he'd felt when he lost his daughter.

He hadn't wanted to talk initially. Not to anyone, his then wife included. Tony imagined Emily wouldn't want to talk to him or even have him in her home. So, he sat silently on the opposite side of the couch, waiting for any signal she might give to console her. But she just sat there, purposely looking in the other direction. After a long stint, Tony broke the silence.

"Have you eaten today?"

Emily kept her head turned the other way.

"No."

"I can go get you something if you want," Tony said, his voice barely above a whisper.

"I'm not hungry," Emily said.

Tony was miserably uncomfortable. He wanted to hold her and tell her the pain would subside eventually, but he thought better of it. It was hard seeing Emily, the go-getter, in a broken state. He remained silent as she sat stationary.

Emily breathed heavily. "I need to go outside ... call my sister." Tony gave her a reassuring look as she slid the glass door open to sit on her patio.

Estella began talking before Emily could. "Emily, hey, are you okay?"

Tears fell from her eyes. Why was it that she seemed to be slightly functional until Estella asked if she was? "No, Stella. I'm not okay," Emily cried. Estella remained silent as Emily sobbed. "How can I be?"

*"You didn't forgive him. You should've forgiven him,"* the intrusive thoughts bullied her. "I didn't forgive him! I shouldn't have ignored him. I should have let it go. What was I thinking? He was sick and I didn't forgive him, I refused to talk to him, and now ..." Emily trailed off weeping.

"Don't do that, Emily. Don't do that to yourself. Dad understood. You were taking your time and dealing with it the best way you knew how," Estella replied.

"But that wasn't the best way!" Emily proclaimed. "I should've forgiven him."

Angelo's advice came to her recollection. *"I know from experience that it's best to forgive quickly."* Her rebuttal also came to mind. *"I know that ... and I'll forgive them just as soon as I get past my anger."* Had Angelo experienced this? Refusing to forgive someone and that someone dying? Was that why he was so adamant about her forgiving her parents? Their past conversations whirled in her mind before Estella snapped her back to the present.

"Dad wouldn't want you beating yourself up. You know that. He loved you and always wanted the best for all of us."

Emily paused. She thought about how Estella must be taking the loss. *"She's with child for crying out loud!"* Emily thought. *"You have yet to ask her how she's doing."*

"Estella, I'm being so selfish. How are you doing? And the baby?" Emily didn't know much about pregnancy, but she figured grief couldn't be easy while carrying life.

"I'll be okay. We'll all be okay … Oh goodness, I sound just like Mom," Estella said with annoyance. Emily let out a small chuckle. She thought it weird that she could do such a thing in that moment.

"You do. You sound just like her." Emily paused in reflection. "And you're right about what you texted earlier. She's going to need us now." The reality of her mom being a widow settled in and crushed her even more.

Estella sighed, "I know. I wanted to stay the night with her, but Reggie doesn't think it's a good idea with Mom being around Dad and all … she'll have to get retested for covid again."

Emily hadn't thought about that. She hadn't thought about anything. All she wanted to do was sleep and escape the harsh news of the day. Yet, there she was again. Ignoring her mom who may also have coronavirus just like she ignored her dad. Ignoring her sister's grief in her delicate condition. *"You're self-centered. If that had been a potential client calling ..."* The intrusive thoughts returned and challenged her love for her family. She shook them off.

"Of course," Emily replied. "Lord, I pray she's negative."

"Me too, sis. Me too," Estella breathed.

Emily remembered Tony was still in her home and sighed. "Well, Stella. I guess I should head back in. My babysitter is waiting for me."

Estella scoffed. "Don't look at it that way, Emi. We all need people from time to time whether we realize it or not."

Emily rolled her eyes. "I guess so. I'll talk to you later. I love you."

"I love you too," Estella said before the call ended.

Emily took a deep breath and re-entered her home. Tony sat in the same place, but the TV was clicked on.

He looked at her, "A little TV to get your mind off today?"

Emily nodded her head and walked toward him. She sat a few inches away from him, but Tony inched closer and pulled her into his arms. She laid her head on his chest as a few more tears slid from her eyes. He didn't say a word. He let her tears wet his shirt as they watched more classic cartoons.

## THE FUNERAL
## MAY 2020—SAVANNAH, GEORGIA

Benjamin was a man of preparation. He had filed life insurance on himself and his dear Elena well before his kidney failure. "I ain't gonna have you grieving over me *and* stressing about how you'll afford the funeral," he said to his wife years ago. Elena was grateful for his proactive thinking. It allowed her the opportunity to simply grieve and remember the good times.

She had tested positive for covid. Fourteen days in quarantine, the day after losing the love of her life, was the worst experience of Elena's life. Her daughters were sweet. They checked on her every day. "I don't feel bad at all, praise God," she told them on a group call. "I'm ... what do they call it? Asymptomatic?" She reassured her daughters she was fine—and covid wise, she was—but her grieve nearly swallowed her alive. There wasn't a place in their home that didn't remind her of Benjamin in some way.

She was thankful the funeral was today. "It'll be closure for all of us," she said to her daughters dressed in royal blue—Benjamin's favorite color.

"Don't wear black to my funeral," Benjamin had also said years ago. "That's depressing. Wear something vibrant. Wear my favorite color, and don't be boo-hooing either. I don't want no sad funeral. Be joyful that I lived a good life. I want it to be a celebration. A 'going-up-a-yonder party'!" Elena smiled at her late husband's request.

She wanted to give him all that he had desired, but the covid restrictions placed limitations on his request. It broke her heart to inform much of their family that they couldn't attend the service. "No large gatherings they say," she explained. They all understood, but breaking the news was nevertheless difficult. And for the ones that could attend, those restrictions were also heart-breaking to abide by.

"Social distancing will be enforced, and please wear a mask," she stressed to the mere ten guests who would be present to lay her sweet Benjamin to rest.

Emily's struggle with her dad's death, her mom's quarantine, and her berating intrusive thoughts may've proved enough to consume her if Tony hadn't refused to leave her home. "I know depression when I see it, Emily. I'm not leaving you," he had said. Tony had temporarily sheltered with Emily everyday after the news of Benjamin's death. His presence kept her from hitting rock bottom. Although she hadn't exactly welcomed him with open arms, Emily was thankful for his company.

Celibacy was a thing of the past for her. After so many nights of being in Tony's arms, she succumbed to her desire. Tony initially made it a point to avoid such a thing given her state of sorrow, but Emily assured him that she was an adult capable of making her own decisions. She yielded, and she wanted to yield. No thoughts of what God thought of her choices weighed on her conscience. No prayers went up to Him either. Emily was numb and started to believe that maybe her intrusive thoughts were right. Sick and tired of being sick and tired was an understatement.

No amount of sleep, cartoons, workouts, cleaning, rendezvous with Tony, or even money could ease her mind. *"Closure, huh?"* Emily thought after Elena spoke. Closure would be nice, but would it take the pain away? Her mom opened the front door to the house that was once full of love and laughter, now stained with grief and Benjamin's lingering essence. Elena turned her head back to look at her daughters and son-in-law.

"Ready?" she asked.

Solemn nods were given by Emily, Estella, and Reggie. Elena walked out first, and the family followed her one by one in a single-file line. They marched down the porch steps and headed for their cars parked in the cul-de-sac in front of the house. The black limousine that Elena requested for the family was denied.

"Funeral transportation services don't allow for social distancing," the funeral director instructed her.

"It'll only be my daughters and son-in-law. We're all in the home together less than six feet away. It won't make a difference if we sit in the car together," Elena had argued.

"I'm sorry, ma'am, but it may put the limousine driver at risk. I sincerely apologize for the inconvenience," was his rebuttal.

So, they drove, instead of being escorted, to their loved one's funeral. The director did, however, permit the use of the hearse, which was parked directly ahead of the car they piled into. Emily grew sick to her stomach knowing her daddy's body lay in the vehicle. She felt even worse knowing that her dad wouldn't have been happy if he knew he alone was riding in style to his going-away service. She later learned that Benjamin had also died alone.

Once the hospital diagnosed him with coronavirus, the staff prohibited Elena from remaining by his side. "You let him die alone?" were the last words Emily had uttered to God. Nothing was right about this. From Benjamin's death, to the cruel isolation the family had to endure following his death, to the restrictions placed on his requested funeral wishes, nothing was right. And Emily couldn't understand for the life of her how a God who claimed to love her, and her family would allow them to go through unfair agony.

Reggie carefully rolled away from the house and made the trek to Healing Rose Church. Upon arrival, Elena again led the family through the doors and they gravely walked toward the front to view the body before they sat in their respective seats. Emily barely glanced at Benjamin in the casket. She couldn't. She followed Elena to the first pew and sat six feet apart as mandated.

Six feet apart from her mother. Six feet apart from her sister. Six feet apart from anyone at all who cared to extend their condolences or comfort in this comfortless time. *"What kind of 'going-home' celebration is this?"* Emily thought. *"Ten people? Separated from one another? No handshakes? No pats on the back? No hugs?"* What was supposed to be a celebration felt cold and distant. *"Closure,"* she huffed at the thought.

Emily wrestled with her anger toward God. At this point, she questioned if there really was a God. And if there was one, was it too hard to allow her dad to go away as he requested? Was it too hard for Him to allow her mom to hold his hand as he took his last breath? No, nothing's too hard for a sovereign God is what she was always told. A God that breathed life into man and spoke the stars and heavens into being surely can do anything. So, why did He choose to do this?

Emily shifted in her seat at her inner questions. She glanced at the picture of Benjamin resting on an easel at the front of the church flanked by blue and white floral arrangements. *"Such a handsome man,"* she thought. Brilliant smile—the same smile she always thought she's inherited. Everything was beginning to feel too heavy to bear. She breathed deeply as the service began.

A song selection, prayer, reading of the Word all proceeded Pastor Peoples mounting the pulpit, none of which felt celebratory to Emily.

"I stand here today to eulogize a dear old member, companion, and fellow servant of God." Pastor shifted his weight behind the podium. "This is no easy task as I am grieving along with you all. Mrs. Waters, Emily, Estella and family you have my deepest sympathy."

"I won't be before you long. But I would like to briefly come from Romans 14:8–9. If you have your Bibles, turn with me and if you have your phones, scroll with me to the referenced text. Emily reluctantly opened her Bible app. If apps could collect dust, Emily's Bible app would be rather grimy. Pastor Peoples proceeded.

*"If we live, we live for the Lord; and if we die, we die for the Lord. So, whether we live or die, we belong to the Lord. For this very reason, Christ died and returned to life so that he might be the Lord of both the dead and the living."*

"You know, when we read scripture, we see that God views death differently than we do. Death to us feels final, but death, to God, is temporary. We know this based on how God addresses death when He spoke of Lazarus. When Lazarus was dead for four days, Jesus said he was sleeping. When the people stoned Stephen to death for preaching the gospel, the scripture states Stephen slept." Pastor Peoples carefully scanned the crowd as he normally did when attempting to make a point.

"Sleep is by no means permanent to us just as death is by no means permanent to God. As we ought to view things the way God does, shouldn't we also consider death temporary? Plus, we see here it says if we live or die, we belong to the Lord ... don't you all see that nothing will separate us from the love of God? Not life, nor death? If we live for God, we belong to God. And if we die *in* God, we not only belong to God, but we get to be with Him after life on earth has ended. Either way it goes, we belong to the Lord ... though in grief it may be hard to hear, that's something to be joyful about."

Emily stretched her neck and repositioned her seating. Pastor Peoples hadn't said a thing she hadn't heard before. Emily was, after all, attending a 'going-home-celebration'. She understood the meaning of the phrase. But none of it made her pain disappear. She only wanted this godforsaken funeral to be over. Pastor Peoples finished his eulogy. Family and loved ones were then allotted their time to briefly express their sentiments about Benjamin.

A couple of family members gave a few words, none of which, in Emily's opinion, adequately explained the beauty and complexity that was Benjamin Waters. So, on a whim, Emily hopped up to defend her dad's honor and save what she could of his funeral. Elena, Estella, and Reggie all looked on in appalled concern. Emily ignored their looks and proceeded toward the center of the church, in front of the casket and next to Benjamin's portrait.

Her amber eyes lingered on the curved smile on his picture. She turned to face the minute congregation. "Not too long ago I discovered Benjamin Waters wasn't my biological father," Emily blurted out. Although her eyes were concealed by darkened sunglasses, Elena's eyes burned into hers. Emily could feel it. She knew Estella, Reggie, and the remaining six guests also disapproved. But she had to say her piece. It was her last opportunity to do so.

"I didn't know how to process that—I still don't." Emily dropped her head but continued speaking. "So, I shut him and my mother out of my life. I shut my sister out too," Emily paused. "I was hurt, and I didn't forgive him before he left. He left this world knowing that I hadn't forgiven him. And that hurts the worst." Emily lifted her head, blinking back tears. "But I want you all to know that Benjamin Waters was a good—no, he was an outstanding man. Nothing you or any of us will say or have said today will do him justice."

"I want it known to you all that I love Benjamin Waters. I couldn't have asked for a better dad. A better role model or encourager. My dad meant the world to me," Emily said, clearing her throat. She glanced over at Benjamin's face in the casket. She swallowed and breathed deeply. "I know you didn't mean to hurt me. You did the best you could. And it was good enough, Daddy. I declare it was good enough. I love you. Rest well," Emily concluded as she walked back to her seat. There was an uneasy silence in the room as she took her seat. Pastor Peoples stood and asked for any more final words. No one stood.

Emily watched in a suspended reality as the funeral home personnel closed the casket on Benjamin's face. Numb. Emily's whole body went numb. A few men lifted the casket and exited the building. The funeral had ended. The family grabbed the floral arrangements, along with Benjamin's portrait, and proceeded to the outside of the church where the burial was due to take place.

"Ashes to ashes. Dust to dust," were among the few words Emily heard at the graveside. Her detachment prevented her from remaining focused. Emily watched as they lowered the casket into the ground. Slowly, they lowered it. With each passing second, she became more aloof. Her mother sent up her final wails for her beloved Benjamin.

Estella whimpered into Reggie's arms. But Emily's numbness had managed to lull her into silence.

They rode home. They went through the motions of being a supportive family in grief. Emily's detachment eased a bit after a few hours. She shared her new career standing and financial status to the family—just to make conversation. A frail attempt to lighten the mood. They were proud of her. But without Benjamin's congratulations, which would have been overtly extravagant, the applause wasn't as gratifying as Emily hoped. She thought about her final words at the funeral. She apologized to the family.

"Mom, I wasn't thinking about how that made you look. For all they know, you were unfaithful to dad. I shouldn't have talked about a private matter in public. I'm so sorry."

Elena nodded her head, accepting Emily's words. "Emily, I won't lie. I wanted to slap you silly. I didn't think that was the right place or time for that. But then I realized that you needed to release. I can't imagine your pain, and I won't pretend that I understand it. Benjamin would have wanted you to have your final words. Besides, honestly baby, what people think about me ain't my business. I know the truth and that's all that matters." Emily smiled at her mother's words.

"Well, family, if you don't mind, I think I'm going to go lie down for a while," Emily stated.

Estella nodded her head "I was thinking the same, sis. I'm drained."

Elena rose from her seat. "Y'all go ahead and get some rest. I'll settle down eventually." Emily rubbed Elena's back before she ascended the stairs. In the silence of her old bedroom, she shed herself free of her funeral attire. She folded the dress and stuck it in the furthest corner in her closet. She vowed to never wear it again. It reeked of pain.

After an intentionally cold shower, Emily crawled into bed and awaited the escapism of sleep to arrive. Besides the infrequent shuffling of feet, the house was silent. Mirroring her emotions, it was as if the walls leaned in, and the ceiling hung lower. The doors creaked in mourning and the foundation seemed unstable. Emily knew homes died when they sat empty for too long. Although it seemed much too soon, she reckoned it could feel its host, its leader, was gone. As if the presence of the rest of the family did not matter. Its depreciation had prematurely begun. And so had Emily's.

Rolling thunder woke her from her slumber. The red numbers on the nightstand illuminated a late-night hour. A crack of lightning startled her as slanted rain pelted her window. She beckoned for sleep's return—to alleviated her from her pain—but it refused. She sat up in bed groggy from too much sleep. She pulled the covers back as flashes of lightning temporarily lit her path as she walked out of the room.

The stairs faintly creaked as she walked, barefoot toward the kitchen for a drink of water. To her surprise, Elena was sitting at the dining room table with her chair turned in the opposite direction, watching the dark precipitation through the curtain-drawn window.

"Mom?" Emily whispered. Elena snapped around, face as wet as the window she was staring out of. She quickly wiped the tears away.

"Emily, hey. What are you doing up?"

"Weather woke me up, I guess," Emily said as she grabbed a seat next to her mom. Elena rose just as Emily sat.

"I'll get you some water."

Emily watched her mother pour her a glass of water as her heart tumbled. She couldn't wrap her mind around her own grief—let alone her mother's. More thunder rolled as they sat in silent darkness.

"Emily, I've been thinking about whether to do this now or give it more time."

Emily studied her mother's sunken face. "But if I haven't learned anything else, I've learned that time isn't guaranteed to any of us. So, while I'm still given the time, I want to tell you what I know about your biological father ... that is, if you want to know ..." Elena waited for Emily's response. She uncomfortably shuffled her feet under the table before she gave her mother a hesitant nod.

"His name is Allen Gray. We only dated for three or four months. He was a good guy. Funny, vibrant, loved to party." Elena fiddled with her fingers as the recalled the past. "He never knew about you ... I was back with your dad before I found out I was pregnant." Emily breathed as Elena continued. "I felt so terrible about how I ended things with him. Well ... I never really ended things. I kind of just stopped answering his calls. He caught my drift and never bothered me again."

Emily waited for Elena to divulge more information. "I'm not sure, and of course this was over twenty years ago, but last I heard, he moved somewhere up north. Detroit or Chicago, I think. I remember him saying he'd moved down south to live with his grandma to get away from the street life." Elena once more rose from the table. This time she walked toward the antique China cabinet.

She bent down, pulled out a drawer, and retrieved what appeared to be old mail in an envelope. Settled back down in her seat, she shuffled through the folded papers until her hands landed on an old photograph. Her eyes gazed across the still picture briefly before she slid the photo in front of her daughter. Emily's eyes fell on the withered photo. Its corners were curved, white cracks slightly distorted the image. A young Elena sat under the arms of a caramel-complected man with amber-brown eyes.

His leather jacket and slick smile exuded style and confidence. His eyes shone with the same fire and zeal Emily saw every time she looked into a mirror—though they hadn't shone as brightly recently. Her heart skipped a beat and simultaneously dropped as she realized she was the spitting image of a man named Allen Gray, not Benjamin Waters. Emily slid the photo back to Elena and finished her water.

"Looks like y'all were having a good time," she said. Partygoers were seen in the background along with strobe lights and a dancefloor.

"Like I said, he loved to party. He really was a good man ... he just wasn't the man for me." Emily nodded in silence as the storm began to calm outside.

"And you never heard anything else about him?"

Elena shook her head. "Only speculation. Nothing concrete."

Emily grabbed her mother's hand. "Thank you for this."

"You're welcome," Elena said with a weak smile.

Emily stood up and tucked her chair under the table. "I'm headed back up. Love you, Mom." Emily slowly walked back up the stairs and threw herself back into bed. The man in the photograph was etched in her brain like a hot brand. Her eyes floated to the mirror that stood on her dresser. Her eyes adjusted to the darkness to see a photo of Benjamin proudly beaming at a 16-year-old Emily who had just won a gold at her first track competition.

She wondered why people said funerals brought closure. To her, it only solidified the dismal fact that she'd never see or hear from her dad ever again. The house felt as if it had caved in just a tad more since her short visit downstairs. *"Allen Gray,"* her mind said as her heart grieved for Benjamin. It seemed inappropriate to think of this Gray guy when Benjamin was all the father she'd ever hoped for. Yet, a twinkle of hope had settled on Emily's heart despite its persistent grief.

Life was fleeting as Elena had stated. Though conflicted, Emily deemed it only best to find out about Allen Gray, the other part of her, while she had the chance. She turned over on her pillow and cried herself to sleep with Benjamin Waters, Allen Gray, and a cyclone of depression heavy on her mind.

Emily managed to roll out of bed and eat breakfast with the family before curiosity moved her to investigate. She excused herself from the dining room table amidst a trivial discussion. With her bedroom door closed, she began her research. Allen Gray wasn't the most uncommon name she soon discovered. Her search proved to be a bit more extensive than she had anticipated. Yet, eventually, Emily ran across a profile picture that made her pause.

"*He's too young to be ...*" Emily initially thought when she stared at the young man in the profile picture. But those were her eyes—Allen Gray's eyes—in the picture, she was sure of it. It took all of a split second before she concluded that she'd stumbled upon what could only be her brother's, Allen Gray Jr, social media account. She hesitated to click on his page. Nerves built within her torso like a hill of fire ants.

Without another thought, she clicked on the page. *"Lives in Detroit, Michigan"* Emily read. She carefully scrolled down his timeline. Allen Gray Jr. appeared to be a lover of music, some sort of producer from what she gathered. He didn't smile much ... or at least from the few pictures she'd come across he didn't. Emily scrolled down his page for quite a while. Yet, she didn't see any signs of Allen Gray Sr.

She stopped scrolling and clicked on his photo gallery. Pictures of Allen Jr at parties and social events reminded her of the withered picture Elena had showed her the night before. She finally came across a smiling photo of him. He looked so much like his dad—her dad. Like her. Her heart broke knowing she'd gone her entire life without knowing her dad or brother or without them knowing her. Anger briefly surfaced but was immediately replaced with regret. She couldn't remain angry at Benjamin or Elena, or she shouldn't, she reasoned as she continued through the pictures.

Emily stopped on a photo, a digital flyer, that Allen Jr had posted roughly six months ago. *"Please call 313-587..."* Emily read in silence. Contact information sat below a photo of an older gentleman with the same amber eyes. Her dad, Allen Gray Sr, had aged, but not gracefully. Concern wrapped around Emily as she discovered Allen Sr was apparently missing. She read the caption below the flyer.

Allen Jr had written, "Some of you know. Some of you don't. This ain't easy to admit, but my father (pictured) has battled addiction for years. He was doing good for a while but I'm inclined to believe that he has relapsed since I haven't been able to locate him. I thought we had gotten past this nightmare. I need your prayers and your eyes on these streets. Please let me know if you've seen him."

Remorse filled Emily's lungs. She'd opened pandora's box and it was stuffed with cracked hope and bad dreams. *"A missing drug addict? That's who my father is? That's my lineage?"* Emily asked with disdain. She closed the webpage and sat on the edge of her bed both shocked and distraught.

Life couldn't be this hilariously awful she told herself. She'd just attended the funeral of one dad. This new daunting discovery begged her to reach back into the corner of her closet and pull out the funeral dress she'd worn two days ago. Because this revelation felt like the second death to the second dad she never knew.

*"Emily Gray doesn't sound right anyway,"* she thought as she threw herself back on the mattress. Against her wishes, tears poured. A headache accompanied her as she slowly wiped them away. She was exhausted. Tired. Tired of praying. Tired of crying. Tired of being met with bad news. Tired of life beating her up. Tired of waiting for a silent God to talk. "Do you not see me? Hear me?" Emily asked out loud.

She waited for a few seconds. For what, she wasn't sure. Perhaps for God to respond audibly or to show some sign that He saw her. To confirm that relief was on the way or a clue as to why one thing after another kept happening to her. But she was met with silence. In that moment, Emily felt her faith breaking, and the point of pressing on felt more obscure.

She was confused as to how she could feel completely numb, yet completely sad. A brief knock at the door was followed by Estella's voice, "You okay in there, Emily?"

Emily sat up and instantly lied. "Hey, yeah, I'm fine. Just got caught up watching a show on my phone." Her lie was received well. After a few more words, Estella stepped away from the door and left Emily to her faux entertainment.

Hopelessness surrounded her. Her mind and body ached from stress and anguish. Tears flooded her face as she cried silently, careful not to alert anyone in the house to her breakdown. Despair seemed to insist on being her best friend. To nuzzle next to her no matter how much she tried to resist her. She couldn't stand her, and she was tired of fighting against it. She wanted to wake up from her sadden emptiness or at, minimum, sleep it away. But whether she slept or not, depression just wouldn't let her be.

Yet, she put on the mask of being okay—or well enough for a grieving daughter—in front of her family. She didn't bother to tell Elena about Allen Sr. There was enough sadness in her mother's eyes as it was. *"Just hold it together until tomorrow,"* Emily told herself. She was due to fly back to California the next day. Although she didn't know how she could go the next minute, let alone the next day, without crumbling into nothingness, she willed herself to pretend that she could do just that.

As Emily headed out the front door, her mother hugged her one last time. "I love you Emily," she said, holding her firmly.

"I love you too, Momma." If only Emily could bottle up her warm embrace and release it when needed it, like a fresh aerosol. Or if she could've saved pieces of Benjamin on a hard drive or ... Emily's mind gasped. She remembered that she did have a piece of Benjamin saved. The voicemails. The unheard voicemails her dad and mom had left on her phone. Surely, they would provide some form of psychological therapy.

Emily said her goodbyes, made her way to the airport, and boarded her flight back to California. She dismally walked through the check-in process and eventually jetted into the clouds. She slept through the ride. Sleep, when it came, still felt far better than being awake. The plane landed on the strip and again Emily bleakly followed the standard procedures to disembark. She walked to her car, cranked it, and headed home.

The sun was high, sky was clear. *"Such a gorgeous day,"* Emily thought. *"Why can't I feel it? It's just grief,"* she told herself. *"You'll get passed it."* She kept driving. *"But will you? How long will you have to go on like this? The pain only stops when you sleep ... if you can sleep ..."* Emily ignored the thoughts, but they persisted, and appeared to be accurate. *"You have everything ... a successful career, money, an attractive man, beauty, a nice place, a nice car. If you aren't happy now, will you ever be?"*

*"Will I?"* Emily thought. Life seemed meaningless. The acquisition of things. The pursuit of success. She felt as if she were merely floating through life. Existing, but barely living. She looked up. The Golden Gate Bridge was on the horizon. The city still resembled an apocalyptic

movie scene. She slowed down her car as she rolled over the bridge and silenced the useless mumbling on the radio. She'd never viewed the strait that flowed just below the bridge. She brought her drop-top convertible to a complete stop on the side of the overpass.

Emily stepped out of the car and breathed in the air. She felt the sun on her skin as she shielded her eyes from its brightness. The voicemails. Emily needed to hear those voicemails. The sound of Benjamin's baritone voice would allow her to feel something. Anything besides the threatening cloud of misery that hung dangerously low over her head.

*"Hey, Emi baby. Just calling to check on you. I know you want your space. I just need to know you're okay in this crazy pandemic. Love you."*

*"Emi, I know you're fine. Stella told us you were. I guess I just want to hear your voice... I'm so sorry for everything. I love you."*

*"I won't bother you anymore, Emi. I'll give you your space. I'm so sorry for this, baby girl. I pray you can find it in your heart to forgive me. I love you."*

Cinderblocks fell into Emily's heart. The sound of her voice. That's all he'd wanted to hear. Emily loathed herself for not giving that to him. Especially since she was gifted with the opportunity to hear his voice past the grave through what he had engraved in her throughout the years. She paced the bridge. Up and down. Back and forth. Tears blinded her vision.

The weighted reality of her circumstances folded her core. Benjamin was gone, and the thought of her missing biological dad somewhere on drugs, or maybe even dead, added to the immense weight. The threat of continued isolation, loss of companionship, confusion, and God's silence all buckled her. The pressing thought of life not seeming worth the effort chilled her soul. Everything felt too heavy. Much too heavy to continue on. Hope seemed as distant from her as grass was from the galaxies. *"This is too much,"* Emily thought. *"I can't do this. I can't do this."*

She paused as her body trembled from uncontrollable sobs. She took a few deep breaths and walked toward the edge of the bridge. *"It would be easy to do,"* the intrusive voice returned. Emily was weakened. She was exhausted. Another inner voice told her to turn around. A nudging at her soul told her to stop, but the intrusive voice was so loud. *"It's all meaningless anyway. It'll all go away. In one second, it will all go away. The pain. The worry. The uncertainty. Gone. Then you'll have peace."*

Emily grabbed the rusty red metal. She leaned over to peer at the water below. Her heart crushed into tiny, jagged pieces at the thought of her actions. She breathed. Inhale. Exhale. Inhale. Exhale. She closed her eyes. Images of Benjamin, Elena, Estella, and Reggie ran through her mind. An uncommon rush of longing and anguish overtook her.

Still pictures of Allen Sr, Allen Jr, Stacey, Tony, Chelsea, Victoria, and Angelo flashed in and out of her head in short spurts. Memories—old and new, good and bad—flooded her. Tears trickled. Her lips quivered. "Have mercy on my soul, dear God," Emily whispered. She opened her eyes and looked toward the sun.

*"Leap, Emily. Leap."*

Emily obliged.

## ACT III

"Caw! Caw!" Just as Emily began to loosen her grip on the eroded metal, the sound of a bird caught her attention. The squawk was unusually loud. Her eyes darted like fire across the crystal blue sky to locate the bird. "Caw!" One more croak made Emily snap her head up vertically. "Oh… my…goodness…" An eagle circled directly over her head.

Its wings were stretched out wide, gliding harmoniously. Emily's breath caught in her throat. Though it didn't compare to the size and majesty of the bird in her dreams, the sight of an eagle, soaring in the big empty blue sky, had to signify something. Her essence knew it.

She watched as it tilted and flew from over her head. It swooped on its side like a jet as it soared from the left side of her vision to the right. Smoothly, peacefully it flew. And then, as quickly as it came, it was gone. Emily stared into the horizon, still gripping the bridge. Her heart thumping in her ears.

She slowly stepped down from the bridge and loosened her grip on the railings. Once again suspended in what felt to be an artificial reality, Emily walked back to her car. She was stunned at what had just occurred, utterly shocked that she had listened to the hideous, intrusive voice urging her to end it all. She was even more so astonished that God had sent her a ram in the bush—or rather an eagle in the sky. *"That was God. That was nobody but God,"* Emily's thoughts whispered.

She sat in the stillness of her car, perched on the bridge free of traffic, for a few more moments. Death was not something Emily wanted for herself. This she was certain of. The moment before the eagle appeared, she knew death was not the answer. It couldn't be. Buzz. Buzz. Her phone went off. Incoming call from Tony.

*"He's worried,"* Emily thought. Tony had agreed to meet Emily at her house after she landed and she was running late.

"Hello. Hey, Tony. I'm sorry. I just needed a moment to digest everything … I need a rain check … I know it isn't raining … yeah, you're a jokester as always … I just need some time alone." Emily convinced him to give her the day to settle in before he visited. As she ended the call, she flicked the radio on.

"Get ready to tread on your brand-new Fit6000 Treadmill! Burn calories, tone muscles, and get fit. You will tread." Emily froze at the phrase. *"You will tread ... where have I heard that before?"* Emily's mind worked backward through time before the origin of the phrase popped into her head like a jack-in-the-box. "Pastor Peoples' sermon … he said, 'You will Tread'," Emily stated.

A tingle surged through her body. Surely, God was speaking to her. Wasn't He? But through a treadmill radio ad? *"Confirm it with the Word."* She heard her dad's voice emerge from her mind. Benjamin always taught his girls that God talked to His people through the Word of God. *"Always ask God to confirm it through scripture. The mind and heart can't be trusted, but God's Word can be."*

Emily blinked back tears in confusion and desperation. "God, I haven't talked to you in a while. I've been angry with you. I was hurt. Please forgive me. Thank you for sending that eagle. I know that was you, but I don't know if this is you. Lord, if you are talking to me through this radio ad, please make it plain. My mind has been scattered. My emotions—or Satan, or maybe both—have gotten the best of me. I need you. I *need* you. Please, help me. I don't know what to do with my life or myself. So, I surrender. I surrender it all. My life, my will, my plans. They are all yours. Have your way. I welcome you. Please, God, have your way."

The ride home was peculiar. It was evident to Emily that she'd hit rock bottom. An attempt at suicide was both triggering and alarming. She understood she needed help. But who could she tell without judgement? How could she tell her mom that she had almost taken her own life? That would fracture her widowed heart all the more. *"Stella wouldn't understand,"* Emily thought. God forbid she tell Tony.

The thought of seeing a therapist was none too appealing. Too impersonal. Undignified. *"Prayer. Prayer'll do it,"* Emily thought. She made her way home and settled in with a shower. She received a few check-in calls. One from Elena. One from Estella. Emily claimed that everything was fine, that her flight was decent and that she had just arrived safe and sound. The standard "I'm okay" reply rolled off her tongue naturally as it does for most. How could she admit that she wasn't okay?

She received one more unexpected, yet well welcomed call.

"Emily, I'm so sorry. I just heard the news. I didn't know. I would've called earlier had I known. Are you okay?" The sincerity of Stacey's voice was uplifting.

"Hey, umm, I'm making it I guess ..." Emily trailed off. If there was anyone who wouldn't pass judgment, it was Stacey.

"You don't sound okay, Emily. I saw Reggie's post asking for prayers for the family. I'm sorry I missed the funeral." Stacey sounded as if she was going to cry.

"It's okay. Only ten people were allowed to attend anyway." Tears rolled as Emily's emotions resurfaced.

"I'm so sorry, Emily. I wish I could've been there for you. You've been on my mind so heavy lately. I just thought it was because I missed our friendship ... I should've checked on you."

Emily broke into a half smile. "That's okay, Stacey. I thank you for calling now. It means a lot to me."

Stacey paused before she continued. "I actually called Stella before I called you. She told me about what happened between you all a few months ago—about the family secret. You know, blood couldn't have made him love you anymore."

A painful smile spread across Emily's face. "I know. I know, Stace."

Emily held back from chatting too much with Stacey. She wasn't sure if this was a pity call or if Stacey wanted to rekindle their friendship. She didn't think she could handle assuming the latter if it was the former.

"Emily, you can talk to me if you want. I'm here for you. I love you. Regardless of what I said, at the end of the day, you're my girl." Emily knew then that Stacey wasn't only showing sympathy. Knowing Stacey for over 20 years allowed Emily to decipher that a friendship was still in the cards for them. Yet, Emily wasn't ready to confess her low moment to anyone.

"I believe you, Stace. I'm glad to know I can call you. I'll be in touch." They said their pleasantries and ended the call.

The remainder of the day forced Emily to peep into the dark crevasses of herself that she had so long ignored. As she observed them, she saw that they ran over with pulse and gore. But she stared at her wounds until she accepted them as part of what had caused her to make such a drastic attempt. Her lacerations, coupled with the devil's schemes, would have proved fatal if it hadn't been for God's saving grace. She sat in the uncomfortable parts of her being. She faced her demons and declared that they would never consume her again.

*"But how?"* she thought. *"How will I keep this from happening again?"* Emily went to bed with mixed emotions. She was still rattled about what had occurred, yet thankful for God's provision. She was proud of herself for addressing her wounds, but still unsure of how to do so on a continuous basis. She was confident that God would hold her hand, but uncertain if she would hold on to His.

"Lord, I don't trust myself, but I do trust you. Please rescue me from this pit and show me how to never fall into it again." Emily rambled off her fears and thanks until her eyes grew heavy and she fell asleep.

Confirmation. Emily woke up with confirmation that God had spoken to her through the treadmill radio ad. Of all people, Pastor Peoples called her as the sun peeped through the morning clouds.

"Hello, I'm trying to reach Emily," he said when she answered on the fourth ring. She sat up in bed, instantly recognizing her childhood pastor's voice.

"Hi, Pastor Peoples, you've reached me." She grew anxious. *"What could he have to say?"* she thought.

"Hey, Emily. I just wanted to check in with the family. How are you holding up?" Emily didn't want to lie, but she didn't want to tell the truth either—at least not the entire truth.

"I guess I'm doing okay considering the circumstances ..." She grabbed her covers tightly around her as if she was exposed, as if he could see right through her lie.

"You know, Emily, before he passed, your mom and dad came to me about what you revealed at the funeral. They didn't know how to deal with the pain they caused you."

Emily remained silent as he continued, "I counseled them the best way I knew how, but they were heavily burdened. But you know what Benjamin told me?" Emily tensed at Pastor People's question. He continued before she could reply. "He told me that he knew you'd come around sooner rather than later. He said you didn't have it in you to never talk to him or your mother again. He said you were too full of love for that.

"You should've seen how he lit up talking about you. He was so proud of you ... which is why it crushed him to hurt you. And I know now that he is gone, it is crushing you that you didn't reconnect with him ... that you didn't get to forgive him while he was alive. But I'll tell you what I told him and your mother, and if I'm not mistaken, you were present when I delivered this message. So, this is just a reminder. Psalm 91:13 says, 'You will tread on the lion and the cobra'."

A single tear of joy rolled down Emily's cheek at Pastor Peoples' words.

"No matter what is thrown at you. You can overcome it if you abide under the shadow of the Almighty. I want to encourage you to read Psalm 91 in its entirety and let it dwell in your mind because it's true." Emily wiped the tears away as he continued to minster to her.

"Thank you so much for calling, Pastor," Emily said. "You have no clue how much I needed to hear this."

"Well, praise God," Pastor Peoples said with a gleeful laugh.

Emily eventually ended the call and sat in the bed, amazed. "God, who am I that you would answer me like this? I can't believe you would answer me like this." She fell into crying and worshipping. It was like God knew exactly how to speak to her. It was as if He had actually heard her request. How could she take that as a coincidence?

Emily proceeded to get out of bed and shower. She prepared a steaming cup of creamed coffee before she stepped outside onto the back porch. She breathed in the crisp morning air. The sound of birds chirping made her smile. God's confirmation made her smile even more. *"God is real,"* she thought to herself. *"What am I to do with that fact?"* Settling down on her barely used patio set, she began to read Psalm 91 on her Bible app.

She read it at least three times and meditated on it before her phone dinged. It was a business-related email.

Good morning, Emily. I wanted to confirm our closing videoconference for Angelo Heights, scheduled this morning. Please reply to this email as confirmation.

*"Goodness, that is today,"* Emily thought. The idea of seeing Angelo felt awkward to her. Last she saw him, she wasn't with Tony. *"Why does that matter?"* she thought. *"Angelo has never expressed any real feelings for you. Get over it."*

Speaking of Tony, she would have to postpone their meeting once more for the closing. "We can maybe have lunch afterwards?" Emily asked when she dialed his number.

"Sure," he had replied.

So, Emily prepared for the virtual closing with Angelo. She coiffed her hair, added a touch of makeup, and threw on standard business attire. At 10:00 a.m. sharp, the closing began.

"Hello, Ms. Waters. How are you this morning?" the mortgage lender inquired. Emily greeted him along with the seller before Angelo entered the conference. Emily composed her breathing at his entrance. He was just as purely beautiful as she remembered.

*"How can his essence be felt through a monitor?"* she questioned.

"Good morning, Angelo. Good to see you again," she stated.

Angelo smiled, "Likewise."

Emily peered at his surroundings. *"Where is he?"* she thought. He was outside for sure. Walking it appeared. He passed by a few red brick buildings.

"I'm sorry if my walking is distracting you all. I'll be seated momentarily. Please proceed."

Emily listened to the lender and seller give their spiel as she frequently darted her eyes between them and Angelo. He had just passed a few more buildings and crossed the street in front of a coach bus.

Angelo finally seated himself on a bench. When he angled the camera toward his face, his location became obvious. He was perched in front of the Golden Gate Bridge. Emily breathed deeply, hoping no one had noticed the rhythmic change of her heart. The closing proceeded. No one had noticed Emily's panicked moment … except maybe Angelo.

As he settled on the bench, Emily could have sworn he saw her brief state of panic. It was as if his eyes peered right into the well of her dark secret. Or maybe she was just paranoid. Either way, the meeting continued forward without a glitch. The videoconference ended with all parties agreeing to electronically sign the required documents. Angelo was officially a homeowner.

"Congratulations, Mr. Heights. It's been a pleasure serving as your agent. I'll contact you once we end this call about handing you the keys to your brand-new home," Emily said.

"Yes, ma'am. Thank you," Angelo replied with a smile and nod.

The seller and lender offered their best wishes and ended the call. Emily immediately phoned Angelo. "Hi, so I can drop the keys off in the bushes or mailbox if you'd like," she stated.

"Umm," Angelo said. "May I request a different delivery option?" Angelo questioned.

Emily hesitated. "Uh, yeah. Sure. What do you suggest?" She checked the time. Not quite lunch time yet. She had time to spare before Tony arrived at her home for lunch.

"Will you come meet me in front of the Golden Gate Bridge?"

Emily bit her bottom lip. *"Don't go. Tony wouldn't approve. Shoot, do I even approve?"*

"Umm, you want me to give you the keys in person?" she asked.

"Yes, I do." Angelo plainly confirmed.

"Angelo ... I don't know if I should," Emily stated. "I think it's best if I just drop them off with no contact." She waited for Angelo's response.

"I figured since it appears our time together has ended, it's only right to see each other one last time in person."

Emily remained reluctant, "Angelo, can I be honest with you? If this is strictly a client-agent relationship, I don't understand why we need to see one another for this exchange, especially given the nation's current request to social distance."

Angelo's voice remained steady. "Who said this was strictly a client-agent relationship?"

Emily gave an exasperated sigh. "Angelo, I'm seeing someone ..." There was a stint of silence in the air. She continued, "I didn't think you were interested in me. If you would've made it known, maybe things could've been different."

Angelo preceded with his request. "I understand that, Emily. I really do. My request still stands. Will you meet me at this bench in front of the Golden Gate Bridge? One last point of contact before I bid you farewell? I have a mask and I promise to socially distance."

Emily thought it over. Why couldn't she shake him? Something about him continued to persuade her—urged her to see him one last time against what she considered to be her better judgment.

"Yes, I'll meet you," Emily sighed.

"Great, I'll see you in a bit," Angelo said as he hung up.

Emily hopped in her car and sailed down the empty streets to meet Angelo. The more she drove, the more frustrated she became. *"What kind of games does he think he's playing? Showing interest, then pulling back, then kind-of-sort-of showing interest again."* She slowed as she drove past the same, red-bricked buildings she had seen Angelo pass as he walked towards the bench. She spotted the oddly parked coach bus that sat adjacent to the bench and settled on parking her car a few feet in front of it.

Emily gathered her thoughts and composure before she exited the vehicle. *"Just tell him the truth."* As she climbed out of the car, her eyes landed on the beautiful man who sat alone on the bench. Her mind rewound to the second time she had seen him, perched on a bench alone, at her cousin's wedding. Angelo was just as mysterious then as he was now, if not more so currently.

He turned his attention to her as she walked toward him. His smoldering eyes refused to leave hers. She looked away, around at the scenery, attempting to remain focused on what she wanted to tell him, but his aura chipped away at her hardened exterior. She reached into her purse for her mask, thankful for its ability to camouflage her expression. Angelo followed suit and positioned his mask over his mouth and nose as well. Emily stopped just in front of him.

His eyes lingered on her face "Aren't you going to sit?"

Emily shook her head. "No, it wouldn't allow us to social distance." She fished into her purse for the small manilla envelope that read 'Congrats, Homeowner' across the front. "Here you are," she said. "Again, congratulations. It's been a pleasure assisting you."

Angelo removed the baseball cap from his head, exposing dense, tight kinks. "Has it been a pleasure, Emily?"

"We both received what is expected out of the deal, right? You have your home and I have the sale. We both win," she said with a tight mouth.

"You said over the phone that our relationship was strictly a client-agent relationship," Angelo said, raising from the bench. "Is that all you view me as? A client?" he asked. "Please sit, I'll stand," he added.

Emily considered opposing him, but she didn't want to compel him to insist. She sat down as Angelo loomed over her. She peered up at him, squinting from the blinding sunlight. He moved in front of the blazing rays, blocking the sun from her vision, casting a glowy outline around his frame.

"What else am I supposed to view you as, Angelo?"

He folded his arms in front of his chest and stared into the distance. "You said you're seeing someone else. Do you think he's right for you?"

Emily scoffed. "What? Are you right for me? Why does it matter? You said yourself that our time together is over."

Angelo remained still. "It is. But do you think *he's* right for you?"

Emily laughed. "You are hilarious! First you act like you're interested in me, inviting me over to your place, cooking for me and whatnot. Then you play as this righteous advice giver, and then—"

Angelo interrupted. "Was my advice wrong?"

Emily became indignant.

"Whether your advice was right or wrong, it was unsolicited."

Angelo nodded. "I see you've failed to answer my question. You know he's not right for you. You're settling because of your loneliness."

Emily rose from the bench and faced him. "Again, what difference does it make. You're not offering to replace him, right?" Angelo's eyes bled into Emily's, pleading with her to understand, but she didn't.

"What aren't you telling me? If you don't want to be with me then what do you want?" she asked, her sincerity replacing her anger.

Angelo looked up toward the blue skyline, grabbed his baseball cap from the bench, and placed it snuggly on his head before answering.

"I've always had your best interests at heart. And my intentions—no matter how mixed they may seem—are only good."

Emily saw that he wouldn't give her a deeper explanation. It was as if he was fighting within himself, struggling to keep the truth from her. She'd had enough of Angelo's ambiguity. Their time together was indeed, as he stated, over.

"I've got to go, Emily. You take care," he said as he walked away. But he stopped mid-stride as Emily's eyes burned into the back of his head. He turned back around, dropped his mask below his mouth, and violated the six-feet social distancing rule. He grabbed her arms, pulled her closer to him and peered deeply into her eyes before he planted a kiss on the top of her ginger-brown curls. Then, he walked away without another word.

Emily watched him as his silhouette disappeared into the distance. She stood in awe, in confusion, muddied with emotions. Angelo Heights had managed to come into her life and leave without even so much as a clue as to who he was or what he wanted from her besides a house. Her heart burned within her. His touch seemingly electrocuted her. His kiss, though only on the top of her head and completely devoid of lust, had to be the best kiss she'd ever had.

She sat down on the bench, trying to make sense of what had happened between the two of them. She glanced backward at the Golden Gate Bridge. *"Of all places,"* she thought, *"Why here?"*

Emily's phone rang. Incoming call from Tony. She stared at her phone as it rang. Frustration settled in at Angelo's words. *"How dare he tell me who is or who isn't right for me? Who exactly does he think he is?"*

Emily tossed her purse across her shoulders and headed toward her car. She walked past the coach bus once again, reading the logo on the side of it.

"Malach Coach," Emily read aloud. It wasn't uncommon to see tourist buses around, but the empty coach bus only amplified the abnormal solitude of the city. She hopped in her sports car and zoomed across the bridge, praying for the day she could drive over it without feeling trauma's ghost breathing down her neck. In the meantime, she had a lunch date.

That same tantalizing cologne encased Emily's nostrils upon opening the door. Tony stood in the doorway with a bottle of rosé and a warm smile. He bent down to embrace her, and she succumbed to his warmth.

"How you been holding up?" Tony asked as he shut the door behind him.

*"I found out my biological father is a missing, or possibly dead, drug addict. Oh, and I almost plunged off the Golden Gate Bridge yesterday"* didn't seem to be much of an icebreaker. So, Emily gave a basic reply.

"I'm making it I guess," she said. "What should we order? I forgot to thaw the meat," she asked.

Tony gave a sly smile. "Good, that gives me a chance to showcase my culinary skills."

He ran out to his car and returned with a few bags of groceries. "Just relax. Let me take care of you today."

Emily smiled at him, gave him a peck on the lips, and moseyed over to the couch. She took a couple of grateful glances at him while he prepared their lunch.

She rolled her eyes at Angelo's advice about Tony. She rolled them again at herself for thinking about Angelo and his stupid advice while in Tony's presence. She clicked the TV onto a show she knew Tony would like. Although she didn't want to, her mind kept comparing the two. Tony versus Angelo. Who did she really want to be with? But that didn't matter, right? Angelo hadn't given her that option. But what if he did ...?

Emily shook the thoughts away as Tony brought their plates over. *"I'm not settling,"* she thought as Tony joined her on the couch. *"He caters to me, he likes me, and for goodness sake, look at him."* Emily's disdain toward Angelo pushed her further into Tony's arms. But her consistent intrigue of Angelo, no matter how much of an infuriating enigma he was, caused her to second-guess if she was in the right arms.

"Mashed potatoes and gravy." Emily cocked her head to the side at her mom's answer.

"No meat or veggies?" Emily asked. Elena normally whipped up hamburger steak, green beans, and a perfectly flavored tea to accompany mashed potatoes.

"No. I don't need to cook all that food. This'll do."

Emily read between the lines. With Emily and Estella long gone from the nest, and Benjamin's absence, Elena had no one to serve her plates of love to.

Emily tried to put herself in her mother's shoes—the shoes of a widow. Living in the same home she'd shared with the same man for over 30 years. There couldn't have been a single space in that house that wasn't filled with Benjamin.

"Mom, I've been thinking ..." Emily led. Elena raised an eyebrow and eyed her daughter.

"About?" she inquired.

"I'm lonely here, and I could use some company. I was thinking about taking a leave of absence from work. Maybe we could quarantine together for a few weeks?"

Emily knew this was partly true. She wasn't alone verbatim. She had Tony's company. Yet, she wanted some time away from him to think clearly. Because though she didn't want to admit it, what if Angelo and his unsolicited advice was right? Plus, her emotions were still scattered and fighting her depression was still an intense battle. She figured having company would do her and Elena some good.

Elena's face lit up as Emily's suggestion. "Emily, I'd love if you stayed with me for a while. It'll mean the world to me."

Emily gave a short smile. "Actually," she stated, "I'd prefer it if you stayed with me."

Elena looked away from the camera and gazed around her home. "It's bittersweet ... being in this home. Some days it's too much, and I want to sell it. Maybe move into an apartment. Other times I can't imagine letting go of all the memories shared here." Elena looked back into the camera with a sweet smile. "Getting away from it all will help me clear my head."

Emily smiled. "I'll book you a flight today if you want?"

Elena nodded, "Then I'll get packed."

Emily ended the call, realizing that she'd never spent significant alone time with her mother as an adult. Even as a child, she'd clung to Benjamin. She wondered how long Elena would stay or what they'd do together in isolation. Per the purchased airfare ticket, Emily would find out in two days' time.

Silent dancing. That's the waltz Emily and Elena whirled around in for the first couple of days. They'd cook together, clean together, and watch TV together. But they hadn't talked in depth nor confided in one another. They simply danced around one another in separate, silent mourning. Until the seeds and soil came in the mail.

"They're here, Emily. You want to plant them today?"

Emily shrugged her shoulders. "Why not?"

Emily and Elena made their way to the backyard to plant the squash and tomato seeds that Elena ordered.

"Now, don't have me plant these seeds for nothing," she had said while purchasing them online. "I want you to help me plant them and when I'm back in Georgia, I want you to send me pictures of our little harvest." Elena's request sounded like a challenge to Emily's ears. She'd never planted a garden before.

"Not a problem," Emily had responded.

Elena dug out circular holes in the soil while Emily followed suit. "Have you thought any more about what you're going to do with the house?" she asked her mom.

Elena answered without looking up. "I'm keeping it. Benjamin worked too hard for that house for me to just give it up."

Emily didn't disagree. "Isn't it too hard though, Mom? To be in that house?"

Elena grabbed the seed packet and ripped it open.

"Yes. It's downright depressing sometimes."

Emily looked at her mothers' older hands as they cupped and sprinkled the seeds. "So, you're choosing to stay in a place that depresses you?"

Elena stopped, mid-sowing, and looked at Emily. "If I stay in the home, I am a widow. If I move, I am a widow. I can't run from the grief. No matter where I am, I have to deal with it. And I choose to deal with it in the home that I shared with not only him, but you and your sister."

Emily struggled with her mother's answer. "It sounds like we don't have a choice in the matter. As if being depressed is just something we have to deal with ..."

Elena gave her daughter a tight smile as she continued to plant seeds. "Well, I'd like to count myself as a child of God. Just so happens that many children of God in the Bible dealt with depression. Times were so rough for some of them, they wished they were never born. Shoot, Jeremiah wished he was never born and Elijah even asked God to take his life from him."

Elena emptied the seed bag and began to gather soil in her hands. "So, now I have to ask myself, how did they deal with their depression?"

Emily waited for her mother to answer, needing to know the response. Elena continued, "Usually, they cried out to God in their despair. They told God how depressed they were and acknowledged their need for Him to see them through. But no matter how bad off they were, they knew God was their answer and that He'd see them through. So, I'm trying to follow that example." Emily sat there unmoved by her mother's simplified answer.

Elena felt her daughter's eyes glued to her. She looked up from her sowing to examine Emily's face. Elena knew that look. It was that same inquisitive face she'd always make when an answer given wasn't enough. She slowly kneeled down in the dirt and sat face-to-face with Emily as she peered at her from underneath her gardening hat. Tears were streaming down her daughter's face.

"Mom, what if I know that God is the answer, but I can't feel Him or what if I won't feel Him when I'm at my lowest moments?"

Elena grabbed Emily's face.

"Sweetheart, you're in good company. Even when the prophets didn't *feel* like He was the answer, they *knew* He was. You have to keep in mind that your feelings aren't always factual. Emily stared at the ground and nodded dully. Elena knew her answer still wasn't enough. Her mind flickered to Benjamin. He would've had the right response for his Emi.

"You know, after you stopped talking to us, your dad and I had a hard time coping with it. We knew all the scriptures. We knew God would see us through. But we needed something else... an outlet. So, we talked to Pastor Peoples. Maybe, you should talk to someone too."

Devil's advocate tapped on Emily's shoulder. "If God is the answer for everything, why did y'all need to talk to someone else? Why not just read your Bible and pray about it?"

Elena smiled at Emily and replied, "God *is* the answer to everything, but *how* He answers could be through earthly remedies. You know that. Isn't that why you wanted Benjamin to have the transplant? Why didn't you just pray for a healing miracle instead of insisting that surgery was the way to go?"

Emily glanced her mother over. "Talking to someone won't lessen the pain."

"But maybe it'll help you work through it," Elena countered.

Emily dug in her heels. She couldn't tell anyone what happened. *"What if they have me committed?"* she thought.

"Yeah, you're right. Let's work through finishing up this garden. I'm getting an appetite for that meal you promised," Emily deflected.

Elena knew Emily's tactics but wasn't well-trained on maneuvering them. So, they continued sowing seeds and gathering soil until the small garden was completed.

Aaaagghhh!!"

"Breathe, baby. You've got to breathe, remember? You got this," Reggie said as he rubbed Estella's back. There wasn't enough time to make it to the hospital she'd argued.

"No, I think he's coming now!" she'd yelled as Reggie ran to the nursey to get her hospital bag.

"Okay, I'll dial 911," he said with a relaxed exterior but a frenzied interior.

"No! Run some bathwater and get me in the tub NOW!"

Reggie's hands shook as he filled the porcelain bathtub with warm water. He reached inside the linen closet and pulled out a stack of clean towels. Bullets of sweat dropped down his brow as he dashed back to his wailing wife.

"The water's ready. C'mon, I've got you."

Estella grabbed on to Reggie's broad shoulders as they carefully made their way to the tub. Another contraction seized Estella's body before she could submerge herself in the water. She yelped and buried her head in Reggie's shoulder.

"Jesus!" she yelled.

"You're doing good, baby. C'mon, let's get you in this tub before another one comes."

Reggie aided Estella as she lowered her body into the water. She swayed and moaned. Grimaced and cried. Reggie coached her out loud while motivating himself inwardly. A home birth was not their original plan. He'd told Estella that they should've gone to the hospital an hour ago when her contractions appeared to be more frequent and severe, but she insisted that she had time. That was until she had the urge to push.

Reggie and Estella had watched a water birthing video together on YouTube a few months ago just for kicks and giggles. Estella had jokingly said that she'd never do anything like that. God must've laughed at her declaration. Reggie was refocused on the present when another contraction racked his wife. He saw her bear down and push.

She reached down and gasped. "His head! I can feel his head!" Reggie's eyes widened. He desperately wanted to dial 911, but knew Estella needed him to stay in position.

*"Breathe, Reggie, breathe,"* he told himself. "Okay, okay, we're almost there, baby. Once his head is out, we're home free. You ready?"

Estella gave him a bewildered, nervous nod before she bore down once more. She gave several hard pushes before she huffed out an otherworldly gasp as she pulled her newborn baby from underneath the water.

She propped him up in her forearms as she and Reggie gazed upon new life in amazement. Sweat and tears sang a beautiful symphony of joy on their faces as their hearts danced. An ethereal presence fell over them and time stood still as they took in the beauty of their precious baby boy. After time began again, they contacted their families.

Elena's phone rang as she and Emily relaxed on the couch after cleaning up from planting the garden. She answered the FaceTime request and covered her mouth in shock. Emily threw her a puzzled look. Elena turned the phone in her daughter's direction and Emily yelped.

"Oh my goodness, Estella! He's here? He's beautiful!" She scooted closer to her mom. "Wait ... are you at home? You done had the baby and been discharged and you're just now calling us? Estella, you—"

Estella cut in before Emily could continued, "I had him less than an hour ago at home, for your information. We're heading to the hospital shortly to make sure we're both okay. None of this was planned."

Elena finally peeped out a few words. "He is the most beautiful baby, Estella. My goodness, I'm so proud of you!"

Emily smiled. "Yes, we are, sis. I can't wait to hold him! Ugh, this pandemic needs to end today. Hey, little Reggie Jr," she cooed into the phone.

Reggie popped his head into the screen. "What's up, fam?"

Emily smiled. "Congrats, bro! I see you didn't faint from the sight of my sister giving birth … or did you?" she smirked.

"Nah, sis. Real men don't fold under pressure," Reggie bragged. "But I really just wanted to correct you. His name isn't Reggie Jr."

Elena's and Emily's eyebrows furrowed.

"Yeah, we changed it," Estella confirmed as she looked caringly at Reggie.

"Well, what's his name?" Elena asked anxiously. Estella smiled warmly at her mother.

"His name is Benjamin Reginald Jones."

Elena gently placed her hand over her heart. Emily's lips stretched into a soft smile.

"Pops meant more to me than y'all will ever know," Reggie chimed in. "He was the best father figure I ever had. It was my idea to rename our son. It just felt right." Elena wiped away a few tears as Emily stifled hers.

"Well, then," Emily said, "I can't wait to meet little Benjamin."

Elena nodded her head in agreement, "Me either." Estella shared her birthing story to her mother and sister. Excitement of fulfilling auntie and grandmother duties consumed Elena and Emily. They all laughed and shared joy with one another until it was time for Estella, Reggie, and Baby Benjamin to set off for the hospital.

Seeing new life evoked a surge of energy in Emily. She figured if God could bring forth life, He certainly could handle hers. Optimism swelled within her. She could feel it. It was in her lungs. It was in the air all around her. It was undeniable. Newness of life was on the horizon. And she couldn't wait to meet it either.

"Girl, I had to leave him."

Emily paused a beat before responding. On one hand she was happy that Stacey wasn't going to commit her life to a nonchalant prick. On the other hand, heartbreak was never easy, even if it was for the right reasons. "I'm sorry, Stace. I know that couldn't have been easy for you."

Stacey shrugged her shoulders while leaning into the camera phone. "Yeah, it hurt, but I knew he wasn't right for me ... and you better not say 'I told you so' either Ms. Thang," Stacey said, playfully waving her finger.

Emily raised her hands up as if surrendering to the police. "Never," she said.

Stacey continued, "It's been hard though, Emily. I can't lie. Being in quarantine and dealing with this breakup hasn't been easy ... which made me think of how difficult things must be for you right now."

Emily nodded her head. "Yeah, it's been tough, but I'm making it." Stacey stared at her. Emily knew Stace wasn't buying it.

"I was just reading online about how many couples are divorcing and how many people are depressed due to the isolation. It's taking a toll on so many people."

Emily kept nodding. "Yeah, it's been crazy."

Stacey pressed on. "Yeah, it has. Believe it or not, I was so tired of being cooped up in this house with my rollercoaster emotions, that I looked into counseling."

Emily remained silent. Stacey continued, "I never thought about counseling for anything other than premarital counseling. But when I called to cancel those sessions, the counselor mentioned the other services she offered.

"I turned her down at first, but as time went by, I thought about it some more. She's a Christian counselor, she's a sista, and I think I'll feel comfortable with her. So, I'm starting my first session this week." Stacey smiled and crossed her fingers at her last statement. Emily offered a smile in return.

"That's great, Stace. I hope it works out for you."

Emily knew what was happening. At this point, it wasn't a coincidence. This was the third time someone suggested counseling in some shape, form, or fashion. First, Pastor Peoples, then her mother, now Stacey.

Yet, no one knew of her bridge encounter. She hadn't told a soul. Only God knew. And it appeared He was pointing her in the direction of a remedy through an unexpected avenue.

Stacey broke through her thoughts. "Yes, girl. Ain't nothing wrong with prayer and a little extra help. Shoot, if I broke my ankle today, I sure wouldn't just pray over it. I'd pray *and* go to the doctor. My heart is broken girl. So, maybe this counselor can help. We have to take care of our hearts and minds just like we would take care of our bodies."

Emily smiled. "Okay, Oprah."

Stacey laughed. "I'm being real. I'll let you know how the session goes. It's all virtual so I think that'll make me even more comfortable."

Emily nodded. She knew Stacey could see through her mask. She appreciated her ability to always see her pain and help her without making her feel insecure.

"Yeah, let me know how that goes," Emily said.

"For sure," Stacey replied as she casually eased the conversation onto a different subject. Neither said it aloud, but they were both delighted to be back in each other's graces.

## JUNE 2020—SAN FRANCISCO, CALIFORNIA

Emily pressed the lock button on her keypad as she and Elena exited the car. Elena was due to board her plane back to Georgia in the next half hour. They grabbed her bags from the truck and made their way into the building. Before boarding, Elena hugged her daughter tightly. Emily returned the snug embrace. Elena had only stayed two weeks, but it was enough time to spark a new mother-daughter relationship that they both needed.

"Call me when you're home, Mom," Emily said.

Elena nodded and walked to her exit. She gracefully waved one last time before she disappeared behind the doorway. Emily also made her exit through the airport and back towards her car. She fished for her keys while in motion but couldn't locate them. She dug around in her purse for several more seconds after she made it to her car but had no luck in locating her keys.

She let out a sigh and began taking out a few items out of her purse one by one. *"So, they just disappeared into thin air, huh?"* Emily thought in frustration. As she pulled out lipsticks, lotions, and pens, her hand grazed across what felt like an envelope. She pulled the envelope out and examined it. 'Congrats, Homeowner!' it read. Emily's face scrunched into confusion. She didn't have any closings coming up anytime soon.

She opened the manila envelope and recognized the golden key instantly. *"How did this get in here?"* she asked herself. Emily specifically remembered handing Angelo the envelope. No way it should've ended up back in her purse. Plus, that was two weeks ago. How could he have gone two weeks without noticing the keys to his brand-new home were missing?

Emily didn't want to call, let alone see Angelo, but she had to give him his keys. *"Why hadn't he moved in? He couldn't get into the home without his key ... He hadn't even bothered to visit his house since closing?"* Emily pondered. *"He's so weird."* She dug around in her purse yet again to locate her own keys and her hand immediately landed on them. She pulled them out and sarcastically scoffed. *"Oh, so now I find them."* She rolled her eyes, tossed the other items—including Angelo's keys—into her purse, and pulled off from the airport parking lot.

Emily drove until she turned into the pristine neighborhood of Angelo's new home and sighed in relief when she didn't see his old Chevy truck in the driveway. She reached into her purse for the envelope, exited her car, and headed toward the front door. She knelt to put the key under the doormat.

*"I'll just text him,"* she thought.

Yet, when she bent to put the key under the mat, she noticed the door was ajar. Emily slowly rose with the envelope still in her hand. No one should've had access to the home. Fear settled upon her as she considered a possible break-in.

Her eyes dropped down to a small tag that was on the door handle. She stepped closer to read it. 'Emily' is all it said. She flipped it over on the back. 'Letter on the dining room table.' Emily recognized Angelo's handwriting from the Hassen's paperwork. She stood in the doorway, confused. *"How could he have left anything on the dining room table without a key?"*

She contemplated whether entering the home was a wise decision. She reasoned that it probably wasn't. Yet, her inquisitive mind got the best of her. She doubled-back to her car to grab her keys that held her pepper spray and said a silent prayer that she wouldn't need anything more forceful. Emily stepped into the home and shut the door behind her.

Mac & Sons furniture had spruced the place up beautifully. *"He ought to love this."* she thought, though she still found it ridiculous that he wanted or needed such a large home for himself. She walked over to the dining room table where a neatly folded letter lay in the center of it. Emily rolled her eyes and breathed deeply.

"Angelo, are you here?" she asked loudly. "I don't have time for your games if you are." She waited for a reply but was met with silence.

She snatched the letter from the table, unfolded it, and began to read.

*Emily,*

*I know I haven't been easy to understand. I've left you unsure of what to think of me and my actions. What I have to say to you in this letter are things I hid from you because it was ordained that way. It was difficult passing up on the opportunity to love you. It was never easy to deny you. But it was necessary.*

*Do you remember the song that was playing on the radio when we went to B.A. Burgers? Do you recall the name of the package I opened that time you FaceTimed me? The package that had Guardian's toy inside? What about the Malach Coach bus you saw at the bench in front of the bridge? Don't you know what Malach means? Or the scripture that was read in church when you saw me that Sunday after the wedding? Psalm 91? Don't you remember what it said?*

Emily paused in reading the letter. *"Yes, I know what it says,"* she thought sarcastically. *"I read it not too long ago. And what's up with the 21 questions?"* She pulled out her phone and read the Psalm 91 again but was still confused. *"What song was playing on the radio at B.A. Burger's?"* Her mind flashed back. The rhythm of the song re-entered her mind. Anita Baker's *Angel* ...

She paused. Emily glanced down at her phone to read the scripture again, specifically verse 11.

*For he shall give his angels charge over thee, to keep thee in all thy ways."*

Emily's heart caught in her throat. Her mind tracked back to Guardian's toy package. It was an Express Envoy package. Emily remembered the familiar packaging. *'Envoy' as in messenger?"* she thought. And the oddly placed coach bus? "Malach Coach," Emily whispered as she Googled the meaning of Malach.

The search results showed: Hebrew name for Malach: Angel or Messenger. Emily's heart pounded as her head whirled. She pulled out a seat from the dining room table, attempting to congeal the facts, the evidence that lay before her. It was clear, yet impossible. *"There's no way ..."* she thought as she breathed hard and continued to read the letter.

*Your kind is quite oblivious at times, which is why my Father sent me to you. I had an assignment to complete. A work to do. Emily, be of great cheer, for your heavenly Father loves you. He foresaw your confusion, your sorrow, and your deepest pain. He dispatched me to aid you before and during your lowest point. Did you not see me on the Golden Gate Bridge, fighting an entity you could not see?*

*Emily, God has blessed you with a gift. You dream dreams that peer into spiritual realms. I was combatting your demons, your intrusive thoughts. They were cast on you and many others from spiritual wickedness in high places. They can be powerful and quite effective, especially when the victims are unaware that they are under attack.*

*But praise be to God! Glory hallelujah! Hosanna in the highest! I was able to defeat your enemy in just the nick of time. Upon victory, God beckoned the eagle to fly, as a sign of the battle won. He knew the eagle would be symbolic to you because of your reoccurring dream. Speaking of which, don't you know the meaning of it by now?*

*You looked into its eyes. You recognized its familiarity, and yet you didn't realize who it was or what it represented. Emily, the eagle is you. Didn't its eyes glow like yours? The first time you saw it, the eagle was submersed in dark waters, chained, bound down by something you couldn't see. Likewise, there are matters in your life that hold you back. Your wavering belief, your failure to surrender to God, some of the company you keep, your own flesh, Satan and his schemes – all are things that have bound you.*

*And yet, upon breaking free of its chains, you saw how massive the eagle was. It was bigger than you expected. Its beauty and majestic essence surprised you. Similarly, you are bigger than you think you are. Your purpose is greater than what you have imagined. God has a great work for you, but it can only be revealed upon your release of all things that prohibit you.*

*As the eagle was ornately decorated with multiple stones and jewels, you are wonderfully engraved with multiple talents and gifts. You possess the power of influence, which is why you are a great saleswoman. You possess passion and grit. Love and excellent stewardship. All of which will be used mightily for God's glory and your good if used correctly.*

*Fight the good fight of faith, allow God to order your steps, and He will lead you and guide you in the way you need to go. The crimson gash on the eagle's wings represents your trials. Every loss you endured, every pain you felt, was needed to develop you into who you are called to be. The eagle's injury never stopped it from flying. Neither will your deep pain stop you from soaring.*

*So, fly Emily. I'll be watching from up north.*
*Love,*
*Angelo Heights*
*Your Guardian*

P.S. My Father told me I'd feel His wrath if I or any of the other heavenly host mingled with the humans and produced giants on earth again. Though I was tempted, I couldn't take that chance.

Also, I promised you that I would play the trumpet when it was my time to do so, and I will. At the last call, I will blow my trumpet before all men and heavenly host with purpose. That, Emily, I can promise. But remember our deal. You promised to use your gifts for God if I blew my trumpet. I will uphold my end. See to it that you uphold yours. Take care, Emily. Be vigilant. Use wisdom. We're rooting for you from above.

The letter shook in Emily's grasp as her hands trembled. She moved the paper backward to prevent her tumbling tears from ruining the ink. *"Jesus ... Jesus ..."* was all she could utter. Emily sat at the table, her mind working in reverse, thinking of her previous encounters with Angelo. Hadn't other people seen him? Was she absolutely losing her mind? They ate at a restaurant together; they spoke to one another in the grocery store. *"Surely other people noticed him,"* she thought.

Emily snapped out of her trail of thoughts when she heard scurrying footsteps coming down the stairs. Startled, she jumped up from her seat but broke into a wide smile when she saw Guardian bounding towards her.

"Hey, boy! What are you doing here, huh?" she asked as bent down to pet him. His fluffy fur comforted her, yet his presence brought forth more questions. *"Why had Angelo bought this enormous house if he wasn't going to live in it? And who would care for poor Guardian?"*

She continued to rub Guardian's black and caramel-brown fur when her hand clashed against his collar. Emily peered at the silver engraving that read,

Guardian
8634 5<sup>th</sup> Ave, San Francisco, CA 94107
415-550-3333

Emily breathed. It was her address and phone number. *"I always wanted a dog ..."* she remembered telling Angelo. He had responded, *"Maybe you'll have one of your own one day,"* with that divinely stunning smile. Emily's own smile stretched broadly across her face. She grabbed Guardian's face and mashed her head into his. He nuzzled against her, and her heart melted.

She sat on the floor, mind racing a mile a minute, with Guardian's head in her lap. Her phone rang. Incoming call from Tony. She watched as the call went to voicemail. Part of her didn't want to leave Tony. She enjoyed his company and their chemistry. He had borne his soul to her, and she was confident that he only wanted to love her despite his flawed way of initially pursuing her. Yet, how could she soar with God while dancing in sin?

Emily rose from the floor, grabbed the letter off the table, and beckoned Guardian to follow her. He trotted behind her as she walked through the foyer and out of the front door. She reached down in her purse for the keys in the manilla envelope, locked the door, and headed toward her car. Guardian leaped into the passenger side of her two-seater. She smiled at him, shook her head at the impossibility of the day, and put her car in reverse.

Just as she was backing out, a silver Altima blocked the entrance of the driveway. Emily put her car in park and watched the older model car from her rear-view mirror. The passenger door of the vehicle flung open, and a familiar face arose from the seat. Mrs. Donahue. Emily's brows furrowed as she watched her step out of the car. She was followed by Mr. Donahue who spilled out of the driver's seat. They both looked toward the house in astonishment and walked hand in hand toward the driveway. They slowed their stride as they approached Emily's car and stopped.

Emily stepped out of the car, unsure of what to say or do.

"Mr. and Mrs. Donahue, I—"

Before Emily could conclude composing an intelligent response, Mrs. Donahue wrapped her arms around her.

"Thank you. I can't thank you enough Ms. Waters. I know nothing is guaranteed, but I also know you said you wouldn't show clients homes that are out of their price range. So, thank you!" Mrs. Donahue yelped. Mr. Donahue stood back with a wide grin on his face.

Unsure of what to say, Emily uncomfortably rubbed Mrs. Donahue's back.

"I'm sorry, we're supposed to social distance," she apologized, pulling back from Emily. "Ms. Waters, we were bad off. Before the pandemic, I lost my job and was having a hard time finding employment. We thought about postponing searching for a home, but honey here," she said pointing to her spouse, "said we couldn't stay in our neighborhood anymore. Things were getting too dangerous out there. We had already lost one son to the streets … we couldn't afford to lose another."

Mr. Donahue nodded his head in grave agreement. "But when honey lost his job too because of the pandemic layoffs..." Mrs. Donahue shook her head, "I just didn't think things could get much worse.

"I'm sorry for my nasty attitude towards you, Ms. Waters. After that gang took my son from me, my heart grew cold. I started to snap at everyone and everything." Mrs. Donahue took a deep breath. "When we met you, I guess I looked at you as our saving grace. I knew God had led me to you, but I was counting on you to help us instead of Him." Mr. Donahue rubbed her back as she bit her lip underneath her mask, struggling to get her story out.

"God had to show me myself. He showed me my bitterness and how He wouldn't bless me if I continued in my nasty ways. So, I repented and asked God to have mercy on me, to take that anger out of me." Emily's eyes welled up as she listened to Mrs. Donahue's sincerity. "God did just that, but I didn't understand why He hadn't answered my prayer on getting us out of that wicked neighborhood. I knew our income and credit score wouldn't allow us to move, but I was walking by faith. But when you told us you couldn't help us, I thought maybe I was wrong to believe such a foolish thing."

"But I told her to remember that nothing is too hard for God," Mr. Donahue chimed in. "Everything is possible for the one who believes."

Mrs. Donahue looked up at her husband and smiled. "And Lord knows you are right. Ms. Waters, I don't know if you are married, dating, single, or indifferent, but if you're looking for a spouse, make sure he's the type of man that can speak life when all you see is death. Make sure he knows and loves God because you'll need someone who can pray when you can't..."

"Anyway, long story short, we ran into a man in the grocery store the night before the county shutdown ... I think he said his name was Antonio Heights, but I can't remember. I just call him Mr. Heights," Mrs. Donahue said, blinking rapidly.

"Angelo. You mean Angelo Heights," Emily stated.

Mrs. Donahue snapped her fingers. "That's it," she said. "I don't even know how we ended up talking about home buying, but he said that he had a connection with a realtor that could help us. I'll admit, when he mentioned your name, I initially refused. But he said he knew about our situation ... something about him being your coach or mentor or something like that."

Emily dipped her head to prevent her face from showing any emotions. She nodded and continued to listen.

"He said that he was sure—positive, in fact—that you had a home that would be perfect for us." Mr. Donahue chimed in. "I asked him if we needed to contact you to confirm anything, but he said he'd work out the details. He wrote down this address, date, and time and told us you'd meet us here."

Mr. Donahue shrugged and cocked his head to the side, "We had our doubts because what were the odds of us running into your mentor in the grocery store? Plus, we thought you would eventually confirm the home showing ... but you never did. Instead, Mr. Heights called us and told us you had some personal matters to take care of, but that you'd be here today. We figured the least we could do was show up, and if you were here, then we'd know he was the real deal."

"And since you are here ... we know Mr. Heights was in fact the real deal," Mrs. Donahue added with a wide grin, exposing a beautiful face that Emily had failed to notice before.

Emily drummed her fingers against her upper leg and took a deep breath. "Yes, of course," she said. "Allow me to let you all in to take a look." She reached back into her car to pull out the keys encased in the envelope. "I'm sorry. I'll just put my dog in the backyard for now if you all don't mind."

"Oh, that's fine. Take your time," Mrs. Donahue smiled.

Emily returned a quick smile and walked Guardian to the back. She fished out the secondary key to the picketed fence and unhooked the lock. Emily gasped in amazement at the backyard scenery. Stringed lights, paper lanterns, and a healthy-sized banner stretched across the fully furnished patio. She read the banner as Guardian strolled the backyard, 'Congrats Mr. and Mrs. Donahue! It's Yours!'

Emily noticed a blue folder carefully placed in the center of the patio table. She opened it and skimmed the document. She smiled and walked back toward the gate, searching her mind on how she would explain that her 'coach' had given them the deed to his house. She looked up toward the afternoon sky and breathed. Her quick mind and clever tongue couldn't think of a logical explanation to offer her waiting clientele.

"... I suppose I'll blame it on you, God." Emily whispered looking up towards the sky as she cracked open the gate and walked toward her new unexpected homeowners.

Emily had run the conversation through her head countless times, *"I just need to focus on myself", "I'm not in the right headspace to be with you right now", "It's not you, it's me"*, none of which would be easy to relay.

"Well, we have nothing but time to talk," Tony said in his easy-going way. They made their way over to the couch where Emily sat down with one leg tucked underneath her, gripping a pillow for security. Guardian's warm belly on her toes added an additional sense of comfort.

Tony sat down, eyes still on Guardian. "So, what's the long story?" he asked pointing at Guardian. Emily looked down at her dog and back up to Tony.

"He was a gift," she stated matter-of-factly.

"Well, that isn't a long story," Tony said leaning forward. "A gift from who?"

Emily didn't want to explain why a client would give their dog to their realtor. It wouldn't be as easy as yesterday's explanation to the Donahue's.

When she had escorted them to the backyard and their eyes fell on the banner and decorations, their tears and gratefulness was enough to make Emily shed a few tears herself. Mr. Donahue had asked why. Why had Mr. Heights left them this home? He didn't even know them. Mrs. Donahue had hit the nail on the head when she said, "Because if we knew him, maybe we wouldn't give God credit. God did it this way so we'd know without a doubt that this ... this is a miracle!"

But Emily couldn't explain Guardian's presence as a miracle or gift from God. Yet, she'd always been quick on her feet to give a response.

"My client had to return home, —back to his original station—military man. He couldn't take his dog with him, so I took him off his hands."

Tony nodded. "Well, that didn't take that long to explain at all. How was quarantine with your mom?" Emily wiggled her toes under Guardian's fur.

"It was nice," she said, squeezing the edges of her pillow. "Um, Tony ... I really don't know how to say this but—"

Tony cut her off. "But you don't think this is going to work?"

Emily stared at him, struggling to read his demeanor. Was he mad? Disappointed? "It's okay, Peach. You have a lot on your plate. A lot to take in." He stretched out his legs. "I didn't forget what you told me ...

how I was pretty much a distraction for you." Emily dropped her head, unsure of how to respond.

"Don't feel bad about it. I knew where your head space was, and I stayed around anyway because I wanted to."

Tony rose from his seat, headed to the kitchen, and returned with two wine glasses. He popped open a bottle of wine and poured them each a glass. Emily sipped and settled back on the couch.

"Thank you for being so understanding."

Tony tasted his wine before responding, "I always knew there was a chance you'd pull the rug from underneath me ... I was just hoping it wasn't going to be so soon.

"So," he continued, "how do you want to go forward. Friends? Co-workers only? Friends with certain benefits?" he raised his eyebrows on the last question. Emily gave a sarcastic smile.

"I'd say friends if I trusted you to keep it purely friendly, but we both know that's not your style."

Tony shrugged. "You know me well."

Emily appreciated his honesty. "So, I guess cordial co-workers it is."

Tony finished his glass and nodded his head. "Yes ma'am," he said as he stood. He looked down at Guardian once more. "Looks like I've been given the boot, man. Take care of her for me."

He bent down, grabbed Emily's chin, and gave her a smooth kiss before turning to leave. "I'll see you around, Peach." Before Emily could make it to the door, Tony was climbing into his Jeep. Without a handwave or a beep of the horn, he was off.

Emily plopped down on the couch. She knew she had done the right thing but she felt terrible about it. She found it ironic that she was in the same boat her mother had been in years ago. *"He was a good guy, just not the one for me."* She recalled Elena's statement about Allen Sr.

She grabbed Guardian's toy and tossed it across the room. He eagerly bounded across the wooden floor and pounced on the orange rubbery toy before bringing it back to her. Her mind drifted to Angelo. He had said a lot to her in that letter. She must've read it 50 times since discovering it. And yet, some questions were still left unanswered.

Like why did she still suffer from depression and loneliness? When would the pain of losing her dad, discovering bad news about her biological dad, and the regret of not knowing her brother go away? How would she defeat the intrusive thoughts? Emily thought of all the people who had successfully jumped from the bridge. All the people who had allowed the intrusive thoughts—just as she had—to get the better of them. Why was she saved? Why not them? Survivors' remorse asked questions that Angelo's letter didn't answer.

Perhaps God would provide clarity sooner or later. Emily prayed it would be sooner.

## AUGUST 2020—SAN FRANCISCO

Emily logged off the live-stream and hopped up to tidy up her place. She'd attended more virtual church services in the past few months than she'd attended church in the past year. Hearing worship and the Word of God preached every week was refreshing. It encouraged her and filled her spirit. But the once-a-week filling up wasn't enough. She needed a daily dose, and her quick morning devotions weren't doing the job. She needed more.

So, Emily changed her schedule. She became more intentional about her morning devotionals. She was consistent, determined to seek God. It was her new goal. She pursued God with the same laser focus she usually put toward her career. She didn't just read the Word, she studied it, meditated on it. As a result, her prayer life became more sincere. Emily found that the newness she felt in Christ was worth more than any commission check she'd ever received.

She'd never felt so close to God. She'd never felt so light. She chuckled while she swept the same floor she'd crumbled on a few months earlier. Amazed at God was an understatement. She was still grieving and had questions about her identity amongst many other unanswered questions, yet, her burdens didn't feel as heavy when she tossed them on His shoulders. God promised her perfect peace if she kept her mind stayed on Him. She discovered this to be true.

Yet, she knew that even though God had allotted her an unspeakable peace, He'd also pointed her toward therapy a few months ago. She'd ignored the signs. Therapy just wasn't ... it wasn't her style. She was uncomfortable with the vulnerability of it or maybe she was embarrassed by its stigma. Either way, she'd avoided counseling until her soul kept nudging her about it.

Although she was sure of His instruction, Emily went to God for confirmation once more. And once again, He pointed to earthly help. The same day she prayed for guidance was the same day she ran across a random video promoting Christian therapy. So, today was her third session.

Emily sat clutching her journal as she waited for Dr. Harris—or Lisa as she preferred to be called—to dial in. So far, Stacey's good report of her seemed accurate. Lisa had given her some great pointers and advice on how to navigate the complexity of her emotions in the midst of isolation and grief. What Emily really loved about the counseling sessions was Lisa's skill, or her anointing, to tie in sound scriptures to support her professional advice.

When Lisa addressed depression, she spoke of the woes of Job and reminded Emily there was a time and a season for everything—a time to weep and a time to laugh, a time to mourn and a time to dance. Yet, she also advised her to maintain a routine, to stay connected with others, and she also suggested she find a hobby or craft to occupy her mind.

Emily admitted that her small garden of squash and tomatoes, that Elena had recently approved of, helped in idleness. She even helped Emily navigate her feelings on whether to reach out to her newfound family. She was still undecided, and Lisa assured her that the feelings were valid and perfectly okay.

But there was one piece of advice that particularly piqued Emily's interest—something that she hadn't considered. "Many people find purpose and fulfillment in helping others in need. Whether it's helping the homeless or feeding the poor, helping others can aid us in feeling uplifted ... and it's biblical," Lisa had said. Emily thought about how enriched her soul felt when Mr. and Mrs. Donahue had discovered the home was theirs.

Their tears, their gratefulness, had filled Emily in such an interesting way. They pelted her with thanks as if she was the one who had and gifted them the home. Seeing the power that the gift of giving possessed, sent a surge through Emily. She hadn't thought much more about the idea of giving since then. She was much too consumed with her own problems.

"Thank you, Lisa," Emily had replied. "That makes sense. I'll look into that." She ended the call with Lisa and dwelt on what she'd said about purpose. She had always known there was more of herself she could offer the world. That she had purpose outside of being Hassen's best. And if she could give but a fraction to others of what Angelo had given to the Donahue's, she knew she'd feel purposeful. Maybe Lisa was onto something.

## DECEMBER 2020—SAVANNAH, GEORGIA

Emily bounced Benjamin Jr. on her knee and made silly faces at him. He laughed gleefully as Christmas tunes played in the background. She'd waited six months to see her nephew and she didn't plan on putting him down anytime soon. Estella and Reggie smiled at her finally fulfilling her auntie role as Elena pulled the glazed ham out the stove.

Christmas would never be the same. Despite Elena's traditional decorations strung throughout the house and the smell of southern comfort food permeating the air, Benjamin's empty seat left a hole in all their hearts. It was odd. It was hard. But they were thankful for the break in isolation.

"Benjamin wouldn't want us moping 'round," Elena had announced after the food was laid out on the table, "so, in honor of him, we will be glad and celebrate," she said as she lifted her glass of sweet tea.

"So," she continued, "I'd like to present a toast. A toast to the good times. A toast to the memories shared, and a toast to new memories we will create." Elena smiled genuinely. The heaviness in her eyes, though still present, had somewhat lifted as the months passed. They all lifted their glasses in unison and toasted in agreement with her.

It was one wild year, and the uncertainty of the global pandemic was still looming, but all things had strangely worked together for her good.

"How's things going over in Cali, Emily?" Reggie asked after he scoffed down a thick helping of roasted vegetables.

"It's going pretty well. I managed to sell a few more houses and I'm doing a little something on the side—getting my hands dirty in the homelessness crisis going on in the Bay Area."

Estella raised an eyebrow. "Really, Emily? What made you want to take that on?"

Emily hadn't told her family about her counseling sessions. Nor had she told them about the bridge incident. It had taken her months to finally confess the incident to Lisa.

Lisa had followed up with a series of questions to evaluate Emily, which left Emily initially uncomfortable with her confession. But ultimately, she was glad to have divulged her truth. She felt a lifted weight after unpacking herself. Maybe she'd tell her family one day. But for now, God and counseling would have to do.

"I just want to help others. It makes me feel better knowing I'm trying to do something to help," Emily answered.

"So, what exactly are you doing to help?" Elena asked, intrigued.

"Well, turns out the same woman I sold a home to earlier this year is the Executive Director of the Department of Homelessness in San Francisco." Emily had been thoroughly surprised when Ms. Leona Fletcher's face had popped up on her screen when she researched how to assist homeless individuals during the pandemic. She shot Ms. Fletcher an email and expressed her desire to aid.

"Ms. Waters! What a surprise. It's good to hear from you. Absolutely, we can take all the help we can get." Ms. Fletcher explained how Emily could help pack care packages for the homeless in the safety of her own home and where to drop them off. She also threw out obvious hints that she could use someone with her persuasive touch to jump start the non-profit she was in the works of creating.

"I'm calling it Beauty for Ashes. It may sound corny to some, and I don't know your personal beliefs, but I want to show others that, through God, we have the power to give others beauty in our own way," Ms. Fletcher had said. Emily instantly thought of the powder-blue Beauty for Ashes shirt the young woman at the medical clinic had on the day she had filled out donor paperwork for Benjamin. It was as if God had been leaving her breadcrumbs in the forest leading her to purpose.

"I'm in 100% agreement with you Ms. Fletcher. Please let me know how I can help," Emily had offered enthusiastically.

Elena nodded and smiled proudly as Emily explained her involvement in the community.

"That's what's up, Emily," Reggie said. Estella agreed.

"Benjamin would be proud," Elena added.

Emily flashed a smile at her mom. "Enough about me. How's parenthood going?"

They conversed and communed at the table with one another until dinner was well over with. Eventually, the traditional Christmas family movies started and before long, evening turned into night. Reggie and Estella had passed out on the couch about an hour ago. Emily was on baby duty while Elena cleaned the kitchen and put away leftovers.

"Little man," Emily said to Benjamin Jr, "you done wore your mommy and daddy out, haven't you?" He gave Emily a cute gummy grin.

She scooped him up in her arms and gently rocked him until his little eyes closed in a peaceful sleep. Elena walked into the room and offered to take him.

"Here, I'll put him down. There's an art to it. Gotta make sure he doesn't wake back up." She winked as she took him. "You look tired too," she added.

"Yeah, I'm going to head on up." Emily rose from the couch and kissed her mom on the cheek. "Good night, Mom."

Emily slowly took the stairs up to her old bedroom. She looked around the room. As usual, Mom kept it clean, but exactly as it was years ago. Her golden trophies gleamed, and pictures of old memories remained tucked in the frame on the mirror. So much had happened since she last left. So many questions still floated through her head.

Life had proven itself to be tough, and the global pandemic had introduced a new normal that still felt ambiguous. But oddly enough, Emily felt more certain of who she was now, amid uncertainty, than who she was in the midst of her normality. If she wasn't sure of anything else, she was certain God loved her, that He cared, and that she was here for a purpose. She was certain she was a daughter of the King and saved by grace.

Emily freshened up for bed, climbed under the covers, and stared at the ceiling. She thought about Benjamin and how he would come talk to her on the edge of the bed when he could sense something was wrong with her. Her heart longed for him. A few tears dropped from her eyes before she went into prayer. Before Emily could say "amen", she was lost in a world of slumber.

*The eagle with the fiery amber eyes soared high in the horizon, displaying its mutli-colored gem-studded wings. Emily watched it as it flew to heights unimaginable.*
*"You look at it as if you're surprised. I'm not."*
*Emily turned toward the voice. Benjamin sat beside her in a grassy field watching the ethereal eagle soar.*
*"I can do a lot of things, Daddy, but that's mighty high."*
*"Yeah, it is. You need some power to go that high."*
*A cool breeze rustled the grass. They sat in silence as they watched the sky together.*

*"You're on the right track, Emi. Take over California for me, okay?"*

*Benjamin rose from the grass and Emily followed suit. He wrapped her tightly in his arms. His warmth engulfed her. The sunlight blinded her eyes. She shut them tightly, holding on to Benjamin and his words.*

The blinding sunlight flooded through the thin curtains as Emily stirred. She turned over and regretted waking up. No dream should feel that real, she reasoned. Her phone dinged on the nightstand. Her hand fumbled around on its surface until her palm landed on the device. She slid the phone into bed with her and pulled up her notifications. It was her daily Bible app ding. She popped it opened and read the verse of the day.

*Now unto him that is able to do exceeding abundantly above all that we ask or think, according to the power that worketh in us,*
*Ephesians 3:20*

*"You need some power to go that high."*

Benjamin's words bounced around in her head. She relived the warm embrace and closed her eyes to the memory. Tears dropped and rolled into her pillow. She sat in bed awhile longer and stared at the ceiling until she heard shuffling in the other rooms. She tossed the covers from her body, swung her legs over the side of the bed, and walked out of the room in what could only be her God-given power.

## ABOUT THE AUTHOR

Quin Arrington was launched into her unexpected writing career in 2020. Though it took 30 years for its revelation, writing for Christ has proven to be her life's passion.

In addition to composing books, Quin writes weekly Christian inspirational articles and actively posts edifying content on her social media platforms.

Quin is the wife to Barry Arrington and the mother to their sweet daughter. She resides in Sweet Home Alabama. *According to the Power* is her 1st fictional piece but her 3rd literary work.

CONNECT WITH THE AUTHOR

Quin Arrington is the owner of the Bible-based blog "Now, That's A Word! LLC. If you enjoyed this book, visit her website at
**www.nowthats-aword.com.**

She is active on the following social media sites:

Facebook: @nowthatsaword
Instagram: @quin_nowthats_aword
Twitter: @NowThatsAWord1
LinkedIn: Quin Arrington
Medium.com: quin-a

# Acknowledgements

God, thank you for allowing me to write for you and to your people. I never would have written fiction on my own accord. I didn't think I had it in me, but you reminded me that you created me. You know my potential even when I am doubtful. Thank you for reassuring me and for gracing me the opportunity to complete this work. No greater honor do I have than the position I have been allotted in servitude to you. Thank you.

To my husband, my editor, my lover, my friend, my great debater, you, dear sir, are awesome. I do not say it enough, so I'll say it here. You are well appreciated and loved. Thank you for all that you are, have been, and will be. I love you.

To my daughter, I love you little girl! You keep mommy on her toes. I thank God for you, and I appreciate your spunky, loving ways. You are special. You are beautiful. You are loved immensely.

To everyone who aided in the completion of this project—editor, cover designer, photographer—thank you for offering your services.

To my family (special shoutout to my mother!), friends, and supporters, thank you for your continued support. I am grateful for every article, post, or book you've read. I appreciate your words of encouragement and affirmation. It does not go unnoticed.

Again, I thank God for this opportunity. Three books down… only God knows how many more to go.

## *Leave a Review!*

Hi, Quin here 😊 I would very much so appreciate it if you would leave a review on Amazon if you enjoyed this book.

Simply go to www.amazon.com/author/quinarrington click on the title of this book, scroll down, and leave a review.

This book is also available on the Goodreads website (www.goodreads.com); thus, you can leave a review there as well if you feel so inclined.

Thanks for your time!
Be blessed!

Made in the USA
Columbia, SC
23 March 2023